ANG POMPANO

Diet of Death

The Reluctant Food Columnist Mysteries

LEVEL BEST BOOKS

FOR MY WRITING GROUP OF 25 YEARS
Christine Falcone and Roberta Isleib a.k.a. Lucy Burdette

Chapter One

An early morning call from my boss, Archie, was never good. I answered anyway.

"Tolzer wants to end his feud with you," Archie said.

Dr. Alan Tolzer, the inventor of the Westport Diet, has held a grudge ever since I panned his weight loss plan.

"Why the change of heart?"

"He's looking for publicity for his new book, *The Enhanced Westport Diet with Miracle Kopi Berries.* He actually admitted he needs 'Cooking with Betty.'"

"Fair enough."

People will give anything for a mention in "Cooking with Betty." It means instant success for all things food related. And that makes me the reluctant Oprah of the cooking world. We all sell our souls one way or another in the cooking industry.

I looked at the clock on the nightstand, 7:00 a.m. I scoffed.

"Fine. I'll shoot an email with some questions over to him. Coffee first."

I could hear Archie clearing his throat on the other end of the line. "It has to be a face-to-face."

Archie must have gone out of his mind.

"How am I supposed to pull that off?"

I wrote "Cooking with Betty," a food column in *On-Topic Magazine.* That's quite an accomplishment for someone as culinarily challenged as I was. I managed it with recipes given to me by my neighbor, Mary Ticarelli. As if that wasn't enough on my plate, so to speak, I had to hide the fact that I was Betty. No way could I do a face-to-face interview.

"You'll think of something," he said. "And there's one more thing. He wants the interview this morning. You have a nine o'clock appointment."

Before I could say anything, Archie disconnected.

After my divorce, I moved to Norwalk. It's a few miles down the Connecticut shoreline, but a universe away from my hometown of Sachem Creek. One day, I ran into my old college friend, Archie Monahan. He convinced me I needed to save him from his Siberian tiger of a father, the publisher of *On-Topic*. All I had to do was fill in for a couple of columns until Betty moved up to the New York area from Philadelphia.

He assured me that after Betty transitioned from her current job, he'd create an investigative reporting job for me.

A couple of columns led to four when Betty needed to wait for her kids to finish school. Four led to eight when her husband got sick. Every month, it was one excuse after another. The column took off, and before anyone realized it, it was translated into six languages.

Then Archie informed me that Betty wasn't going to be moving to New York after all. In fact, she was dead. A car accident. Her car hit a cow. On the way up from Baltimore. When I heard Baltimore instead of Philadelphia, I realized the truth. There was no Betty. But Archie assured me there was. Me, a.k.a. Quincy Lazzaro.

* * *

Dr. Tolzer, the diet guru, had a reputation for being difficult, but I tried not to let that intimidate me. I've held my own with more than one prima donna celebrity since I started writing "Cooking with Betty." But for the thousandth time, I questioned the time and effort my job required.

The ta-thump, ta-thump, ta-thump of the tires on my '68 Camaro on the wooden bridge to Canfield Island did nothing to reassure me. Nor did the sight of homes I couldn't afford if I worked until I was one hundred. My stress stemmed from Archie's insistence that no one was to know that Betty wasn't real, especially his father. It was getting harder and harder to make excuses when people wanted to see Betty in the flesh. My only hope was to convince Tolzer that I was Betty's assistant.

I looked for the ivy-covered wall that marked Tolzer's Westport Diet Institute. It was almost 11:00 a.m. when I approached a wrought iron gate decked with the letters WDI. I pressed the button on the call box.

"Betty Ann Green's assistant," I said into the intercom.

A giggle came through from the other end, and someone buzzed me in. It was clear that Archie's publicity rumor that I was Betty's boy toy, as well as her assistant, preceded me.

I cursed Archie as I drove up the copper-beech-canopied driveway to the main house. The greystone mansion had more chimneys and leaded windows than a palace. Beyond, Long Island Sound lay calm as a kitten on Paxil. No wonder they called this the Connecticut Gold Coast; prime real estate indeed.

I parked next to a Lexus convertible and followed a boxwood-lined path to an arched door. It opened as I was about to knock. A well-dressed woman charged out, slamming into me.

"He's such an ass!" the woman said.

She gave me a withering look, as if the collision was my fault, and hurried past me to the Lexus. After some hard thinking, I put a name to the face. Irene White, the wife of state senator and gubernatorial hopeful Jonathan White, sped down the copper-beech tunnel.

"Do come in." A stunning woman with a single thin braid in her long, golden-brown hair stood in the doorway. It took me a second to collect my wits.

She motioned for me to enter. "You are Betty Ann Green's assistant, aren't you? You said so when I buzzed you in. I'm Megan Hawkins, assistant director of the Westport

Diet Institute. I didn't catch your name. Mister?"

"Lazzaro. Quincy Lazzaro. She sure was in a hurry."

I could see the puzzlement in Megan's almost violet eyes. Finally, she seemed to understand I was talking about Irene White.

"I am sorry about that. It's a long story. Will Betty be here soon?"

I wanted to tell her that she was here. "I'm afraid she can't make it. As her frontman, I'll gather the facts, and she'll write the interview later."

"I see." Her voice trailed off.

"Is there a problem?" Of course, there was a problem. There always is at first, even in phone interviews. But then the interviewee realizes it's in their best interest to go along with it, and everyone is happy.

"Not with me, but Dr. Tolzer may be a different story."

She led me to a study where she left me to wait for Tolzer. The room was a shrine to the man himself. Every inch was chock-a-block with awards, mementos, and pictures of him with celebrities. While I was reading a framed thank-you note from President Bill Clinton on the wall, Megan returned carrying a tray with a silver pot.

"Isn't that awesome? Dr. Tolzer devised a food protocol after the president's heart surgery."

She put the tray down and directed me to sit in a huge leather chair.

"It will be a while before you can see the doctor. I thought you'd like some civet coffee while you wait."

"Civet?"

You know, Kopi Luwak from Sumatra. It's acceptable. It's on the diet." She poured a cup and then pushed a plate of baked goods toward me. "Try one of these almond flour muffins."

"They look too healthy for my taste. I could use some sugar, though."

She looked at me as if I were a heretic. "I'm afraid you won't find sugar at the institute. It's absolutely forbidden on The Westport. I could get you some cream, though. That's allowed."

"Cream? That's my kind of diet."

"Definitely. With Westport, fats are actually encouraged. I'll be right back," she said.

Tempted to Tweet, "Take that, Mayo Clinic!," I took a bite out of one of the muffins instead. That was a big mistake. It was like a mouthful of sawdust. I gulped the coffee, spilling some in the process, making a big wet spot on my lap.

I went to find a bathroom and some paper towels. I could hear talking down the hall and walked in that direction. As I drew nearer, the voices got louder with each sentence.

"You can't fire me. I am the image of the Westport Diet. Me and only me!"

Chapter Two

I knew that could only be Jordy Ponds. He was the Olympic gold medal tennis champion who blew up to over three hundred pounds after he retired. After losing a hundred and fifty of them on the Westport Diet, he became its spokesperson. I'd seen him in dozens of commercials for the diet plan. From the sounds of it, Dr. Tolzer had given him the boot.

I stored that information in the back of my mind. It might be of interest to my readers. I returned to the study still troubled by the wet pants. I rubbed my hand over my lap in the hopes of making the spot disappear. I heard the same giggle I heard over the intercom at the gate, and I looked up. Megan stood wide-eyed in the doorway.

"Spilled," I said. I smiled and shrugged my shoulders.

She lifted the plate with the muffins. "Here, use this." She handed me a cloth napkin. How did I miss that? I dropped it over the wet spot as she gave me a sympathetic smile. "You tried the coffee?"

"Not yet." I loaded the coffee with cream, picked up the cup, and breathed in. Unless I was mistaken, it smelled a little musky. I sniffed again. It smelled a lot musky. I hate musky.

"Smells good," I said. I took a large sip. This time, I noticed it was syrupy and strong.

"But do you love it?" Megan was beaming as if she were a proud parent. I didn't want to hurt her feelings, but what I would have loved was a cup of Dunkin' sweet and light.

"It's good." Not for me was it good, but I imagined some people would like it.

"At five hundred dollars a pound, I would hope so," she said.

Was she kidding? Even Starbucks doesn't cost that much. For that price, I'd expect it to come in a gold-plated souvenir mug. I couldn't hide my shock. "Who would pay that for coffee?"

"The people who follow Westport. That's what makes the diet different. It has all kinds of fine ingredients that make the people on the diet feel special. It's easier to handle hungry if you've paid through the nose for it."

That statement was wrong on so many levels that I had to mention it in the column. I knew it would elicit quite a reaction from my readers. "It's a lot of money," I said.

"It's not that exorbitant when you consider the process. I'm told that plantation workers have to pick the beans out of the feces of the Sumatran palm civet."

"You mean that coffee came out of the ass of the Giant Rat of Sumatra?" I looked at the half-drained cup.

"I love your Sherlock Holmes reference. I'm a fan too. But it's a marsupial, not a rat. They eat only the finest coffee beans." Then she topped off my cup.

I closed my eyes for a second as I suppressed a gag.

"Oh dear," Megan said.

That seemed to be her catchphrase. At first, I thought she was referring to my reaction to the coffee. She jumped up and rushed out. Curiosity made me follow. She dashed toward a woman in the hall. The woman's short stature reminded me of Mary Ticarelli, but the resemblance ended there. Mary has dyed brown hair, which tends to redden between beauty parlor visits. This woman had a bushy salt-and-pepper hairdo. Her mature but pretty face wore a troubled look. She wore an oversized Hampshire College sweatshirt.

Megan spoke in a soft, patient voice as if to a disobedient child. "Jeanette, what are you doing here? You know what the doctor said. He doesn't want you on the property. I'm sorry, honey. But you'll have to leave."

In contrast, the woman had a tone of near hysteria. "But I want to see his holiness!"

Megan remained calm. "Dr. Tolzer will be very angry with me if I let you stay. You will have to leave immediately." She touched the woman on the shoulder.

"Okay, okay. I'm leaving," Jeanette said in an even louder voice.

That brought Tolzer out into the hall. I recognized him from his pictures, even though he looked at least ten years older in person. I judged him to be in his early seventies. His plugged hair looked like an army of blackened spider legs marching across the top of his head, his face lifted and nailed in place.

It ticked me off when someone deceived the public like that. But then, who was I to talk about deception when Mary was the real brains behind my column?

Tolzer was nowhere near as conciliatory as his young assistant director. "Why the hell are you here? If you don't get out right now, I'll have you arrested."

Jeanette was persistent. "I want to talk to you."

"There's nothing to talk about." Tolzer raised his voice to the point where he could have stroked out if he wasn't careful. "Get out. Now!"

"I swear you're crazy, Alan." Jeanette huffed and marched toward the door.

Megan looked very troubled as she called after her. "I'll call you later to check on you."

As Jeanette left, Tolzer glared at Megan. "I took her key card away weeks ago. Did you buzz her in?" To his credit, he didn't otherwise reprimand her for offering support to the woman. Not that Megan seemed the least bit intimidated.

"No. I have no idea how she got in. You should know that when I spotted her, she told me she would leave."

"This place is out of control, from staff to patients. I'll get a handle on it if it kills me."

Megan realized I was there. "Dr. Tolzer, you have a guest waiting for an interview."

"I'm not doing any interviews today."

"It's for the 'Cooking with Betty' column. We scheduled it," she said.

Tolzer glanced at me. If he wondered who I was, he didn't ask.

"Betty? Okay, introduce me to her." As he brushed his jacket, he immediately became a different person. It was as if he were brushing away his natural persona to expose his public personality.

Megan, arms crossed, dug in. "She's not here. This is Mr. Lazzaro, her frontman."

"Well, then, first I'm going to go finish my lunch. I'll see him in half an hour."

He went into his office and slammed the door. Megan turned to me red-faced. "Let's go back. Dr. Tolzer is running behind. He's had several crises to deal with today."

I guess he did. First Irene White's rant, and then his firing of Ponds; and now this. "No worries. I've never yet had an appointment with a doctor who was on time."

Megan paused as if something struck her. Or she wanted to change to a lighter subject. "You don't remember me, do you?" The look on her face told me she wasn't quite sure herself.

I studied her face. She looked familiar, but I couldn't place her.

"I spent a summer in Sachem Creek years ago. My parents rented from your father."

"Megan! Of course! You." I held my hand about waist high, indicating how small she was then, which made her smile.

"Yes, we all tend to grow up, don't we?"

She sure did. I remembered the pesky little kid who always seemed to show up when Brooke and I wanted to be alone when we were dating.

"I had a crush on you," she said. "Isn't that the funniest thing in the world?"

"Small world," I said. I suppose I could have told her that Brooke took up with her tennis instructor and kicked me out, so I left Sachem Creek. But that would make me sound like a loser. As would telling her that I was the real Betty and I was writing the column with Mary's help. She might have found it funny that I slip in Brooke's recipes every once in a while, as a bit of sweet payback.

She looked at her watch. "Dr. Tolzer should be ready. You can bring the coffee."

Despite the offer, I left the coffee cup on the table as she led me out of the room.

"Down there. Third door on the right," she said as if I didn't already know.

I walked down the hall and knocked on the door with Dr. Tolzer's name. A muffled voice told me to come in. I found myself in a large, paneled office furnished in leather and mahogany. The views of Long Island Sound were spectacular. This room also seemed to be a shrine, decorated with mementos. No one was in the room. To amuse myself, I studied the pictures of Tolzer with every celebrity from Adele to Jay-Z.

"Where's Betty?" came a voice from beyond a door standing ajar.

"Dr. Tolzer?"

"Well, who the hell do you think it is? It's me you came to see, isn't it? I'm in here."

I realized the voice was coming from the bathroom. "Excuse me, sir. They sent me in. I'll come back."

"What's the problem? Johnson gave interviews from the bathroom all the time."

"Who?"

"Johnson. Lyndon Johnson. He was the president of the United States once. How old are you anyway? You sure you can handle this?"

I looked out the window at the khaki-colored beach. "What was that?" I asked.

"I said, 'Are you sure you can handle this?' Where the hell is Betty?"

"Betty's a very busy lady. I'm her assistant. She prefers to have me do the legwork."

I would have snuck out, but I needed that interview. My "Cooking with Betty" deadline was coming up in a week. I paced around the office, spotting a food tray on a table near his desk. On it were the remains of three lamb chops and a side of cauliflower. Next to it, a small paper cup held a white pill stamped with AJP 254. What would the great diet guru be taking? A supplement? I took a picture of it with my phone so I could look it up later. I thought I'd even add it to my column if it was newsworthy.

"I understand you have a new Westport Diet book." I slid the phone into my pocket.

Tolzer's voice boomed out from the bathroom. "It's more than another diet book. It's *The Enhanced Westport Diet with Miracle Kopi Berries*. I repeat: *The Enhanced Westport Diet with Miracle Kopi Berries*! She'd better get that right for God's sake."

"I will. I mean, I'll relay the information to Betty. She's a stickler for accuracy." I walked over to a weigh-in scale at the far side of the office and fiddled with the sliding weights along the beam. I was about to step on the platform when Tolzer shouted from the bathroom.

"You're not touching my scale, are you? That's an antique. It was a gift from Herman Tarnower, the poor bastard. Nobody uses it except me."

"Nope. Not touching," I said.

"Thank you!" he said. I felt as if I were a reprimanded kid.

Tarnower? I heard that name before. He'd been another diet guru back in the day. I moved to a bookshelf and picked up a book, The Sugar Revolution, by Dr. Alan Tolzer.

As I looked at the book, a gray tabby cat with green eyes jumped onto a nearby counter. I put out my hand. He sniffed, pulled back, and jumped to the floor. He circled me a few times, then rubbed against my legs.

I crouched down and wiggled my fingers at him, then looked away not to challenge him.

"Hi there," I said in a soft voice.

"Did you say something?" Tolzer called from the bathroom.

"I was talking to your cat."

"Menu doesn't like strangers."

I noticed the striking "M" on Menu's forehead, a patterned marking found on most tabbies.

"Menu is the perfect name for you," I said to the cat.

I slowly extended a curled finger. The cat bumped his nose against my knuckle, then sniffed my fingers again. Before I knew it, he was cheek rubbing my hand and headbutting my arm as if we were old friends. When Menu had had enough, he went on his way, and I went back to flipping through the book.

Tolzer came out of the bathroom making a face that exposed his teeth. "Take my advice, floss. If I'd known I was going to live this long, I'd have flossed more diligently."

"You were brushing your teeth?"

"Yeah. What did you think I was doing?"

No wonder he had been so hard to understand. He sat at his desk, his eyes falling on a picture of him and Barack Obama. If he wanted me to comment on it, I didn't. This doctor was the personification of vain.

Tolzer gestured toward a seat on the other side of the desk, and I sat. Menu jumped on my lap and curled up. I gave him a few gentle pats, and he purred.

The doctor cleared his throat and called Menu. The cat looked at him for a few seconds, tilting its head from side to side.

"Come on." Tolzer clicked his tongue several times.

Menu stood in my lap as if he were about to jump on the desk and walk across to his owner. Instead, he leaped over to the table with the food tray. Tolzer patted his lap, and Menu jumped off the table, knocking over the paper cup with the pill.

Tolzer got up and retrieved the medication. "Damn! I should have taken this before I ate." He realized he was thinking out loud, and he palmed the pill. He then popped it into his mouth washing it down with a swig of Perrier. He nodded toward the book in my hand.

"*The Sugar Revolution* started it all," he said. "That was back in the early seventies when I invented the low-carb diet. I beat Atkins by two years. You didn't know that. Did you? Why would you? Nobody gives me credit for that. You do Westport?"

I grimaced. "I'm afraid it's out of my league. But Betty finds it interesting."

"Okay." His dismissive tone told me that he didn't care what I thought as long as Betty was on board. She was the one who could help him push his books.

To my surprise, he retrieved two cannoli from under the napkin on his tray. This was the man who wrote *The Sugar Revolution*? He held one out to me. "Take it. It's one of Betty's recipes."

I raised my eyebrows as I recognized the pastry featured in a column a year or so ago. Getting that recipe from Mary was like pulling teeth. "I'm Italian," she said. "We don't need a cannoli recipe. We just make them." I finally got her to write it down, but I suspect she left something out because they're not quite as good as hers.

"Sir?" I eyed the cannolo.

"I know, I know. The diet. It has an escape clause. You think the rich people who buy into Westport are going to settle for a diet that doesn't have an escape clause?"

I waved it off. Tolzer gulped the pastry down in two bites and sat. I turned on the recorder on my cell phone. "May I?"

"Of course not. I want to talk to Betty. I don't want this article botched up. I have a sure-fire publicity gambit already, but a good mention in "Cooking With Betty" will mean millions in additional book sales. So, tell me, what's she like?"

I kept the recorder running. "She's a good boss. Nice to work for."

"Bull shit. She wouldn't be successful if she were nice to work for. But that's not what I want to know. What's she like?"

"Like?"

"Don't play dumb, man. You know what I mean. Forget it, then. I already know. Betty and I go way back. She was good then. I'll bet she's still good now."

The remark pissed me off. Sometimes I forget that Betty doesn't exist, and I become defensive about her. For the sake of the column, I tried to be diplomatic with this delusional egomaniac. "Well then, you already know how she is. Busy, busy, busy. That's why she sends me to gather information. I'm sure you want her to write the best article possible. As you say, it could be worth millions. Now, what Betty would like to know is—."

From somewhere in the room, a cell phone rang. Tolzer looked quite surprised. He went to a closet where he retrieved the phone from a jacket pocket. "Hello!" His face paled a bit. "Lucky? What now?"

The volume was loud enough for me to hear a man's voice on the other end, but I couldn't make out what he was saying.

"More? I paid you an hour ago." Tolzer listened. "All right. But that's it." He flipped the phone shut. "Wrong number," he said.

Tolzer's face changed from pale to red. He threw the phone on the desk and slumped back into his chair. "Look, I've had enough. My assistant director will give you a fact sheet."

"I was hoping for an interview."

"And I was hoping for Betty."

I tried to reason with him. "Betty sent me to get the facts. I'm happy to come back."

Dr. Tolzer thought for a nanosecond. "Okay, tomorrow then at nine. But bring Betty."

"I'm not sure if she can make it."

"Then make sure. Call her to confirm. Now."

I knew that sooner or later someone would demand to see Betty in person. "Call?"

"Yes. Here's the phone." He picked up his desk phone and held it out to me.

"I'll use mine, thanks." I rubbed my finger across the face of my phone, then touched the picture of Mary I'd taken in her kitchen. Don't pick up. Don't pick up. It went into voicemail. I breathed a sigh of relief.

"Guess she's not available," I said to Tolzer and disconnected.

Before he could say anything, my phone rang. It was Mary. "What's the matter? You too good to leave a message?"

"You didn't answer," I said.

"I'm screening. And where are you? You went out early."

I don't know why I have to account for my whereabouts to my eighty-four-year-old neighbor. But she feeds me well and gives me recipes, so I make allowances. Besides, I could never pull off writing "Cooking with Betty" without her.

"Betty, I'm at the interview with Dr. Tolzer." I held my phone tight to my ear and turned away so Tolzer couldn't hear Mary's side of the conversation.

"Betty? Are you hopped up on something?"

Hopped up? Where does she get this stuff? "I'm not right now, Betty. But

I may be later."

"Tolzer? Westport? You mean that diet guy? I thought he hated you, or at least Betty."

"Not anymore."

"So, are you in drag or something?"

"Of course not. Betty, he wants to meet you."

"He wants to meet me?"

"Yes, Betty. The interview is so important that he wants you here in person tomorrow morning. Nine sharp. I told him you were very busy and most likely couldn't make it."

"Ahh, so you need me, huh?"

I was holding my phone so tight against my head that I could feel my ear getting hot. "That's right, Betty."

"Let me talk to him." There was excitement in her voice.

Tolzer was standing and shifting from foot to foot. "Well?" he said.

I put a disappointed look on my face. "So, you can't make it, Betty. That's too bad."

Mary was getting agitated on the other end of the line. "I can make it. Tell him. I made eggplant parmigiana, none for you if you don't tell him. No more recipes either, if you want to be stubborn about it."

Most old people hold their wills over your head. Mary holds her recipes. I know when I'm losing a battle, so I decided to go along with it. "You'll squeeze him in tomorrow morning. At nine? Okay. I'll tell him. Thanks, Betty."

Before I could say goodbye, she hung up. I turned back to Tolzer with a sigh. "She'll be here tomorrow." I cringed at the thought of the prepping I was going to have to do with Mary that evening. "I'm going to be asking most of the questions, you understand." I held up my hands as if to say, Don't shoot the messenger. "It's the way she does it. She's eccentric that way."

I didn't think Tolzer was going to buy it, but he did. "Whatever. As long as she's here to make sure that you don't screw up the interview."

Megan, as if on cue, entered the room. Had he signaled her somehow?

"Mr. Lazzaro is leaving. Show him out. But first, give him a fact sheet so he can ask some intelligent questions when he comes back with Betty. Better yet, give him the damned book so he knows what the hell he's talking about."

Megan nodded. "Come back to my office, Mr. Lazzaro. I have some advance copies."

I had no choice but to leave with a sullen, "I'll see you again in the morning."

"With Betty," Tolzer added. I could see he had to have the last word even when he won.

Back in her office, Megan pointed to a stack of three cardboard boxes by her desk. "We received a shipment of books this morning," she said as she struggled with a carton.

I helped her open the box, which contained a couple of dozen hard-covered books. The covers displayed a prominent but Photoshopped picture of the doctor. *The Enhanced Westport Diet with Miracle Kopi Berries* was in gold letters. Megan held out one of the books.

"I'm sure he'll want to sign it," I said with more than a bit of sarcasm in my voice.

Megan smiled. "He may seem a little self-centered, but actually, he's very caring."

I was about to make a wisecrack when we heard a loud crash. What now? I thought. Turmoil seemed to be commonplace at the Westport Diet Institute.

Megan dropped the book from her hand and dashed down the hall. I followed. A dapper man with a mane of white hair poked his head out of the office across from Tolzer's.

"Mr. Richardson, what was that?" Megan shouted.

We all ran into Tolzer's office to find him sprawled on the floor by the antique scale. My first thought was that Tolzer had fallen off. A dizzy spell? Heart attack? I immediately began giving him CPR.

"Call 911," Megan shouted at Richardson. "I'll get Dr. Lang."

I looked up long enough to see her bolt from the room. I continued the CPR, but Tolzer was not responding. Still, I didn't stop until Megan returned with a balding man in a lab coat.

"I'm a doctor," he announced as he nudged me aside.

I stood by Megan, who had a look of terror on her face. Richardson, too, looked as if he were in shock.

Dr. Lang checked for a pulse, then worked on Tolzer a bit longer. Once more, he checked for a heartbeat. Finally, he stopped and looked up at us. "Dead," Lang said.

Chapter Three

"No!" Megan cried. I gave her a gentle hug, and she buried her head in my shoulder. The first EMTs were entering the room, and we moved off to the side.

Megan stood with her hand to her mouth. Tears welled in her eyes while Dr. Lang and the paramedics did their thing.

"Let's go back to your office," I said. "You don't want to watch this."

I tried to edge her away, but she pulled back.

"Don't tell me what I want to do. I want to stay." I backed off, not wanting to frustrate her more.

"Of course," I said.

She also refused the chair I brought over for her. She stood there, never taking her eyes off Tolzer's body. Helpless, I turned my attention to the paramedics. One of them was moving aside the toppled antique that Tolzer had said nobody but him was to touch. I recalled that Dr. Tarnower's lover had shot him dead. At least Tolzer escaped murder.

All I could think of was that Tolzer lived by the scale, and he died by the scale. I snickered at the stupid pun in my head.

"What are you doing?" Megan seemed perturbed by what she perceived to be my disrespect.

Embarrassed, I looked away. That's when I noticed Menu cowering under a cupboard. I got down on the floor and coaxed him out. Whatever happened in Tolzer's office must have scared the poor fellow out of his wits. I scooped him up and handed him to Megan.

"He can sense Dr. Tolzer is dead," Megan said. Then she tried to tell the frightened feline that everything would be all right. I don't think she believed it herself. Menu twisted and struggled in her arms until she let him jump down. Then he darted back to his hiding place.

A few minutes later, the police arrived, led by Sergeant Nina Estevez. She raised her eyebrows when she spotted me but otherwise didn't acknowledge me. The fact was that we had been in a relationship.

"What happened?" Nina asked.

Richardson, the man with the white hair, spoke up as if Nina had directed the question only to him. "I was on my way to Dr. Tolzer's office to confer with him when I heard a crash and ran in. He was on the floor. I yelled for help. They arrived a short time later." He nodded toward Megan and me.

We had all gone into the office at the same time, but there was no point in making a big issue out of it.

Nina was stone-faced. "I take it that's Dr. Tolzer they're working on."

"I told you who he is," the man said. If he thought his condescending tone was going to intimidate Nina, he didn't know who he was dealing with.

"You said it was Dr. Tolzer's office. You didn't say who was on the floor. And you are?" Nina took out a pad.

He seemed almost insulted that she didn't know. "Stephen Richardson. Dr. Tolzer's attorney."

I noticed a fleeting change in Megan's expression. I suspected that Richardson was more than an attorney at the Westport Diet Institute. I made a mental note to ask her about him later.

As the paramedics put Tolzer on a stretcher, I chimed in. "I gave him CPR while Megan ran for help. I kept it up until the doctor got here." My voice almost cracked. "He wasn't responding."

Nina gave me a look that told me I would have my turn when the time came. She turned to Megan, who was watching the paramedics' every move. "You must be Megan."

"Yes. Megan Hawkins. I'm the assistant director here."

"I see." Nina wrote in her pad. "And I do know this is Mr. Lazzaro."

Mr. Lazzaro. So, this was Nina Estevez in police mode. I'd never seen this side of her. She was all business; as well she should be. She turned back to Richardson. "You came here to talk to Tolzer about what?" Nina said.

"I didn't come here. I was about to go to his office to talk to him. My office is across the hall. What we had to discuss is irrelevant."

I could tell Nina didn't like the answer or the tone of it. "I'll decide what is relevant. Are you saying your office is at the institute?"

"I'm on the board of directors as well."

The paramedics wheeled Tolzer out with Dr. Lang close on their heels. It surprised me that they didn't even cover his face. I wondered if that was something they only did in the movies. I tried to stand in Megan's line of sight, but she moved to watch. I don't think she believed the doctor was dead.

Nina turned to Megan. "Where were you when the incident occurred?"

In a shaky voice, she said, "Mr. Lazzaro and I were in my office." She then told how we heard the crash, ran down the hall, and when we saw the doctor on the floor, she ran to get Dr. Lang. "I'm guessing that was the doctor who was working on him." Nina eyed Richardson, almost daring him to challenge her choice of words. Then she looked around. "Where did Dr. Lang go?"

"He went out with the ambulance crew," I volunteered. I knew she was wondering what I was doing at the Westport Diet Institute, so I offered up the information. "I'm here to do a preliminary interview for Betty's column. I had a brief conversation with the doctor."

She didn't seem impressed. "Did he look sick when you spoke to him?" Her question to me was almost an afterthought.

"He was fine."

"No complaints?"

He had plenty of complaints, but not about his health. I wasn't about to get into that. "He didn't say he felt ill. In fact, he ate his lunch a little while before. He even offered me some cannoli."

The mention of the pastry seemed to surprise her.

"Dietetic, I suppose," Nina said.

Megan became a bit defensive. "It was his only vice," she said.

That I doubted. But then, it wasn't my place to judge.

Nina still wasn't finished with me. "So as far as you could see, he was healthy."

I shrugged. "Yeah, he seemed okay. He did become agitated when he took a call from someone named Lucky. Getting upset like that can give someone a stroke or a heart attack."

Nina paused, then wrote something on her pad.

"You're not a doctor, Mr. Lazzaro." The Mr. Lazzaro thing was getting old.

"Still, there was something about the call that bothered me," I said.

"Such as?"

"I don't know, I'm not a cop either."

Nina gave me a look that could burn down a house. Then she went on. "So, you were interviewing him, and he keeled over with no warning?"

Nina knew that wasn't the case. Was she trying to trick me or test the others' stories? If she'd thought there was anything suspicious, she would have separated us for questioning. She almost seemed to have an ulterior motive.

"As Megan told you, we were in her office when it happened."

"I see," Nina said with more than a little sarcasm.

A skinny blond cop who looked straight out of the police academy called her to the overturned scale. He was holding Tolzer's shirt on a pencil.

"Cooper's a rookie," she said as if that explained it all. "You can go," she said to me.

It was only then that I realized Dr. Tolzer had on an undershirt but no dress shirt when we found him.

"I have to track down Dr. Lang, and then we're finished here," Nina said.

"I'm going to stay with Megan," I said.

"I guess you didn't hear me, Mr. Lazzaro. You can go." Her tone said I didn't have a choice in the matter.

I gave Megan my cards, both my business and my personal, and said, "Call me if you need anything. Anything at all."

As I left the office, I could hear the rookie cop.

"All the buttons have been ripped off," he said.

Chapter Four

I wasn't happy about how Nina dismissed me. Between the shock of Tolzer dying and Nina's rebuff, I was pretty hassled by the time I got to my car. As I drove away, I thought of how our friendship had cooled ever since she made sergeant on the police force.

With a good part of the day shot, it made no sense to go into the On-Topic offices in Manhattan. I decided to work from home instead of driving all the way down to the city.

First, I needed to decompress. If anything can calm me down when I'm over the edge, it's pushing my '68 Camaro to its limits. The car belonged to my brother, Jerry. I was born in 1980, five years after he went missing in Southeast Asia. I've lived in his shadow my whole life. My father entrusted his car to me when I was a teenager, with the warning that I had better take care of it.

I held the car back until I got onto I-95, then opened it up as I headed east with no destination in mind. Despite the semi-heavy traffic, I felt like I owned the road all the way to Fairfield, where I exited onto Black Rock Turnpike. Every once in a while, the crazy fact that Tolzer had died out of the blue minutes after I'd talked to him surfaced in my mind. I shoved it aside by losing myself in the exhilaration of the ride. I headed east when I got to the Merritt Parkway, a beautiful ribbon-park highway that extended from the New York line. I was passing under a WPA-era art deco bridge when a bulletin came over the radio.

"Just in, diet guru Dr. Alan Tolzer is dead, the victim of an apparent drug overdose."

So, it began: the media circus that comes with the death of someone of stature. I should have predicted the hoopla, but labeling Tolzer's death a drug overdose caught me off guard. Did Nina come to that conclusion after she dismissed me?

If the media had the story already, Mary was sure to hear. The only good side of the situation was that I wouldn't have to prep her this evening on how to pose as Betty. I decided I should call her and let her know what was going on. I passed a sign that read phone in one hand, ticket in the other, which made me think twice. The last thing I wanted was a $500 fine.

"Call Mary Ticarelli," I said to my Bluetooth.

The call went into Mary's voicemail as I expected. This time I left a message.

"Mary, it's Quincy. The interview with Dr. Tolzer is off."

With that, she picked up the phone. As I suspected, she'd been screening her calls again.

"No kidding, it's off. He's dead! They cut into my soaps. What did you do...off him?"

"Of course not.'

"You sure? I don't go for that stuff."

If I ever have to go to court, remind me never to have Mary take the stand as a character witness.

"All I know is one minute he was alive, and the next minute he was dead. As dead as the interview I was going to do with him." The truth was that I felt cheated out of the interview, heartless as that may seem.

"What are you going to do about it?" Mary asked.

Was she serious? "What can I do? I'm on my way home to figure out how I can fill the column. I'm thinking of writing a tribute or something."

"That's all? It's not good enough."

"Do you have a better idea?"

"Gotta go, I'm missing my stories. We'll talk when you get home. I'll save you some parmigiana. I used the eggplant from my sister's garden." She hung up without another word.

As I approached the entrance to the West Rock Tunnel, my phone rang again. I whipped off my sunglasses, then turned on the phone.

"Listen, Mary. I appreciate you helping me with the recipes and all. God knows I can't cook, and if it weren't for you, there would be no 'Cooking with Betty,' but I have to handle this one on my own."

There was silence on the other end. Did she finally realize the truth? As I approached the end of the tunnel, I threw my sunglasses back on. At about the same time, my phone came to life again.

"Who's Mary? Is that you, Quincy?" I recognized the voice of Amy, the recipes editor at *On-Topic Magazine*. Crap. "Where are you? Your phone keeps cutting out. All I caught was 'Mary' and you can 'handle something.' "

"Sorry. I was going through a tunnel. Forget it. What can I do for you, Amy?"

"Listen, Quincy. There's a problem with Betty's tiramisu recipe. It's too complicated. I've asked you a thousand times to tell her that the steps need to be short and logical. Assume the readers are dummies. We want our dummies to have success with the recipes. I'm going to have to send it back to her for a rewrite. And please, Quincy, from now on, have her list the ingredients in the order they're used. She's a great cook, but her writing style drives me nuts. I don't know what the story is, but I'd love to meet her to tell her myself. Meanwhile, I know you have her ear." I heard Amy chuckle at what I took to be a reference to the boy toy rumor. "Talk to her, will you?"

"Right. I'll do that. I'll have her get a simplified version to you tomorrow. Later."

After that close call of blowing my cover, I was willing to promise her anything. I didn't need another problem with the column. The tiramisu recipe was one of Brooke's. So much for sweet revenge.

Chapter Five

Amy's call reminded me that I should be working instead of joyriding. I got off the parkway, crossed over the bridge, and got back on the other side heading west, eventually getting off in Norwalk. When I got to my apartment building in the gentrified section of town that we call SoNo, for South Norwalk, I tried to sneak into my apartment, but I heard Mary's door open behind me. Caught. I tried to divert her attention. "You wouldn't happen to have a tiramisu recipe?"

Mary chose to use her selective hearing to ignore the question.

"How did he die?" She pulled me into her apartment. She brought me into her kitchen and put a plate of baked eggplant layered with cheese and tomato sauce in front of me.

"I don't know. He was old, I guess." I caught a glimpse of her gnarled fingers and wished I could have taken back my snarky comment. "It was probably a heart attack."

"Well, that doesn't look good for a diet doctor—to die of a heart attack."

"I guess not."

"Of course not. My cousin Lucy can vouch for that."

"What does your cousin have to do with it?" I shoveled some of the eggplant into my mouth. It was delicious.

"Everything. She had a catering business that she ran from her kitchen to make ends meet. Her husband, Charlie, was a gambler; he never worked a day in his life. He died in the chair."

"The electric chair?"

"No, the kitchen chair. He was eating dinner. So, she dragged him outside and put him in a lawn chair under the grape arbor before she called for help."

"Why would she do that?"

She gave a wave of her hand as if I were a fool not to understand. "People talk! If they found out he was eating dinner, right away they'd say ptomaine. End of business." She slapped her hands in an up and down motion as if they were two cymbals.

It almost scared me that I got her point. I expanded on her scenario. "So, if it turns out that Tolzer died of a heart attack, you think there will be a cover-up."

She heaped more parmigiana on my plate. "You said it. I didn't. Now prove it one way or another."

It took a moment to process what she suggested. It was true that critics of the diet have said it wasn't heart healthy. Even the announcer on the radio mentioned that. "So, what if he got a heart attack from the diet. It has nothing to do with me," I said.

"It has everything to do with you! What if there is something wrong with the diet? Other people, innocent people, could die. I thought you wanted that column your boss has been holding over your head. If we prove Tolzer was killed by his own diet, that column is ours, guaranteed. We save some lives, and we get a better job. Everybody wins."

We? This was not headed in a direction I was comfortable with. "Mary, we've got to talk."

"Right. We'll—how do you call it—brainstorm. First, we have to get hold of his medical records."

"Whoa. We'll do nothing of the sort. First of all, that's not legal. And second, if I do look into this, I'm going to do it myself."

As I stood up to leave, I could see the hurt look on her face. "But we're partners."

"On 'Cooking with Betty, yes. This I've got to do alone. The investigative reporting column, if I get it, is going to be all me."

"It's both columns or none."

She must have thought I was going to back down. I indulged my own sense of selective hearing. "I've got to take Dexter for a walk. We'll talk later."

I got my door open and went into my apartment without asking again for the tiramisu recipe. I would work on it myself. I'd show her that I could cook and handle the investigation on my own.

Dexter flung himself at my ankles, then rolled onto his back for me to scratch his stomach. At least someone was glad to see me.

I won my little buddy, a cockapoo, half cocker spaniel and half whatever, in the divorce. Brooke wanted him because she fancied him a designer dog, but I argued that I was the one who rescued him from a shelter and had kept him fed, walked, and totally spoiled ever since. The victory wasn't without cost. She got the house, the better car, and half of what's vested in my pension if I live long enough to retire.

When he saw me reach for his leash, he jumped on the footstool so I could put it on him. Everything is on Dexter's favorites list, but walking is number one. I had arranged for Mary to take him on walks during the day. When he wants to go out he uses his doggie access and goes across the hall to scratch on her door. I was sure he had been out several times, but I still took him for a run in the dog park.

As Dexter played with a couple of other dogs, I waved to two women and a guy who seemed to be the other dogs' owners. I didn't join them but went to the far side of the field. I had a lot on my mind. First, Tolzer dies. Having failed to revive him sucked, not to mention that my deadline was coming. I'd needed Tolzer's interview as much as he needed "Cooking with Betty."

Next, Nina blows me off. What was with that? It was almost as if she resented me being present when the doctor died. Truth be told, I would rather have been someplace else. Then Amy rejects the perfectly good tiramisu recipe. Now, Mary was giving me grief because I wanted to do my job as I saw fit. What is with people?

"Your dog made a mess." One of the women in the group called over to me.

"My dog?"

"Afraid so." She pointed to the poop bag holder on the fence.

I got a bag and went over to where she was pointing. There were at least four piles of crap in the area. I don't think Dexter goes that much in a week. I picked up the pile that I thought might be his. The woman pointed, and I picked up the rest.

"Thank yooou!" she said in an exaggerated motherly tone as I threw the poop harvest in the trash can.

Her sarcastic "thank you" made me recall Tolzer's reprimand when I touched the Tarnower scale. It also reminded me of the picture I took of the pill that was on Tolzer's food tray.

I went on my smartphone and found the picture of the tablet stamped with the code AJP 254. Then I logged on to a drug index site. I entered the code in the search box. An image of the little white pill popped onto the screen. What I assumed was a supplement turned out to be a medication called Digoxalis. It was a trade name for digoxin, a drug used in the treatment of heart failure and atrial fibrillation. I guess the good doctor did have something to hide. I wondered if Megan could shed any light on what else the doctor was taking. Good grief! I was beginning to think like Mary.

Dexter and I walked back home, my mind filled with questions. I tried to push them aside for the time being, knowing the dreaded tiramisu recipe hung over my head. I had procrastinated working on the column long enough.

I psyched myself into believing that with all the insane events on my mind, tackling the tiramisu problem on my own would be a welcome distraction. I decided to try the recipe and see what was so complicated. All I had to do was follow the steps—kind of like a chemistry formula. How hard could it be to simplify a recipe? What was Amy's problem? She always had an issue with Betty. It was almost as if she were testing. I wondered if she was starting to suspect that Betty didn't exist.

I climbed on a stepstool to reach the top kitchen shelf where I kept the recipe box I "inherited" from Brooke. When she threw me out, she put everything she didn't want in a storage unit and sent me the bill. Most of it was junk, but the recipe box was in there. I assumed it was her way of telling me I was never going to have a home-cooked meal again. If it wasn't for Mary, that might have been true.

I looked through the cards in the box until I found the one with the recipe that I had submitted to Amy. It called for an obscene number of egg yolks. Plus, it required sugar, espresso, rum, ladyfingers, chocolate, and mascarpone. What the hell was mascarpone? I looked it up online and found that it was Italian sweet cream cheese. Huh?

I hated to ask Mary if she had any of the stuff, but I didn't have much choice. No place in my neighborhood sold something like that, and I was too tired to take a ride to the grocery store in the shopping center on the outskirts of town.

I went across the hall and knocked on Mary's door. No answer. She's a little hard of hearing, so I banged harder.

"Mary, are you in there?" I knocked again.

"Yeah, yeah, I'm here." I finally heard from inside.

"Come in. I'm on the phone." I opened the door and peeked in.

"Shame on you! Shame on you! I may be old, but I'm not crazy." She slammed the phone.

No, she was not. Mary may be a pain in the neck at times, but no way was she crazy. "What's going on?"

"Some guy said he was from the bank and he needed my social number. My friend Eleanor got caught like that. Gave the guy on the phone her social number, and they cleaned her out. The woman down at the bank said they have all the information down there. Don't give your number to anybody."

"I thought you were screening calls."

"I didn't have my glasses so I couldn't see the number. I thought it was my daughter."

"Mary.,,"

"Yeah, I know. You're sorry. Don't worry about it.

We'll make the best of it."

I wasn't sure what she meant, and I was afraid to ask.

"Not mad then?"

"No. Here have some anginetti. I made them last night." She pushed a plate of cookies at me.

I couldn't resist and popped one of the sprinkle-covered mounds into my mouth. "Actually, I was wondering if you had any mascarpone. I'll pay you back." As I spoke, cookie crumbs sprayed over the table.

"You need mascarpone? What are you making? A bruschetta?"

"No, a tiramisu."

Mary let out a shout that could wake the dead.

"Tiramisu!"

"That's right. You like it?"

"Naw, I hate it. I don't like cake with rum anything. Napoleon? Forget about it! Give me my rum in a glass."

"So, you don't have any mascarpone."

"I didn't say that. Wait a minute." She headed toward the refrigerator and came back with a round plastic container. "You want a sandwich? Sit down."

Did she forget that she stuffed me with eggplant parmigiana a few minutes before? "I'm all set."

"I just got some fresh cold cuts."

"No, no. Thanks for this." I held up the tub of mascarpone. "I gotta go."

I don't know why, but every time I visit over there I start sounding like I come from New Jersey.

Chapter Six

When I got back to my place and opened the container, I found that it had only a spoonful of the pudding-like cream cheese. I tasted some. It was smoother and sweeter than I thought it would be. All right. Now that I knew what I was dealing with, I'd have to make do with what was on hand.

I went to the refrigerator and found two vanilla pudding snack-packs, clearly marked sixty calories per serving. Out of curiosity, I checked the nutrition facts on the mascarpone container. Sixty calories per tablespoon. The pudding worked for me.

I studied Brooke's recipe. Beat six egg yolks with four tablespoons of sugar in a mixer until thick. Again, I looked through the refrigerator; no eggs. But I did find a tub of Cool Whip topping, ten calories per tablespoon. That sounded better than raw eggs. I emptied the two packs of pudding into the mixing bowl. Then, using one of the empty containers to measure, I added an equal amount of the whipped topping to the bowl.

"Next step, next step," I said to myself. Dexter wagged his tail.

Add one tablespoon of cooled espresso to the mixture and set the rest of the espresso aside. Damn. I hadn't read far enough ahead. I hadn't made the coffee. As it happens, espresso is one thing I do know how to make. It was a family tradition to have an espresso after meals when I was a kid. I also knew it took time for the machine to build up steam. Since I was in a hurry, I made two cups of instant espresso while the pudding and topping blended in the bowl. By the time the mixture got to be thick and fluffy, about five minutes later, the water was boiled and the coffee made. I cooled a small amount by putting in an ice cube and threw it into the mixture along with four spoonfuls of sugar. What the heck, I threw in two more sugars. I let it mix for a while longer. So far, so good. Next step. Put the remaining espresso in a bowl and add two tablespoons of rum.

I got the bottle of rum from the bar. Empty. Now what? I marched over to Mary's place once more. When she called me in, I found her on the phone again. I rushed over and put out my hand. She handed the receiver to me, and I shouted into the phone.

"Listen, you jerk. Stop bothering this woman, or I'm going to find you and beat the crap out of you." I listened. I handed the phone back to Mary. "Your daughter wants to talk to you."

She told her daughter I was "a little nuts" because I saw someone die, then she hung up.

I cleared my throat. "I was wondering if you had a little rum," I said to her in a sheepish voice.

"So, you were drinking! My daughter thought so."

"No, I'm making tiramisu, remember?"

"Tiramisu. I love it. It's my favorite. But I don't have any rum. Try some coffee brandy. Hold on, I'll get it for you."

"But the recipe calls for rum."

"Listen, you see one tiramisu, you've seen one tiramisu. There are thousands of ways to make it." She handed me a bottle about a quarter full. "Try this. You'll like it." She held her thumb to her forefinger and made a little twist by her cheek. "Ummmhuh!"

Back at the apartment, I threw a shot glass full of the coffee brandy into the espresso, then threw in another for good measure. Then I took a shot for myself.

I read the next step. "Dip the ladyfingers into the espresso mixture and then lay them on the bottom of a small baking dish." Ladyfingers? It occurred to me that real cooks gather all the ingredients together before they start to cook. Lesson learned. I thought that was a good hint to give my readers: always read the recipe all the way through before you start.

I knew damned well I didn't have any ladyfingers in my apartment. I grabbed the next best thing, Twinkies. I cut several in half longways. Then I dipped them in the espresso and coffee brandy mixture and proceeded to lay them on the bottom of the pan. Next, I spooned a layer of the pudding and whipped topping mixture over the Twinkies. Then I put down another layer of Twinkies and another layer of pudding. I topped it all off with a helping of miniature chocolate chips. Voila!

Chapter Seven

When I got to bed at 1:30 a.m., I felt satisfied that I had simplified the tiramisu recipe and cooked something on my own. It looked good, and it tasted pretty good too. Although at that point I didn't care.

The next morning, I fell out of bed at six-thirty. Five hours of fitful sleep is not enough, but there was no use in lying in bed. I had an interview at the Westport Diet Institute scheduled for nine. I wasn't going to miss it even if the interviewee was dead. I wanted to look deeper into what killed Dr. Tolzer because something didn't feel right.

Sally's is a luncheonette not far from the railroad station in SoNo. My routine is to have breakfast there, then hop on the train for my schlep into the city. The place is almost part of my DNA now, so I take breakfast there even when I'm not going into Manhattan.

It was about seven o'clock when I walked through the door. Sally poured my coffee, light and sweet, before I even sat down.

"Egg whites on dry whole wheat," she called into the kitchen.

I'm not a healthy eater by choice, but I try to make up for it by having a sensible breakfast. I picked up the heavy restaurant mug and took a gulp. The world came into better focus.

"I need that to go," I said to Sally. "And I'll have a glazed doughnut while I wait."

Sally looked at me like I was mad. "You've had the same breakfast every day for two years. You have to do something to make up for all the other crap you eat. You sick or something?"

"No, I found an escape clause." I looked at my coffee cup. "You ever hear of civet coffee?"

"Nope."

"What about Kopi Luwak?"

"I don't know from Kopi Luwak, but something tells me you've gone wacky."

I waved her off to enjoy my doughnut.

"Hey, guess who's working today?" Sally beamed.

"Newme?"

If you Googled the word proud Sally's picture, as she looked at that moment, would come up. "Bingo! She's home from school for a few days, and she's helping me out."

When her daughter was born on her birthday, Sally joked that the baby was a "new me," and the name stuck. As smart as her savvy businesswoman mom, the child was now pre-med at Yale.

Newme, who looks like a twenty-five-year-old newer version of Sally, waved and put my doughnut on the pass-through.

I'm not ashamed to admit that I wolfed it down. As I licked the sugar off my fingers, I glanced at the newspaper a Brooks Brothers dude at the next table was reading—*The Hour*. On its front page, right beside the headline "Porsche Crashes into Norwalk Home: Rowayton Hose Company Responds," was another: "Diet Guru Dead." I borrowed the paper from Brooks Brothers with an "Excuse me, can I see something quick?"

Dr. Alan Tolzer, whose best-selling Westport Diet became a multimillion-dollar business, died unexpectedly on Monday. Tolzer was found in his office by one of his staff. Attempts by his personal physician, Dr. Bernard Lang, to revive him were unsuccessful.

According to the medical examiner's office, Tolzer's death was due to natural causes. There are no specifics yet on what health conditions the seventy-four-year-old icon suffered. The death is causing a stir in the diet world. Supporters are mourning the loss of an innovator in the nutrition field. But Westport Diet detractors are speculating that Tolzer was suffering from complications of heart disease. They are using the incident to reiterate their contention that the diet is nutritional madness. It has long been said that the high-protein/high-fat diet is not heart healthy.

"To my knowledge, Dr. Tolzer did not have heart disease. Any conjecture is irresponsible," said Stephen Richardson, spokesperson for the Westport Diet Institute. No further details were available at press time.

That article had more holes than the ozone layer. Richardson lied when he denied that Dr. Tolzer had a heart condition. If I knew for a fact that Tolzer was on heart medication, how could Richardson not have? And Dr. Lang had to know. What was that lawyer trying to hide with his spin on the story? I gave the newspaper back and went over to check out the news rack.

"For Whom the Bell Tolzer" proclaimed the Daily News. "The Skinny on Diet Doc's Death" cried out the Post. Despite the colorful headlines, both papers had the same basic Associated Press story. But the News added an unconfirmed report that the doctor had taken an overdose of some yet unknown drug. The Post went one better. They suggested the doctor was found naked, his clothes scattered about the office. I gave the guy CPR and knew for a fact that he had on a t-shirt and pants. I remembered Cooper, the rookie cop, holding up Tolzer's dress shirt on the end of a pencil. But the doctor was hardly naked. What had Cooper said? "The buttons have been ripped off." Still, suggesting the doctor died after a drug-induced mid-afternoon sex orgy was preposterous.

The implication that there was more to Dr. Tolzer's death than indicated by the official line was a problem. I had to get moving before someone else broke the story. I looked toward Sally, who caught on that I was getting impatient.

"Newme, get a move on Quincy's breakfast before he pops a blood vessel." Sally is far from subtle.

I whipped out my phone and looked up the difference between the symptoms of an asthma attack and a heart attack. To my surprise, I found they were similar. They both included chest tightness and shortness of breath. I looked up, and Sally was standing over me.

"Here ya go, egg white sandwich on whole wheat and a light and sweet coffee. Enjoy."

She handed me a brown bag like a mother sending her first grader off to school. I almost expected a Batman Lunch Box.

As I headed for the door, Nina walked in.

"It's like Old Home Week. First Newme, now you," I said.

Nina locked her chocolate eyes on me as she caught my sarcasm. "I've been busy," she said. "Besides, I saw you yesterday."

"Oh, so you did recognize me. I would have never guessed it the way you dismissed me."

"I had a job to do," she said.

I met Nina the first day I walked into Sally's for breakfast. That was a little after Brooke threw me out. After the divorce, I welcomed conversations with the opposite sex without emotional entanglement. As time went on, breakfast took longer and longer. During the day, I found myself making mental notes of things I wanted to share with Nina the next morning.

The fact that she was a cop was my pretense, for a long time, for not asking her out. I was afraid she would be Brooke with a badge. But over time, I saw that as an excuse for not getting involved. The friendship continued for six months before I got up the nerve to ask her to dinner. The reality was that I was ready, ready to get involved, ready to trust—at least to an extent.

Nina and I still date once in a while, but our daily meetups at Sally's ended with her promotion to sergeant. The increased duties of supervising a squad of detectives and her drive to make lieutenant made her too busy for a daily get-together. On my part, if I were to be honest, I was pulling back a bit too, because I was afraid that she was more into her job than me. Sometimes growing apart is the only way to preserve a friendship.

I wanted to ask her why doing her job didn't include suspecting a cover-up, but I didn't. That would only lead to an argument. Then she'd ask me why I felt that way, and I'd have to tell her about everything I saw going on at the Institute. If there was a story there, I wanted it to be exclusive. I didn't see it as withholding information if she didn't ask. I'd get the police involved when the time was right. I held up my bagged meal and forced a smile. "Gotta go," I said.

Chapter Eight

No office today, so I headed in the opposite direction from the train station to where I had parked my car. As I walked, I called the Westport Diet Institute. It was only seven-thirty, but as I thought, Megan was there. "Are you all right?" I asked.

"Yes, I'm fine," Megan said in a strained voice.

Fine she was not. At least over the phone, she didn't sound as though she were. "Are you sure you're okay?"

"Yes. I told you. But I have to get out of here. I shouldn't have come in today. It's all very upsetting."

I opened my car door and sat in the driver's seat. "Want to talk about it? I'm a good listener."

As I started the engine, I could hear her fighting to keep control, her breath coming in short gasps.

"Maybe it would be a good idea if I talked to someone. Would it be possible for us to meet for coffee? Someplace away from here."

Fine. I wasn't looking forward to that passed-through-a-rat's-ass coffee they drank at the Westport Diet Institute anyway. I could talk to Richardson and Dr. Lang later. "Tell me where and I'm on the way."

"Do you know where Common Grounds in Westport is?" she asked.

I had never been there, but I'd heard that Common Grounds served excellent coffee and pastries. That worked for me. "On Main Street, yeah. I'll see you there in about fifteen minutes," I said.

I never did tell her that I intended to visit the Westport Diet Institute to get interviews for a tribute to Dr. Tolzer. I'm glad I didn't. I realized how insensitive that was. Megan was suffering a tragedy, and I was only concerned about the deadline for my column. That and learning about how Dr. Tolzer died.

I decided to take my chances with the traffic on I-95 instead of going on the surface roads. It was not a good move, and I should have known better. An accident choked up the highway. It was a good half hour before I arrived at the modest coffee shop in Westport's tony town center. I found Megan sitting at a rear booth in the cafe. She looked pale. I almost put my arm around her but thought better of it.

"Nice place," I said for lack of anything more intelligent to say.

She gave a halfhearted smile. "I had to get out of there."

I'm glad she felt she could talk to me, even though it had been years since our Sachem Creek connection. At first, we made uneasy small talk, trying to avoid what was on both of our minds. I decided to let her bring up the subject of Tolzer's death when she was ready.

I asked her what had been going on in her life since I last saw her as a kid. I learned that her parents had died. I was sorry to hear that. I remembered them as nice people when they rented from my father. Soon, we couldn't avoid the subject of Tolzer's sudden demise any longer.

"I can't believe he's dead," she said.

"Did he have any health problems?" I asked.

"Not that I know of." She'd hesitated long enough for me to be suspicious of her answer.

"It could have been a heart attack. You sure he didn't have something wrong with his heart?"

"As I told you, there was nothing wrong with him that I know of."

That made sense. If Tolzer was hiding that he had heart problems, he would have kept it from most of his staff. I pressed on. "It wouldn't surprise me if he had a stroke. He was pretty worked up over that situation with Jeanette. What was that all about?"

"He didn't like her for some reason. Jeanette can be pretty abrasive at times. They never got along," she said.

That was a laugh. Like Tolzer wasn't abrasive. Still, that was something Megan should have known about. Maybe she was trying to be professional and keep confidentiality. If that was the case, I had to admire her for it.

Tears formed in Megan's eyes. I was handing her a napkin to wipe them away when the waitress came to take our orders.

"You all right?" the waitress asked Megan as she gave me a sideways glance.

I shifted in my seat, hoping she didn't think I was the cause of Megan's crying.

"I'm fine. I'll only have a coffee, please." She turned away and wiped her eyes.

I could understand her loss of appetite. I had wolfed down Sally's sandwich while I was driving, and it was sitting in my gut like a bowling ball. Still, I felt it wasn't right to take up space at a table instead of sitting at the counter to have coffee. I glanced at the menu and ordered the first thing I spotted. "And add a tiramisu to that, please."

Megan wrinkled her nose at my odd breakfast choice.

"I'm not going to eat it," I said. "I only want to look at it."

I remembered that a look had passed over Megan's face when Richardson told Nina that he was Tolzer's lawyer.

"I'm willing to bet that the spokesman mentioned in the paper was Mr. Richardson, the guy who was with us when we found the doctor."

"Yes, Dr. Tolzer's attorney."

"He seems to be more than that. How does he fit in with the organization?"

"Stephen Richardson is the organization. He's a slick New York lawyer with a background in public relations and advertising. Many years ago, Dr. Tolzer started what he called The Norwalk Diet Institute. He founded it on the philosophy of eating the basics. The business got into financial trouble, and he was about to lose it. Then he met Mr. Richardson, not long after 9/11.

Part of Canfield Island is in Westport, so Mr. Richardson convinced the doctor to capitalize on that town's more stylish image by changing the institute's name. With Richardson's help, the Westport Diet evolved into what it is today."

This was interesting stuff that I could use in the tribute. "How so?"

"He got the doctor to modify the diet by adding exotic foods and expensive supplements so it had snob appeal. The doctor didn't like it at first, but he agreed as long as the foods were natural."

"Let me guess, then Richardson got Ponds to endorse the diet, and the rest is history."

"That's about right."

"I imagine you know Ponds."

"Very well. He's always at the Institute for meetings."

"You like him?"

"Oh yes, he's wonderful. He gave me a free membership to his tennis club. Why do you ask?"

"I heard him getting fired yesterday. It seems he has a bit of a temper." Megan looked puzzled.

"I don't know anything about that," she said. "Are you sure he was fired?"

For being an assistant director, Megan didn't seem to know much about what was going on at the Institute.

"As sure as I can be. I heard it as it happened."

"Well, you seem to know more about what's going on at Westport than I do. Why are you asking so many questions?"

"I'm only trying to get a handle on what made Dr. Tolzer tick so I can give him the tribute he deserves."

"You're writing the tribute, or Betty is?"

I thought about taking her into my confidence and giving up the whole charade but decided against it.

"You know what I mean. It's a tribute in Betty's column. As I've said, I gather the information. What about Dr. Lang? How does he fit in?" I played with a blue packet of sugar substitute, trying to suppress my anxiety about making such a stupid slip.

"He's also on the corporation's board of directors."

The waitress chose that moment to come to serve my tiramisu. This version of the dessert was in a tall glass so you could see the layers of ladyfingers and mascarpone. Topped with raspberries and cocoa, it looked delicious. I could smell rum… rather than coffee brandy, combined with the espresso. I understood what Mary meant when she said that if you've seen one of these desserts, you haven't by any means seen them all.

"That's great," I said to the waitress. I had no urge to even taste it after last night, and besides, I had this morning's doughnut right up to here. "You can take it back."

"What? There's a problem?" The waitress gave me the you ordered it, you eat it look. She must have been somebody's mother.

"No. No problem. I only wanted to see what it looked like. You can take it back. Leave it on the bill."

The words *damned right I'm going to leave it on the bill* went unspoken as the waitress turned on her heels and headed back to the kitchen with the tiramisu.

I got back to the subject at hand. "You were telling me about Dr. Lang."

"His name is Bernard Lang. He works in research at the Institute, and he is—was—Dr. Tolzer's physician."

For a split second, she seemed to struggle a bit, but the moment was fleeting, and she kept it together. I was glad she did. She went on. "Dr. Tolzer brought him in recently to do research and tweak the diet. But I'm pretty sure the two doctors have known each other for years. They may even have been partners years ago. Dr. Bernie is a sweetheart." I didn't quite know what to make of that statement.

"That's cool," I said.

"He's one of those people you can talk to. He like really listens if you're having a bad day. You know?"

I nodded and said, "Yeah, kind of."

"And he's not a complainer. He hasn't had it easy. His wife is in a wheelchair, and he takes care of her, and I never heard him cry, *'Oh poor me.'*"

I could tell she wanted to tell me something else.

"Is there more?"

"Do you know what bothers me? Mr. Richardson only seems to care about what will happen to the company. When he buzzed me in this morning, the first thing he did was call me to a meeting with him and Dr. Lang. He said we have to carry on as if Dr. Tolzer were still here. He even wants to do the 'Cooking with Betty' interview in Dr. Tolzer's place. All he wants to do is push the book. I can't stand how heartless that is."

From what I'd observed of the business world, Richardson's actions may have been callous, but they weren't odd. "I know where you're coming from, but the thing is, corporations live on without the founder. Like Disney without Walt. I don't think Dr. Tolzer would want all his hard work to go down the drain. Right?"

"I guess so."

"Tell him there's going to be a tribute to Dr. Tolzer in the column anyway, so an interview with him would be most welcome."

"If you say so."

"Okay then. Agreed. You know, I have a question about something I read this morning. Was the doctor being treated for asthma?"

Megan closed her eyes for a second as if she were trying to think. "He may have been. I believe Dr. Tolzer had an inhaler, but I never saw him use it. Dr. Lang was so angry that Mr. Richardson put that information out there."

"So, Lang didn't think it was ethical."

"Of course not. Their voices were getting loud. That's why I was so glad when you agreed to have coffee. I had to get out of there."

The sadness in her voice made me wonder if the relationship between Dr. Tolzer and Megan was more than a boss/employee association. Lovers? It wasn't my business, but I hoped not. Tolzer had been at least forty-five years older than her. But hey, like I said, not my business.

"Now that Tolzer is dead, who do you think will take over as head of the Institute?"

"It's always been understood that would fall to Mr. Richardson."

I wasn't surprised at Megan's answer. But I was surprised by her answers to my next line of questioning.

"Do you know of anyone named Lucky that Dr. Tolzer might have known?" The call that upset the doctor so much was bothering me.

"No. Not that I recall."

"That's too bad. I was hoping you could recall a strange character that had been around." I laughed to myself when I realized how ludicrous that statement was. The Westport Diet Institute was crawling with strange people.

"I don't know his name, but there was a man around yesterday I didn't know." I could see the tenseness in her face.

"Who?"

"I told you, I don't know. The doctor was talking to him outside on the lawn yesterday morning before you arrived. I had gone into the office with some files the doctor had requested. When I didn't find him there, I went to the window to see if he had stepped out. Sometimes he likes to get fresh air out on the lawn. I saw him through the window talking to this man. The man hadn't signed in. I would have known if he had, so I don't know how he got on the grounds."

That made me think of Jeanette, who had slipped onto the property. Security at the Westport Diet Institute seemed lax at best.

"Getting past the gate doesn't seem all that difficult. Tell me about this guy."

"I'd say he was in his late thirties, on the short side but built like a weightlifter. You know, wide shoulders like the top of his body belonged to someone taller. He almost reminded me of an ape. His hair was reddish and cut really short like a brush.

"Were they arguing?"

"I don't know. It wasn't my place to interrupt, so I didn't go outside. I left the files on the doctor's desk and went back to my office."

"Did you tell the police about the man in the yard?"

"I didn't see any reason to. What would he have to do with the doctor having a—with the doctor having an asthma attack?"

Was it my imagination, or had she almost said a heart attack? The more we talked, the more I was convinced that something didn't fit. If Megan was going to tell me anything more, I'd never know because I got a text message. As I glanced at my cell, Megan picked up the menu and began to peruse it.

The message was from Archie. It said, *Contact me.*

"I have to go." I touched the menu so she would look at my face. "Are you going to be all right?"

"Everyone doesn't have to keep asking me that. I can take care of myself." She drew in her breath and let it out. "I'm not going back to the Institute for a few hours. I decided to stay here and order breakfast after all."

"Good. I'll call you later to see what time I can meet with Richardson."

I threw the money for breakfast on the table. As I headed for the door, I punched in Archie's number. It rang only once before I ended the call. I walked back to Megan's table.

"That file you put on Tolzer's desk. What was it?"

"It was research on the kopi berry supplement that is going to be such a big part of the revised diet."

"I just realized something. These kopi berries…is that like kopi in Kopi Luwak?"

"Kopi means coffee, so they're the coffee berries that surround the coffee bean."

No kidding. Coffee beans come from berries. I thought I knew it all. "I'd like to get a look at that file."

"You can't. It wasn't on the desk this morning. I looked in the files, and it's not there either. Somehow it's gone missing."

I nodded. I had to get out of there. "I'll talk to you later," I said.

She took my hand. "Why did this have to happen now? He was going to release a new book. He had everything going for him."

That was my question. Why?

Chapter Nine

I was so involved with processing what I had learned that I walked a block past my car before I realized what I had done. I would bet the guy Megan saw with the doctor on the lawn and the person named Lucky who phoned Tolzer were the same. Something in my gut told me if I found him, I'd have a big story.

I heard with my own ears that Tolzer had given Lucky money, and the mystery man was looking for still more. This led me to the conclusion that Lucky was blackmailing Tolzer over the cover-up of a heart problem.

I decided not to get back to Archie right then. I knew what he'd say. Seeing a pill and Megan's almost saying the words heart attack didn't prove the doctor had a bad ticker. And if I couldn't prove that, I couldn't prove that Lucky was blackmailing Tolzer. The only thing that I knew for sure was that I had to find Lucky.

When I got back to the car, I turned to Nina for help. I called her cell as I got into the driver's seat. She picked up right away.

"What is it, Quincy?"

Caller ID takes away the entire element of surprise.

"Do you have a minute?"

"I'm at work, make it quick."

"I'm doing a story on the death of Dr. Alan Tolzer."

"Branching out on your own?"

Once again, I felt a twinge of guilt for not letting Nina in on the secret that I was posing as Betty.

"You might say that. I was hoping you'd be able to help me get some information."

There was a pause on the other end of the line. "What kind of information?"

"A short, muscled type with red hair visited Tolzer a few hours before he died. I was thinking you could let me look at some mug shots to see if I could put a name to him."

There was another pause. When she finally spoke, Nina's voice was flat. "Where is this going?"

"He may be the same guy who called Tolzer. Remember? I told you Dr. Tolzer got a call from someone named Lucky, and he got all bent out of shape. I want to see if there's a connection."

"You're still on that kick that the call from this guy caused Tolzer to become ill?"

"Yeah. That or something else."

If Nina's voice was flat before, it was emphatic now. "I am not going to talk about an investigation."

"So, you did think of it."

"Don't put words in my mouth, Quincy."

"But I only want to get a name for the mystery guy."

"Listen to me, the Norwalk police are very competent. Leave this to us."

"So, I can't count on you for help?" I asked.

"Not even for a second. Word of advice: don't play detective."

Then there was silence on the other end. It took me a bit to realize she had hung up. I started the car and headed toward the highway.

I'd been relying on my friendship with privileges with the most promising sergeant on the Norwalk Police force. Now it was clear those privileges didn't include inside information. Fine. I would rather do it on my own, anyway.

As I drove down I-95, my cell phone rang. I answered with Bluetooth and heard Archie's voice.

"Quincy, I've been trying to get you. You didn't answer my text. Is the column ready? Quincy, are you there? Did you drop the call or something?"

"I'm here, and I can hear you. You don't have to shout."

"How did the interview with Dr. Tolzer go?"

Didn't Archie read the papers or listen to the news?

"Alan Tolzer is dead."

"Holy crap! You offed him? You were only supposed to get an interview."

"Not funny, Archie. There is something fishy going on. I'm looking into it."

"Fishy how?"

"I'm not sure."

"Whatever it is, don't go getting involved. Think about 'Cooking with Betty.' If you put yourself in the spotlight, it's bound to come out that you write the column. If my father finds out there's no Betty, he'll see to it that I never work again! Or you either."

True to form, he was only concerned about himself. If I hadn't yet made up my mind to dig into what caused Tolzer's death, that statement did it.

"Nobody will find out about Betty."

"And what about your deadline?"

"Don't worry, you'll have a column. Instead of the interview, I'm working on a tribute to Tolzer. I'll have it in by Monday. But I'm also going to look into how Tolzer died."

I could imagine Archie reaching for his giant bottle of hand sanitizer and rubbing his hands raw as we spoke. "Make sure you get that column in and keep Betty out of it, or we're both in deep shit."

"You know what your problem is, Archie? You think too much. Listen, I have a file on Tolzer from when he did his first book. It's on my office computer. I labeled it Tolzer Research. I should have put it in my Dropbox, but I never got to it. Send it to me. My password is."

Archie gave an audible sigh, which came over the phone loud and clear. "Super Dude."

"How did you know that?"

"We all know it. It's the office joke. Everyone uses your computer when they don't want to pick up a virus on their own machine."

What the hell. "Just send it, Archie."

"I was on the way out when you called," he said. "I thought I told you I had an appointment. Maybe I didn't. I'll get it to you sometime after lunch. Give me a couple of hours."

Archie wanted the column yesterday, yet he couldn't take a minute to help me out. The guy is a real piece of work. Now he expected me to wait around for him.

When I got home, I went straight up to my apartment. Dexter wasn't there. I try not to be a helicopter guardian, but I like to know what he's up to. Our floor has a small library. He often goes down there to visit with the tenants. I found him sleeping in front of the fireplace next to a cat. Knowing he was safe, I let them be.

I tried to sneak back to the apartment before Mary saw me. I had work to do.

"You're looking for me?"

Caught. "I uh no. I was checking on Dexter." I pointed down the hall toward the library.

"So, you decided to let sleeping dogs stay that way."

"He's fine."

Mary waved me off. "Don't play dumb. You know what I mean. You don't care about what killed that doctor any more than the Man in the Moon. If you did, you'd be out there trying to find out if they're covering something up."

I should have told her to buzz off, but she'd gotten me so ticked that I spilled everything I learned that morning. It was my way of showing her I wasn't slacking off.

"I thought this story would write itself once I proved there was a cover-up of Dr. Tolzer's health problems. Now this mystery man shows up. I don't know which lead to follow."

"Follow the rabbit."

Here we go again. I knew I was in for a story. But experience has taught me that as convoluted as Mary's anecdotes can be, they usually make a good point. "What rabbit?"

"My cousin Dolly was in the woods hunting mushrooms, and what runs by? A rabbit."

"So, she shot it?"

"No, she didn't have a gun. But she followed it. Do I have to explain everything to you?"

"Look, I have to go."

"Hold on. She follows the rabbit, and what does she find?"

"Her husband was in the rabbit hole with the next-door neighbor?"

"What are you, a sicko? She finds more mushrooms than she ever dreamed of. It goes to show, sometimes you get sidetracked, but it brings you where you want to be. Find Lucky. You won't be sorry."

My phone rang. "I got to take this." I headed back to the apartment.

"Follow the rabbit!" Mary called after me.

It was Megan on the phone. She said Richardson would see me in two hours. Archie still hadn't sent me the file, so I figured it would be a good time to channel some of my energy into working on the novel.

I opened my laptop at the kitchen table and stared out the window as it booted up. My apartment is only one bedroom with a kitchen that opens to the living area, but it has a nice view of the river. The rent is a little more than I'd like to spend every month. But I figure now that I'm doing well with the column, I deserve to live well. Especially after Brooke cleaned me out in the divorce. I missed Sachem Creek. But SoNo was halfway to Manhattan, which made it convenient to both work and visit my friends at home. Besides, Mary depends on me to help her out with different little errands she can't handle herself.

I heard Dexter come in through his access door. I guess he had had enough of the cat. He sat at my feet. I was itching to get to work, but first I checked my inbox for messages, hoping for one from my literary agent: none. I got up and went to the kitchen to get a cup of coffee from a pot I had made earlier: cold. Back at my computer, I checked Facebook: what a time suck. Then I checked the inbox again: still no message. I resisted the temptation to check Facebook once more. Instead, I opened the file labeled "Work in Progress." The screen filled with the first of forty-five thousand words of my baby, *Killer View*. It was almost halfway finished. If I could only find the time to work on it. I navigated to my "left off" bookmark and re-read the pages I wrote last time.

My protagonist, Mark Adams, was trying to solve the murder of the richest and most hated woman in Stony Creek, a town I patterned after Sachem Creek. When I left off, three elderly denizens of the local barbershop had come up with a suspect list to "help him out." They had everyone in town on the list, including the protagonist. The problem was I didn't know any more than they did. I had no idea who committed the murder. I had written myself into a corner.

Then a brilliant idea hit me. No sooner did I put my fingers to the keyboard than the doorbell rang. I bit my lip and went to answer it, never expecting to see the Ice Queen, AKA my ex-wife, Brooke. I had forgotten that she was coming to get Dexter. Her niece, Michelle, who is the only person I like in my ex-wife's family, was going to take Dexter for a two-week training program. She's going for her Ph.D., and she's doing experiments with reading therapy dogs. Her theory is that if kids with reading problems have a dog to read to, they can improve their skills because dogs are nonjudgmental.

I've read Dexter parts of my novel, and he's fallen asleep every time so I'm not sure if he's the best candidate for that job. But hey, if it helps Michelle out, I'm all for it. Besides, I thought it would be good for Dexter to get out of the apartment for a while.

As soon as the dog saw Brooke, he headed for the bedroom. She thinks I've tried to poison Dexter's mind by talking badly about her, but that's not true. Dogs may not be good judges of writing talent, but they're excellent judges of character.

Brooke was still wearing her tennis outfit. I wondered if she had been on the courts with Rob. Robert Chase is her tennis instructor and lover.

Brooke shoved a copy of *On-Topic Magazine* in my face.

"What's this?" she demanded.

"You shouldn't wrinkle your forehead like that. I'm no longer paying for your Botox. And it's a magazine."

"The magazine your boss writes for. You, you stinking boy toy!"

"So, what of it?" I flexed my bicep to irritate her.

"She put my cookie recipe in her column. You son-of-a-bitch! You gave her my grandmother's chocolate chip cookie recipe. My recipe."

I had been wondering when the merde was going to hit the ventilateur. In fact, I was a little surprised that it took her this long to catch on. Wasn't she a regular reader?

"Betty didn't claim it was hers. She said someone gave it to her. A lot of people make those cookies."

Was I nuts? I was referring to myself in the third person and the opposite gender. But I couldn't let Brooke find out my secret. If Archie Monahan were here, I'd kick his ass from here to Cordon Bleu for getting me involved in the column in the first place.

"Don't give me that. I know she got it from you. I can't find my recipe box. Do you have it?"

"I have whatever junk you put in that storage bin. There may have been a recipe box in there. Besides, you copied all those recipes into that new book."

"I want it back."

"Why? Like I ever saw you cook."

"It's mine, that's why. Give the recipes back."

"Listen, I didn't ask you to put my things in storage while I was at the gym and then have some ox of a moving van driver drop off the keys to me in the locker room. Do you know what he said to me in front of all the guys? 'Don't bother going home. This is where your stuff is.' Talk about childish."

I was getting pissed thinking about how the goon handed me a card with the address of the public storage shed.

"To top it off, he said, 'Your wife said good luck with the novel. Have a good day.' Then he handed me a bill for the first six months of storage. If I have your recipe box, which I'm not saying I do, then you owe me for storage."

She rolled up *On-Topic* and tapped me on the chest like a bad dog.

"Fine. Be like that. But I hope you get so fat on those recipes that you need a gastric bypass. Then your slutty boss can feed you soup with a teaspoon."

"Hey. Watch what you say about Betty. If it weren't for her, I wouldn't be able to pay your alimony."

Dexter started whining in the bedroom.

"See. You upset him," she said. "Give me his things so I can get him out of here and away from you for two weeks."

I packed Dexter's duffel bag with his toys and favorite snacks and handed it to Brooke.

Brooke picked up Dexter, made a point of looking me up and down, and finally rested her eyes on my crotch.

"Boy toy my ass!" she said.

I looked her up and down in return.

"I suppose a roll in the hay for old time's sake is out of the question."

"You're damned right it is." She slammed the door on her way out with my dog.

She was beautiful when she was mad. I tried to remember what my brilliant idea for the book was but couldn't. I went back to the computer and shut it down.

Chapter Ten

I still had an hour before my appointment with Richardson. But having the patience of a Sumo wrestler in a buffet line, I hopped in my Camaro and headed to the Westport Diet Institute.

When I hit the button on the call box at the gate with the big WDI logo, I could hear the surprise in Megan's voice.

"Oh, it's you," she said through the intercom.

What did she mean by that? "Caught you at a bad time?"

"Not at all." She buzzed me in. When I got to her office, she was all apologetic and asked me to have a seat. "I'm sorry. It's just that I'm surprised you're here. I was going to call you. When I reminded Mr. Richardson that you were coming, he wanted me to confirm that Betty would be here also."

I should have seen that coming. "I didn't say anything about Betty being here. She has a booked schedule."

"But Dr. Tolzer had an appointment with Betty for 9:00 a.m. this morning."

"Mr. Richardson isn't Dr. Tolzer, so it's all good the way I see it." I screwed up my face trying more for funny than sarcasm.

My attempt at charm seemed to go over her head. "But he gave me orders to make sure. He may insist on seeing her."

Menu came from out of nowhere and jumped on my lap and began kneading my thighs. At least someone was happy to see me.

"Well, that's not how she does things. I've explained that a dozen times. Besides, she's not available. She left town this afternoon, and her orders to me were to get the facts so she could write the interview. "I'm here, she's not. Does he want the interview?"

Richardson wanted to use Betty's column for damage control. Similar to how Tolzer wanted to use it to push his book. That's the nature of the business. I was willing to go along with it to get information from him. I was pretty sure he would see me, and I wouldn't have to go through the hassle of having Mary stand in for Betty.

"All right. Let's see what happens." Megan picked up the phone and called Richardson's number. He didn't answer.

"You're a little early. I'll try in a while," she said.

Menu was still on my lap and enjoying the attention I was giving him. He started pushing one paw, then the other against my stomach. "How's this guy doing?"

"Like the rest of us, he's trying to adjust. Cats mourn, too. He's been a little skittish, but he seems happy to see you." Megan picked up the phone and again tried to call Richardson. When he didn't answer, we went looking for him. Menu followed us.

First, we went to Richardson's office. Megan knocked on the closed door to make sure he wasn't there. No response. I glanced at Dr. Tolzer's office door and recalled all that had happened. I never spoke to the man before yesterday and wasn't very impressed by him. Yet, I was now determined to find out if someone was covering up the real cause of his death. I wanted to try the door and peek in, but before I could do so, Megan led me down the hall.

"Most likely, Mr. Richardson is still in the gym," she said.

Sure enough, we found him on a treadmill. Megan reintroduced us, telling him I was Betty's assistant. Richardson stayed on the machine.

"Where's Betty?" he barked after she left.

Here we go again. "I do the legwork and gather the facts. Betty will write it up. That's the way she works. It was okay with Dr. Tolzer." That last statement was a stretch, but Megan wasn't there to call me on it.

I didn't want to give the impression that I needed the interview. I walked over to a nearby barbell. I looked at the weights: Three hundred pounds. I bent my knees, grabbed the bar with an overhand grip, and with a deadlift brought it waist high. Pretty good for a guy of 180 lbs. I guess all that time in the gym that Brooke resented so much paid off. I put the bar down. Richardson didn't seem impressed by my explanation or my showmanship.

"That's not the way I work. Tolzer was too easy with the press. And everyone else, for that matter."

Menu let out a loud meow. I wondered if he was agreeing or disagreeing with the lawyer's statement. The Tolzer I met didn't seem to be too easy on anyone. I executed another deadlift as he spoke. "No problem. We don't have to do the interview. Thanks for your time." I had to be careful not to overplay it. I wanted the chance to wheedle any information he had about Tolzer's death out of him.

I put the bar down and was about to turn away when Richardson heaved a sigh and shook his head. He seemed to remember that he needed me, or at least "Cooking with Betty," for his damage control plan.

"All right, I guess it doesn't matter. Go ahead. The important thing is that Betty doesn't sensationalize this unfortunate incident."

Unfortunate incident? I know Tolzer wasn't the most likable person on earth, but even Scrooge must have gotten more sympathy when he died.

"So, okay then. It will be a fair story; no more, no less." I looked him square in the eye to show him I wasn't intimidated.

Richardson smirked, showing me that he wasn't intimidated either.

"Let's get on with it then. I have a lot to do after I finish here," he said.

I started with a noncontroversial question. "On a personal level, what is your reaction to Dr. Tolzer's death?"

"We were friends as well as business partners. I was up all night trying to get a handle on what happened to Alan, and I can't," Richardson said.

"Being so unexpected, I can understand that it would be eating away at you." I regretted the words as soon as they came out of my mouth. "I wasn't trying to be flippant. Honest."

Richardson wasn't buying my apology. "Mr. Lazzaro, I was hoping this interview would lead to an article highlighting all the good Dr. Tolzer did for the world of nutrition over the decades. He was the first to advocate a nutritional approach to treating diabetes. Nobody talked about bioflavonoids before him, or antioxidants, or vitamin C, or B-complex. How about choline? And don't forget, people laughed when he said artificial sweeteners are a health hazard. Now it's common knowledge. Fish oil? He was the first to tout its benefits. I could go on and on."

"If you send me details about those, I'll be sure they're mentioned in the column. I have to ask, though, besides the tribute, aren't you also hoping to push the new book?"

"I'm not going to lie to you. I'm hoping Betty's piece will mention Dr. Tolzer's new *Enhanced Westport Diet with Miracle Kopi Berries*. It's the crowning star of his legacy. I'm also hoping she'd say that his work of saving lives with the diet is being carried on here at the Westport Diet Institute. But if you won't pass on that information to her, I don't see how that will happen."

"I have no problem with forwarding that information. But I do have a few more questions." I had questions all right, and they all weren't about the book.

"Dr. Tolzer indicated to me there were going to be some changes. Could you shed some light on what he was referring to?"

Richardson considered for a moment. "Some changes were made in the diet. It is always being fine-tuned. As you know, the new book is about the kopi berry supplement that has been added to the diet."

Talk about not being forthcoming. He knew that wasn't what I was asking. This guy wasn't going to give up any information without a fight.

"Could you be more specific?"

"I'm not at liberty to divulge any more information without approval from the board. That's as specific as I can get."

He was the board, and the board's lawyer for crying out loud. Well, I could get more specific, but first I'd back off a bit.

"How is the kopi berry supplement made?"

Richardson wiped his face with a towel hanging on the treadmill. "That's not my department. Dr. Lang is in charge of research and development."

"From what I gathered yesterday, Dr. Lang was also Dr. Tolzer's physician."

He nodded. "They were old friends and worked together from before

I became involved in the Institute. Then their careers went in separate directions for a while."

"So, you were the new kid on the block."

"Not at all. I suggested Dr. Tolzer bring him in. Dr. Lang's research skills and reputation were impeccable. We needed the best talent available. The two doctors had gained a reputation for their great work in the past. I convinced them that it would be in their best interest to work together again. Is this interview going to make it into the next 'Cooking with Betty' column?" I could see where his priorities were.

"Absolutely."

"And *The Enhanced Westport Diet with Miracle Kopi Berries*. Don't forget to mention *The Enhanced Westport Diet with Miracle Kopi Berries*," Richardson said.

"If you don't mind my saying so, aren't you afraid it's going to sound a little callous on your part to push the book?"

"Let me worry about that. Dr. Tolzer would have wanted it that way." He was wearing his lawyer's smile, and he became animated. "Look, I'm giving your boss a scoop. Nobody at the Institute is talking to anyone else in the media. Don't look a gift horse in the mouth. What else do you need to know?"

Okay, since he started it, I did have some more questions.

"There are all kinds of rumors going around. Has the exact cause of death been determined?"

Richardson studied my face, never breaking stride on the machine. "Officially no."

"What do you think it was?"

"I know a little bit of the doctor's medical history, and I'll tell you off the record, the doctor did have a touch of asthma. He was also under a lot of stress lately with his heavy work schedule. I'm sure you know how asthmatic attacks can be brought on by stress. I believe he ignored the signals because he was busy. I think it's safe to say that Dr. Tolzer felt the message of *The Enhanced Westport Diet with Miracle Kopi Berries* was so important to the public that he gave his life for it."

Asthma. What a crock of crap. "So, the rumors that the doctor had heart disease were false?"

He eyed me with suspicion. "Absolutely."

"But wasn't he taking digoxin?"

Richardson's face paled, which isn't easy for someone with the complexion of snow. He stopped the treadmill. "I don't know where you are getting your information."

I tapped my temple to show that my questions were my own. "I read on the internet that digoxin is for regulating the heart. What was it called?" I pulled a paper napkin from my pocket, the only thing I could find to write on when I looked it up. "Arrhythmia. That means irregular heartbeat. Am I right? So, I thought if the rumors that he had a heart condition were true, then he might take digoxin. And if he was, there was the possibility that he overdosed."

Richardson laughed. "You pulled that out of thin air, or worse yet, off the Internet? You know what they say, a little knowledge is a dangerous thing. Only an idiot would get medical information online. You're searching, and I don't have time for games. But know that as the attorney for the Westport Diet Institute, I won't allow rumors that are detrimental to the corporation's good name."

Was that a threat? Richardson was lying. Still, I wasn't going to say that I took a picture of the pill on the doctor's lunch tray; at least not yet.

"So how would you explain the doctor's actions?"

"I don't know what was going through Alan's head. I do know he was passionate about the benefits that the Enhanced Westport Diet would bring to the public."

He turned the treadmill on again, even faster than before; in no time he was running at a fast clip.

"Oh, and one more thing. Is it true that you'll become the new director of the Westport Diet Institute now that the doctor is dead?"

He shut off the treadmill and lurched to the floor. I thought he was going to explode. His face became red as a stop sign.

"If you're implying that I had anything to do with Alan's death, you'd better have some solid proof."

"It seems to me you will receive some direct benefit now that Dr. Tolzer is out of the way."

"That's ridiculous. The company would make much more money if Dr. Tolzer were still alive to run it. But since he's not, I'm going to do my best to do damage control and save what I can. Dr. Tolzer was struggling to build the Institute when we met at a seminar. He was a genius when it came to his storehouse of nutrition knowledge. But he was a bad businessman, and even worse when it came to matters of law. If it weren't for me, there would be no Institute today. The doctor and I worked too hard to let the company fail now."

Gee, the guy was all heart.

"Did the doctor have any enemies?"

"Everyone has enemies. I'm sure you do. But no." He paused. "Everyone loved Alan."

"That's not the impression I got."

Richardson looked both confused and annoyed. "I don't understand where this is coming from."

"There were at least three people who had a problem with him while I was here, so I was curious."

Richardson spread his hands as if to say he didn't know what else to say to that point. "What else do you want to know about the book?"

"Nothing else. Dr. Tolzer gave it to me after someone named Lucky called. That's when he stopped the interview saying that he had to deal with a problem."

I looked for his reaction to the name Lucky, but it seemed to go right over his head. "What does Lucky do here anyway?"

"We don't have anyone by that name working here."

"Dr. Tolzer mentioned paying him. I thought he was an employee."

"You must be mistaken. I know everyone who works here, and there's nobody called Lucky."

"I guess I heard wrong. At any rate, I'd like to talk to Dr. Lang."

"Lang? What for?"

"I want another perspective on the future of the diet. I mean, if Dr. Tolzer did die of heart disease, it might be a public relations nightmare. Wouldn't you say?"

He brushed my comment aside as if it were a crumb on his tie. "I would say you have an active imagination, Mr. Lazzaro."

"Are you saying that it is not a possibility?"

"Do you know what, Mr. Lazzaro? I believe you enjoy stirring the pot."

"It's my job, Mr. Richardson."

"It's also a good way to get scalded."

Chapter Eleven

Richardson didn't seem happy about it, but he told me how to get from the gym to Lang's office in the research wing. I didn't doubt that after I left, he rushed to call Lang to warn him that I was coming. When I arrived at Lang's door, he was just hanging up the phone.

Dr. Lang didn't seem surprised when I appeared in his doorway. He invited me into his office, which had an IKEA feel to it. I remembered Tolzer's office had been decorated befitting a CEO. I hadn't seen Richardson's. I wondered if it was more like Dr. Tolzer's or Dr. Lang's. When I explained that I was Betty's assistant. Unlike Tolzer and Richardson, Lang did not say that he would rather talk to Betty. In fact, he was quite cordial.

"I understand that you were here interviewing Alan before his tragic death," Lang said.

"That's right. Betty Ann Green was going to do a piece on the *Enhanced Westport Diet*. I was here doing a preliminary interview. I believe that she'll use the space allotted for the interview for a tribute to Dr. Tolzer instead. I was hoping you could give me a statement that I could pass along to her."

At that, Lang screwed up his face. For a minute, I thought that he was going to cry. Maybe I got the wrong first impression when he pushed me aside and announced he was a doctor. He seemed much more human today, now that he wasn't in a crisis. I diverted my eyes to the diplomas on his wall: Yale University School of Medicine 1978, Johns Hopkins 1983, among others.

"I'll be glad to give you a statement. I think he would have liked the idea of a tribute," he said.

"Great. Then, on a personal level, what is your reaction to Dr. Tolzer's death?"

"This is still very difficult for me. Alan and I were like brothers. Beyond that, he was a pacesetter in the diet world. It will be decades before anyone of his caliber will come along again." Lang looked as if he wanted to say something else. He paused for a moment. "I must thank you for your efforts until I got there yesterday. There really was nothing more that either one of us could have done."

That was good to hear from a professional. He seemed really sincere about it. I could see why Megan liked him better than Richardson. Still, compliment or not, I had to go on.

"I heard you tell the police that he died of natural causes. Could you be a little more specific?"

Lang stared at me for a second.

"I really can't talk about that."

"Of course not. I didn't mean to put you on the spot. It's just that some people out there think he died of heart disease."

"I don't know how to respond to that statement."

"Of course. I mean, he was healthy, right? I'm just saying."

"I just told you, I'm not going to talk about a patient's health history. I couldn't even if I was so inclined. I'm sure you know that."

"Right. Confidentiality. I understand. It's just that I was talking to Mr. Richardson about the rumors that the doctor had heart problems and how he may have overdosed on digoxin. I was wondering if you thought that might be an explanation."

"I'm surprised at Richardson, but I suppose he can say things as Alan's lawyer that as his physician I cannot. I'm really not about to speak to you about a patient. HIPAA, you know?"

"No. No. Those are my questions. I didn't mean to imply that Mr. Richardson gave me that information. Actually, he told me that the doctor died of an asthma attack." *But thank you very much for just about confirming that Tolzer was taking a heart medication.* "You're right. That did cross the line of confidentiality," I said. "Moving on, would you say that the diet is safe?"

My pointed question didn't seem to rattle Lang. He responded in a very calm voice.

"Oh yes, it's very safe. It's helped countless people to lose weight. Back in the '70s, the government came out with the notion that fats are bad, and people started to avoid them. So, what's happened in the ensuing fifty years? People are fatter than ever."

"Losing weight and being healthy are two different things. What about the effects of fat on the heart?"

"New data comes out every day that fats are essential for a healthy body. And not speaking specifically about the doctor's case, but in general terms, I could say with confidence that sometimes the correct diet can help a person with a medical problem survive long past his life expectancy."

"I only met him the other day, but I found him to be… quite a character." I didn't want to say that I thought he was crazy. I thought it best to move on to a different subject

"Dr. Tolzer told me some changes were going to be made to the Westport Diet. Would you care to elaborate?"

That brought Lang to life.

"Changes. Yes, we are planning to make a few subtle changes to the diet. You have to stay fresh in such a competitive market, or the next latest thing will make you yesterday's news."

"Are kopi berries part of those changes?"

"Most definitely, a kopi berry supplement is being added. It will revolutionize not only the diet but the whole diet industry."

"How does the supplement work?"

"This is a very competitive business. Unfortunately, we have to be very careful about releasing sensitive information, you understand. But I can say that I found that there are certain enzymes in the pulpy berry that surrounds the kopi bean. I take it you know the process by which Kopi Luwak is made."

"Picked out of the crap of a civet; yeah, I heard."

"Exactly. Some of the pulp clings to the bean after it is expelled from the civet. I found that pulp after being exposed to certain enzymes in the animal is supercharged with antioxidants and other fat-burning properties. I'm sorry I can't tell you more."

"Not a problem. I'm just trying to get a clear picture to pass on to Betty."

I must have gained points by not pushing. Lang seemed to soften a bit.

"I'll tell you what. I'll put together a packet of information about the supplement, leaving out all of the trade secrets, of course, and get it to you. I'm sure Mr. Richardson would agree that we would love to break the story in the "Cooking with Betty" column." I handed him my card.

"That would be great. I'd appreciate it if you'd give me a call when I can pick it up."

Lang glanced at some folders on his desk, giving me the impression that he had work to do. "Is there anything else I can help you with now?

"Just one thing. I heard Dr. Tolzer yelling at someone named Lucky on the phone. Any idea who that is?"

"I don't know any Lucky, and as for the yelling, he could have a temper. The Westport Diet Institute and all that's associated with it isn't easy to run."

"Who'll run it now?" I knew, but I just wanted to see his reaction.

He shook his head. "That's hard to say. Stephen, most likely."

Most likely? That was a surprise. He was leaving some doubt that Richardson would be the new CEO of the Westport Diet Institute.

"What about you?" I tried to make it sound conversational and not as an accusation.

Suddenly, a knowing smile crept across Lang's face, which he made a half-hearted attempt to hide by putting his hand to his chin. He leaned forward in a conspiratorial gesture and spoke in a whisper, even though only the two of us were present. "I'm in charge of research. I like it there. If I didn't, I'd leave."

I got up to go, and my eyes fell once more upon the picture of a woman in a wheelchair.

"Your wife?"

"Yes, Ella."

"I know I'm prying, but I'm curious. Is that a service monkey on her lap?"

"Yes, a Capuchin. She has two of them. You'd be surprised how independent they allow her to be."

"I'm interested because my dog, Dexter, is away for two weeks being trained as a therapy dog. My niece plans to take him to hospitals, nursing homes, and even some schools to give comfort to people."

"Very admirable. I see we share a concern for those in need. The monkeys are a bit more than companions, though; they're trained to perform all of the grasping and turning tasks that my wife's hands can't do.

Chapter Twelve

I left Lang in the research wing. As I headed down a long glass corridor toward Megan's office, my cell phone played George Harrison's "Savoy Truffle." I knew from the ringtone that Amy was trying to get me. I hoped she didn't have another complaint about the tiramisu recipe. I'm getting too old for all-nighters, at least of the working kind. I was going to let it go into voicemail, but I gave in and answered at the last second.

"Listen, Amy, before you say anything, Betty isn't going to make any more changes in that recipe."

"Well, hello to you too. I swear I don't know how Betty puts up with your pleasant personality, Quincy." There was a short pause. "Oh, wait, I can guess."

She broke into giggles. I hate giggles.

"Very funny. I'm tired. I don't have to be nice. What's wrong with the recipe?"

"It's interesting. Twinkies have been getting a lot of publicity now that they have brought them back. People will like it. But that's not what I'm calling about. I was surfing the Internet, and I found some information about Alan Tolzer. I thought you might like to know about it before you turn in your column."

"What is it?"

"For starters, he was born Alphonso Tolzerano in Hoboken, New Jersey, in 1947."

"A lot of people change their names, for all kinds of reasons," I spoke above a whisper, in case anyone was around.

"Right, but most people don't try to pass themselves off as a medical doctor when they're not."

I didn't want to take the chance that anybody might overhear my part of the conversation. I told Amy to hold on and headed for an exit halfway down the passageway. I opened the door and walked out onto the lawn. I waited until I was out of earshot of the building before I said anything else.

"Tell me more, Amy," I said, still speaking in a soft voice as I plopped down onto a bench facing the water.

"People assumed he was a medical doctor because he published under the name Dr. Tolzer. In truth, he held a Ph.D., and his education was nothing like what people imagined. In 1969, he earned a degree from Rutgers University in New Jersey, where his only science course was general biology. He majored in physical education and minored in writing."

"This is all very interesting, but you can't believe everything you see on the Internet."

"Tell me about it. So far, my free iPad has cost me thirty-five hundred dollars. That's why I contacted my friend Denise, who works at the New York State Department of Health. They have a whole file on Tolzer going back to the 1970s."

"And?"

"He started teaching in New York City during the riots of 1970. To supplement his income, he began to write advertising copy for the Au-Natural Vitamin Company in 1972. Are you there?"

"I'm here. Go on,."

"He called himself a nutrition educationalist and hit the lecture circuit even though he had no nutrition or health training."

"None?"

"None. In 1977, Tolzer ran into trouble with the FDA for recommending Au-Natural Vitamin products for various complaints. The FDA said he was diagnosing patients and prescribing vitamins for their illnesses. He got arrested for practicing medicine without a license. He paid a fine of five thousand dollars rather than spend a year in jail."

"This is good to know. I guess there was more to Tolzer than I thought. Go on."

"Tolzer then enrolled in the University of Connecticut. He received a master's degree in education in 1980. After that, he received a correspondence course Ph.D. in journalism in 1985. Although he never took a single course in nutrition, in 1986, he became a chief consultant to Being Well Supplements. That vitamin company ran into trouble with the FDA for misbranding because of false claims for their products. After narrowly avoiding legal trouble in New York, he moved to Connecticut. Then he changed his name and founded the Westport Diet Institute."

"Any more run-ins with the law since?"

"Not since the late eighties. He made connections with the right people, and you know the rest. As he became respectable, nobody questioned if he was an MD."

"I can see that he would want to keep that part of his past secret. Good work, Amy. I owe you."

"Well, be nice to me because if I ever call in your tab, the economies of half the Western world are going to collapse."

I hung up and headed into the building. So, the great doctor had something to hide. The Westport Diet Institute was full of secrets. This new information made me think of that strange phone call the doctor got from the guy he referred to as Lucky. From the side of the conversation, I heard it sure seemed like the guy was trying to shake down Tolzer for money. Could he have been blackmailing Tolzer because of the doctor's sketchy credentials? If Tolzer did have a weak heart, Lucky's call, on top of all the other problems at the Institute that day, could have been too much for Tolzer.

I met up with Megan in the hall outside her office. Menu was walking beside her. When she stopped to talk to me, Menu sat on the floor next to her.

"I'm curious about something. I saw Dr. Lang's diplomas on his wall. Very impressive. But I don't recall seeing Dr. Tolzer's diplomas in his office," I said.

"Some people are prouder of their school than others, I guess."

At that Menu got up and started rubbing against my legs. I knew this marking movement meant he was excited about something. I wondered what he was trying to tell me.

"But it's curious that a man who liked to display mementos wouldn't hang up his medical degrees."

I watched Megan's face. She didn't seem to think my line of questioning was off base.

"Alan was very social. He thought his relationships with others were more important than singing his own praises."

How un-doctor-like. "You did know that Tolzer wasn't a medical doctor, though?"

"I'm not sure I like your tone, but the answer is yes."

"Why didn't you tell me?"

"Because you never asked."

"If I'm going to help, you can't keep information from me."

"I didn't ask you to help me with anything," she said. "Alan was a doctor. He just wasn't an MD. What's the difference? He had a talent for digging out research that had been buried in medical journals for years. He brought it to the public and made it general knowledge."

"Still."

Megan became passionate in her defense of Tolzer. "Still nothing. There's a gap of at least twenty years between the time research is obtained and the medical community accepts the idea. He wasn't practicing medicine; he was distributing important information to the public."

I was about to correct her and say he was fooling the public, but then I realized that I was no one to talk.

I know I could have handled that whole conversation in a better way. I blame it on having so little sleep the night before. I was sorry I said what I did, but I couldn't take the words back.

"It's been a long day. I have to go home," I said.

"Good. And maybe you should stay there." She grabbed Menu up, walked into her office, and closed the door, leaving me to find my way out.

* * *

By 11:45, I was back at my empty apartment. I already missed Dexter. Without my routine of feeding him and taking him for a walk, I had nothing to do but wonder what my next move would be. As far as the police were concerned, Tolzer died of an asthma attack, as verified by Dr. Lang. Most likely, there wouldn't be an autopsy.

Richardson and Lang were denying that Tolzer was on heart medication when I knew that he was. That was proof enough to me of a cover-up of Tolzer's medical history. It also casts doubt on the safety of the diet. Considering Tolzer's checkered past and Lucky's call to him, blackmail was a strong possibility. If Lucky had been blackmailing Tolzer, I wondered if he was now doing the same with Richardson and Lang. There was a story here. I knew it.

I flipped on the TV. The Channel 6 News at Noon was doing a piece on Tolzer. A respected local reporter, famous for her human-interest pieces, was outside the gates of the Westport Diet Institute. As she recapped the details of Tolzer's death, the producer cut to several photos of the doctor with various celebrities. Tolzer would have been proud.

"In an exclusive interview you will see only here on TV 6, we've learned that the world-famous diet guru died of natural causes, an asthma attack."

A clip of Steven Richardson followed. He said the doctor ignored his asthma symptoms because he was so busy with the upcoming release of *The Enhanced Westport Diet with Miracle Kopi Berries*. He said Tolzer, out of dedication to the health of people everywhere, had ignored the advice of his physician. I found it interesting that Dr. Lang was not part of the interview.

"Ask him if the diet is safe. Ask him!" I was shouting at the TV.

She didn't ask. Instead, they cut to a report on all the celebrities, including Jordy Ponds, who had endorsed the diet. Didn't they know Ponds was fired? Finally, at the very end of the segment, they gave a quick mention that the diet had some detractors.

Then the commentator said, "Coming up, a related report from a doctor at UConn Medical Center. Stay tuned."

Damn right I would. I wasn't going anywhere. I couldn't wait for them to get to the meat of the story.

Rather than listen to commercials, I made a quick trip to the kitchen to get something to hold me over until I got to Sally's for lunch. I found only enough orange juice in the refrigerator to fill half of the glass, so I topped it off with Coke. I looked at the orange-brown concoction. It reminded me of one of those health drinks I see people downing at the gym. I took a sip. Not bad; in fact, it was good. Energy plus vitamin C. You can't beat that combination. I should tweak the recipe and put it in the column.

I brought my pre-lunch to the TV as the doctor from the Medical Center came on. I had expected an expert on heart issues to follow up on the lead-in about the detractors of the diet. Instead, with measured words, he spoke about Tolzer's death from asthma. Then he outlined what actions those in the TV audience could use to escape a similar fate. What crap. He had nothing to do with the Westport Diet and most likely never met Dr. Tolzer.

Back in the studio after a commercial, the anchorman read a story about a llama named Bean who had escaped from the Bridgeport Zoo. The energetic animal eluded the Park City police for three days. Channel 6 had hit a new low.

I switched the channel and caught the tail end of a story about a guy who beat up someone in a Norwalk bar. I didn't catch his name, but they flashed a mug shot. If he didn't fit Megan's description of the mysterious visitor to the Westport Diet Institute to a T—buzz cut, ape shoulders, and all—no one did.

I missed his name, and they never repeated it. I went to the station's website, and sure enough, there was his picture and an account of the bar incident. The man's name was Charles "Lucky" Grand. I downloaded the guy's picture to my cell phone.

Now that I had a name and picture for Lucky. I wanted Megan to confirm this was the same man she saw talking to Tolzer on the lawn. I looked at my watch. It was 12:30 p.m. I decided to head over to Sally's for lunch before I went back to the Institute. I hoped Megan wasn't still angry with me.

"You seem kind of antsy this afternoon," Sally said.

"I have a lot on my mind. That's all. This is either going to be a great afternoon or a crappy one. You know what I mean?"

"Not at all. But if you want to tell me about it, I'm all ears."

I looked around the crowded luncheonette. "Not now. A few things still have to fall into place. Did Nina say anything after I left?"

"About what happened with Dr. Tolzer?"

"Well, yeah, that and me."

"She's not going to say anything about you if it involves a case. If you want to know what's on her mind, you're going to have to talk to her yourself."

I let the remark slip. If I told Nina my suspicion that Charles Lucky Grand was the same person Tolzer had talked to before he died, she would only have told me to keep out of it. I ate with one eye on the clock. It was one o'clock.

As I left Sally's, I called Megan.

"Hey, I'm sorry," I said as soon as she answered. I seemed to be saying that a lot lately.

"You should be. Dr. Tolzer was a brilliant man."

"You're right. I misspoke. Friends?"

"I suppose so."

"Good. Listen, I have something important to show you. Is it okay to come down?"

"Sure, it's not busy," she said. "The doctor didn't want…" She took a breath. "He didn't want a funeral. Mr. Richardson and Dr. Lang left for New York at noon. They're arranging a memorial service for next month. I'm holding down the fort in case any clients come in to use the gym."

I was at the Institute in less than twenty minutes. At first, Megan felt relieved when I showed her the picture of Grand.

"Yes, that's him. A bar fight…I had a feeling he was violent." Thank God he's behind bars."

I decided to take Megan into my confidence. "I believe he was blackmailing Dr. Tolzer. I'm trying to prove it."

"Blackmail. Are you still on that kick about the doctor's qualifications?"

I knew I had to choose my words with care.

"Please let me give you a few facts. You saw this Lucky Grand talking to Dr. Tolzer in the morning. A few hours later, I heard the doctor complaining about him asking for more money. Believe me, I'm not judging. But the doctor did have a few things he didn't want to become general knowledge. Perhaps rightfully so. Doesn't that make a case for blackmail?"

"I suppose so. But the doctor is gone. Can't you leave it alone?"

"The doctor passed away, but the corporation still exists. Don't you think the blackmail will continue?"

"Well, thank goodness he's in jail now," she said.

"It was a minor charge. Assault and battery. He won't be in there for long."

Megan had a grave expression. "I'm sure he saw me watching when he was talking to the doctor out on the lawn. I'm the only one who can identify him. I should get a gun."

"No kidding? A gun. Do you even know how to shoot a gun?"

I regretted saying the words as soon as they came out of my mouth. I could tell she resented the insinuation that she couldn't take care of herself. She got up from her desk. "Of course, I can. I used to go to a shooting range with an old boyfriend."

There was resolve in her face. If nothing else, I was seeing a side of her that I didn't know existed. Megan was a woman who didn't rely on others to take care of her. I liked that.

Before she could react, someone came into the office. Megan talked to him for several minutes about his membership. I was getting antsy and needed to get out of there.

"I have a few things I have to do. Catch you later," I said.

The way I understood it, the doctor had asked Megan to bring the kopi berry file to his office. When she got there, he was out on the lawn talking to Lucky. Had the doctor intended to discuss something in the file with Lucky? There was that possibility. I didn't notice the file when I was trying to interview the doctor, but then again, I wasn't looking for it. Megan said it wasn't there the next morning. That meant it disappeared sometime between when Lucky visited Tolzer and then. Could the doctor have given it to Lucky? Had Richardson or Lang taken it? I wanted to check their offices to have a look for myself.

I stole my way down the hall to where the aborted interview took place and tried Tolzer's door first – locked. I looked up and down to make sure nobody was coming. Then I pushed a Borders gift card I carried in my wallet between the latch and the strike plate on the door. I knew that the obsolete card would come in handy someday.

Tolzer's desk looked as I had remembered it: covered with pictures of the doctor and his celebrity friends. I wished I could remember if the file had been on it when I tried to interview him. Next to his desk was the table that had held his food tray and the pill bottle. As I would expect, both were gone.

I hoped that Tolzer at least got to enjoy his cannoli before he died, his escape clause, as he called it. Escape clause indeed. What if someone had loaded the cannoli with something and it became more of an exit than an escape?

That was something to look into later on. Right then, I had to see if I could find that kopi berry file before someone caught me in the office. I looked through Tolzer's desk and file cabinet. Nothing. I was crouched over looking at the lower bookshelf when I felt a touch on the shoulder. I gasped and spun around to see Menu sitting on the counter. If I didn't know better, I'd have thought he was laughing at me. He rolled on his back and showed me his belly.

"Did Richardson take the file?" I asked the cat in a low voice. Menu got up and arched his back. "Yeah, I don't trust him either. But he had the right and every reason to secure anything about the business."

Menu jumped off the counter and walked toward the door. I opened it and looked up and down the hall to make sure the way was clear. Once more, the gift card did its job, this time on the door with Richardson's name on it.

Richardson's office, paneled with exotic wood and furnished in mahogany and leather, reminded me of Tolzer's. Nice to be at the top. I recalled Lang's office looking as if ripped out of an IKEA catalog.

Menu jumped on Richardson's desk. In contrast to the doctor's, it was clear of pictures, thus showing off the fine inlaid leather top. No sentimentality in this office. The guy seemed to be all business. I looked through the files. Nothing on kopi berries. I searched through the top desk drawer. Not quite as neat as the rest of the office, it was the equivalent of the junk drawer in my kitchen. The side drawer was a different story. It was full of neat, ordered file folders. One was labeled Jeanette King. Could that be the same Jeanette who so desperately wanted a meeting with Tolzer?

Inside was one sheet of paper, a letter to the doctor from a Jeanette King dated two days before his death. In the letter, she demanded to meet with the doctor so that they could "come to an agreement." Otherwise, she would have to "seek further recourse." I wondered if that recourse might be murder. Judging from its condition, wrinkled and creased as if balled up and smoothed out again, this letter had made somebody angry. If this was the same Jeanette who wanted to see the doctor a while before he died, it was no wonder Tolzer didn't want to talk to her. I wondered why it would be in Richardson's desk.

I heard people talking in the hall, definitely Megan's voice and another I didn't recognize. As Menu scampered off to hide, I shoved the letter back into the folder and jammed the file into the drawer.

"Fine friend," I whispered.

"Hold on, I have to duck in here for a minute," I heard Megan say.

She walked into the office.

"Oh!" She gave a little jump.

"I didn't mean to startle you," I said.

She closed the door, leaving the other person in the hall. The look on her face told me I was in big trouble.

"I thought I heard something. What are you doing in here?" Her voice was low but harsh.

"I um. Look, I can make up an excuse, but the truth is, I'm looking for the kopi berry file."

"Did you touch anything?"

"Nothing. I just got here."

Her eyes were like slits, and her mouth was set, hardly moving as she continued to speak in the same low tone.

"I'm going to bring that client out there down to the gym. As soon as we leave, I want you out of here.

Understand?"

"Yup."

"I'm beginning to think it was a mistake to confide in you." With that, she was out the door.

That's what I got for trying to lend a hand – the bum's rush. I opened the drawer and noted Jeanette King's address from the letter: 134 Helen Keller Road, Easton. I hadn't been there before, but I knew Easton was a small town in interior Fairfield County. I said the address to myself several times to commit it to memory before placing the letter back in the file. I left the office and headed for the exit.

Megan was walking back as I got to the door. I could see by the look on her face that she still was not happy with my snooping.

"I'll call you," I said.

She didn't respond.

I left.

Chapter Thirteen

I woke up the next morning with my mind racing. Any sudden death without a witness required an autopsy. For now, the police were accepting Dr. Lang's contention that Tolzer died of natural causes due to stress. And Stephen Richardson was giving credence to that theory every chance he got. But hearing of Tolzer's checkered past convinced me that something didn't fit. I was more certain than ever that someone murdered the doctor.

But who had a motive? True, Richardson would become the new head of the Westport Diet Institute. Lang claimed he was happy in research and that he lost a good friend. I wasn't sure if I believed that.

There were still three other people who might have had it in for Dr. Tolzer I hadn't spoken to. Irene White was angry with Tolzer, as was Jordy Ponds, and the woman named Jeanette.

Of the three, Ponds seemed to have the strongest motive for killing Tolzer. The rage in his voice alone when I overheard him getting fired was enough to put him on my shortlist of suspects. Due to his exposure as the spokesman for the Westport Diet, I knew his story well.

After the 2004 Olympic Games, Ponds played professional tennis for a few years. But he never rose to the ranks the sports world had predicted. He had a few mediocre years followed by a couple of bad years. Then he dropped out of the tennis circuit altogether. Reportedly, he turned to food for comfort, ballooning to over three hundred pounds.

He stayed out of public view for a time. He resurfaced when a celebrity blogger found him working at a rundown tennis facility on the Boston Post Road. Outed as an overweight has-been, he went on the Westport Diet, got in shape, and became its spokesperson. Post comeback, he bought the club and transformed it into an upscale tennis center that he named ACE. I decided to talk to him next.

* * *

I had breakfast at Sally's. There, I learned that turkey bacon does not taste the same as real bacon. No matter how much Sally insisted that it did. As I ate, I looked for the hours of Ponds's tennis club on my phone. The website gave everything but.

"Anyone know what time ACE opens?" I said to no one in particular.

"It opened at 5:00 a.m.," Newme yelled from behind the grill. "Like I'd ever go at that time when it's so much more fun to be here flipping eggs."

I looked at my watch; it was seven-thirty. I called to arrange an appointment for a tennis lesson and asked for Jordy. I lucked out: Ponds had a last-minute cancellation at eight, and he could fit me in.

* * *

At 8:05 a.m., I pulled into the parking lot at ACE. I spotted my upstairs neighbor, Fred Simmons, getting into his car.

"I didn't know you were a member here, Man," he said.

"I'm not. At least not yet. I thought I'd check it out."

"It's a great place. I think half of Fairfield County takes lessons here."

I nodded as I saw the On-Topic office intern, Tom Baylor, drive out. I don't think he spotted me. "Yeah, it looks that way. Hey, catch you later,

Fred. I'm running a little late."

I walked into the ACE grand lobby. The place had more marble than a Roman villa.

"Pretentious," I muttered, not realizing how loud I'd said it—or how the marble would make it echo.

The young woman at the desk gave me a quizzical look.

"Excuse me?"

When I told her I was there for a lesson with Ponds, she asked me to sit at a table in the juice bar. I sat away from two women and a guy who were drinking smoothies and talking tennis psychology. One of the women kept glancing my way. I gave her a nod and fixed my eyes on an LCD screen on the wall. It went through several loops, pushing cardio tennis lessons, game analysis, and a tennis social before the desk clerk came. She put some paperwork and a pen in front of me. Five minutes and a three-hundred-dollar charge on my credit card later, she told me I could find Ponds on court eight.

I didn't see Ponds when I heard him getting fired. But his square jaw, intense dark eyes, and wavy brown hair were familiar from commercials. What wasn't evident on TV was that his nose looked like it had been on the receiving end of a tennis ball more than once.

"Welcome to ACE, I'm glad to meet you," Ponds said.

At three hundred dollars for a half-hour lesson, I'm sure he was glad to meet me. This reminded me that one more reason to write a blockbuster story about the Tolzer murder was so that I could write off this lesson as an expense. Carrying on this charade was turning out to be a pretty expensive proposition. I hoped it was worth it.

"So, what are we working on today?" Ponds asked.

"I need a little help with my backhand," I told him as I made a clumsy, slow-motion attempt at a backhand swing with my racket.

"Okay, let's check your backhand grip."

I held the racquet wrong on purpose and had all I could do to keep from laughing.

"Like this?"

"Nope. You have to change your grip for the backhand. Hold it like this."

He held his racket so the space between his thumb and forefinger formed a V on the back ridge of the handle. I did the same.

"Got it."

"Okay, I'm going to hit you a few. Let's see what you can do. Eye on the ball."

On purpose, I hit the ball off into the court beside us.

"Eye on the ball," he repeated. "This time, as you turn, point your shoulder blade at the ball and keep the butt of the racquet in the same direction. Okay?"

"Yup."

He hit me a ball, and I smashed it over his head and out of the court.

"Better. Now low to high. Pivot that foot and bend your knees. Keep your swing horizontal."

"Like this?"

Puck. The ball made perfect contact with the sweet spot of the racquet. My follow-through was a thing of beauty. As well it should be. Tennis is almost a religion in Sachem Creek, and I'd been playing since I was in grade school. I did the same with the next ten balls.

The confused look on Ponds's face almost made me laugh. Finally, he lowered his racquet and walked toward the net. His voice was low but betrayed some anger.

"All right, Mr. Lazzaro. Why are you here? There's nothing wrong with your backhand."

"Everyone can use some work on their backhand. But yeah, there is something else; Alan Tolzer."

Pond's face hardened. "Who are you?"

"An interested party. I want to talk to you about a few things."

"What's there to talk about? He's dead," he said with a cold voice.

"You don't seem all that broken up about it."

"Once more, who did you say you are?"

I explained that I worked for Betty Ann Green, the famous columnist who wrote "Cooking with Betty," and that I did all her pre-interviews.

"A cooking column? When I write a cookbook, I'll give you a call."

He started to turn away.

"That's not what I'm working on now. This is an exposé on Dr. Tolzer's death and the Westport Diet."

That was the first time I admitted to anyone, including myself, what I actually was working on, an exposé more than a tribute.

"What makes you think I'm interested in that?"

"Let's start with you getting fired as the spokesperson for the Westport Diet." His face paled.

"How do you know that? It hasn't even been announced."

I shrugged. "I'm interviewing you, remember? Let me put it this way. This may be the only chance for you to put the record straight. The police are looking into the possibility that Tolzer was murdered."

Yes, that was a bald-faced lie, but sometimes you do what you have to do. I made a note to go to confession.

"Murdered? I didn't hear anything about that."

"You will. Believe me, they're building their case as we speak. Think about it. You get fired by Alan Tolzer, and he dies the same day. If the police decide it was murder, who do you think is going to be the prime suspect?"

"Me? Are you talking about me?"

"You were fired. That doesn't look good. If you can set the record straight before the police question you, it's to your advantage. I know it didn't make you happy to lose the position."

"No shit. I put the Westport Diet and the Institute on the map. Richardson came to me because he needed me, my name."

"Richardson came to you? I thought you went to Westport for help with your weight problem."

"Of course, he came to me. He orchestrated the whole thing. I mean, I gained the weight on my own after the games. And I worked here checking people's passes and giving a few clinics to bored rich people. One day, Richardson came as the guest of a friend. He recognized me. We talked, and we made a deal. He had pictures taken of me working behind the counter. We picked out the most pathetic, and he funneled them to the blogger who claimed he took them with a hidden camera. The joke was that I was in on it from the beginning."

"You posed for the ugly pictures?"

"Yeah, I told you that a minute ago. Then, when the pictures hit the Internet, you couldn't pick up a tabloid or read a blog that didn't mention me."

"But it made you a laughingstock. Why would you go along with that?"

"Why not? You can't have a comeback until you hit bottom. After the blogger tore me down, Richardson had Dr. Tolzer step in."

"I remember the hoopla. Tolzer was going to help you save yourself with the Westport Diet. I saw the two of you on all the morning and late-night shows."

"You got it. We hit the talk show circuit, and I confessed to my eating addiction on Dr. Phil. America loves to give a sinner a second chance, and I went from joke of the Internet to its darling."

"All as planned," I mocked.

"That's right, as planned by Richardson. He made my rehabilitation a media event that evolved into a reality show. I lost a hundred seventy-five pounds, and I became the face of Westport. I wrote books. I was rolling in the dough, and I bought the tennis facility I had been hiding out in. This one."

He glanced around like a proud father. I remembered Megan telling me Richardson was in public relations in another life.

"So, the whole thing was a scam."

"Not the way I look at it. The weight loss was real."

"Why did Dr. Tolzer fire you?"

"He did? Are you sure of that?"

"Of course, I'm sure. I was in the hall and heard it all. You were beyond angry."

"Well, maybe at first. But then Tolzer explained the deal: he and I would have some back and forth in the media. You know, like Kanye West and Taylor Swift or whoever else he's fighting with this week. Tolzer gets publicity for the Westport and his new book; I get publicity for ACE. Plus, a million dollars. I'd like to get fired like that every day. Of course, that ain't gonna happen now that Tolzer is dead. Believe me, I wanted Tolzer to stay alive."

I guess the guy could have been telling the truth. I wondered if this was going to be the beginning of another waddle down the road to obesity for the once-great tennis player. I almost felt sorry for him. Ponds couldn't very well carry on a public feud, real or fake, with a dead man. Although I had been carrying on a private one with a brother I never knew, almost since the day I was born.

"Tell me something. Do you know a guy named Lucky?"

He was quick to answer.

"Sure."

Now we were getting somewhere. "Mind telling me what you know about him?"

"He's an old friend. He's the mascot for the Boston Celtics."

An intercom page calling for Jordy broke his train of thought. Ponds looked at his watch.

"Listen, I have to go. Besides, I shouldn't say anything else without talking to a lawyer. If Tolzer was murdered, I didn't do it. Period. You have some time coming. I've got a new guy who's pretty good. I'll send him over, and you can hit with him." He started to walk away, then turned and stopped. "If you want Lucky's autograph or something, let me know."

I don't think he was kidding.

A couple of minutes later, a guy ten years younger than me, fair-haired and with a well-manicured three-day beard, showed up on the other side of the court. Brooke's boy toy, Rob. He seemed as surprised to see me as I was to see him.

"I hear tennis isn't the only thing you need lessons in, Lazzaro."

He wore a shit-eating grin that made me want to whack a tennis ball into his teeth.

He hit me a powerful slice serve that curved to the left side of the court. I returned it deep. My point.

"Love serving fifteen," I yelled out, even though he was serving and should have been keeping score.

He served, loaded with topspin. I hit it down the line. His volley came back like a rocket. If I didn't know better, I'd think he was aiming for my head. On my return, I came under the ball, giving it an excessive backspin, which made it bounce in his court close to the net. He rushed forward but never got near it. The ball had already bounced back over to my side of the net as he tried to stop short. My point. He turned to avoid the net, but his momentum kept him going until he hit the post full force, straddling it.

Ouch! That hurt to watch. I actually felt sorry for the guy.

"You did that on purpose." Rob croaked as he doubled over.

"Don't blame me for your clumsiness. I play to win." I turned to leave and noticed Nina two courts down.

What was she doing there? She was laughing at the mishap.

Double ouch for Rob.

Then she hurried for the exit before I had a chance to catch up with her.

"Hope the rest of your day is better," I said to Rob, who was still on his knees holding his nuts. It couldn't happen to a nicer guy. I don't know why I hated Rob so much. He didn't start dating Brooke until after the divorce. It's a competition thing, I guess. Kind of like my competition with Jerry. Jerry never did a damned thing to me. How could he? He never knew I existed, but we still have this sibling rivalry. I never liked being an only child by proxy.

Chapter Fourteen

When I got to my car, I was so angry that it took me a couple of tries to punch Nina's number into my phone.

"Are you—" I realized I was shouting and lowered my voice. "Are you following me?"

"I don't know what you're talking about."

"You were at ACE. You were laughing when a guy almost castrated himself. Then you took off."

"Why do you care if I laughed at your ex-wife's boyfriend?"

Nina knew about Brooke and Robert Chase, but she never met him. "I don't care. But I'm wondering how you recognized him as the guy I was playing against."

"I was doing a little unofficial investigating of this Tolzer situation myself to be thorough. Robert Chase's name came up."

"When?"

"Your ex came up in connection with you, and this Chase fellow came up in connection with her."

"You investigated me?"

"Only to be safe. Since you insist on putting in your two cents. I have to know all the players. Don't worry. It looks like you're cool."

"You know damned well I'm okay. We've been dating. Tell me why you were there checking up on Rob."

"I wasn't. I was there to talk to Jordy Ponds. I spotted Chase's name on his picture behind the desk when I got to ACE. I remembered he was your ex's tennis instructor and friend. I was checking out the courts when I saw the two of you there playing. Very progressive of you, I have to say. Don't tell me you didn't notice his picture up there. I'd have thought you'd be more observant. It's a good thing I've got your back."

"I don't need anyone to have my back."

I hung up, wondering why the police were interested in talking to Ponds.

* * *

It occurred to me that I had to make an appearance at the office if I wanted to keep my day job. After a quick trip home to change, I headed for the train station. I had missed the 9:34 and had to wait for the 10:00, which gave me time to think about how I handled the situation with Nina. She told me before that I didn't have to see everything in relation to me. Brooke used to tell me something similar, emphasizing that I was not "the bellybutton of the world." If Nina said that she was at ACE in the line of duty, then I had no right to accuse her of following me. I had to make it up to her. I hoped she would let me buy her dinner.

I still had questions, though, and I thought about them the whole trip in. If she thought Tolzer died of natural causes, why was she investigating? She knew something she wasn't sharing with me.

I got off the train in the dim tunnel below Grand Central and trudged up the stairs with the crowd. Outside, I caught a cab without trouble. Still, it was well after eleven when I arrived at the Ashfield Building on West 26th Street. There the On-Topic headquarters shared space with several other media, arts, and corporate tenants. The stone-and-glass structure occupied an entire city block on the West Side by the waterfront. I ran into the lobby and headed straight to the elevator.

"Hey, hey, hey, Lazzaro. Forget something, did ya?"

I stopped dead in my tracks.

"Geez, Cliff. You know who I am."

The security guard was next to me by this time. For a big guy, I don't know how he moved so fast.

"Sure, I know you. And I appreciate that favor you did, but rules are rules. They want me to have everybody sign in. I have everybody sign in."

I got his nephew, Tom Baylor, a job as an office intern at the magazine several months before. Cliff's a nice enough guy with a wife and four kids, and I knew he worked as a bank security guard when he left this place at noon. It can't be easy to work all those hours, so I didn't want to give him a hard time. I went over to his station and signed the book. Then I bolted for the elevator doors and took the elevator to the On-Topic offices on the eighteenth floor.

I found Archie in his office. With both an Xbox 360 and a Nintendo Wii system, as well as exercise equipment and other toys, a playpen might have been a better word for it. He was sleeping with his feet up on his desk. I slammed the door as hard as I could, and he almost fell out of his chair.

"What the hell. I thought you were my father," he said.

After shaking off the grogginess, he gave his hands a shot of sanitizer and then went to the fridge, where he took out a Red Bull and handed it to me.

"Vodka in it?" he asked.

"Too early."

"Good man." He picked up a Nerf Ball gun and shot at Homer Simpson, who was attacking a doughnut on a flat screen that hung on the far wall.

"Didn't you forget to do something for me?" I asked.

"What?"

"You never sent me the files on Tolzer."

He held up a mock-up of the next issue's cover. Along with the usual Diet of the Month and How to Tell If Your Husband Is Cheating teasers was the headline Betty Ann Green Pays Tribute to Diet Guru Alan Tolzer.

"I got busy and forgot. Some of us work around here. At our real jobs, not sidelines that can get you killed."

I would be touched, but I knew Archie's only concern for my safety was about how it would affect the column. I pointed to the Betty Ann Green Pays Tribute headline on the cover mock-up.

"I couldn't do much without the files, so I went over to the Institute to get some reactions to Tolzer's death to put in the column."

"And…" Archie said. "With you, there's always an and."

"And while I was at it, I tried to see if I could find out how a guy named Lucky, who called Tolzer while I was there, fits into all this. I talked to a lawyer named Stephen Richardson, who's more or less in charge now, and a Dr. Lang, who's responsible for research. They both deny knowing anyone named Lucky."

"Did you say Stephen Richardson?"

"Yeah, you know him?"

"If he's the same one, I've met him at various social functions. He's a hard-nosed New York lawyer who used to be a spin doctor. I'd watch out for him. I always had the impression he was bad news. What happened when you talked to him?"

Archie was beginning to soften on the idea of me looking into the case. For one thing, he knew he couldn't stop me, and for another, he was afraid that if I came up with something, I could give it to a rival magazine.

"He was more concerned with the image of Westport than with Dr. Tolzer's death. I found out Tolzer had a cardiac issue, but Richardson didn't want to hear it. If it got around that Tolzer had any heart trouble, people might say the diet caused it. It could create a nightmare for the company. Off the record, he is willing to concede that Tolzer may have overdosed himself because of stress. As you said, he's trying to put a spin on the situation. He wants to use 'Cooking with Betty' as part of his campaign to save the company."

"I wouldn't trust him if I were you." Archie hit the pump on the bottle of hand sanitizer again as if talking about Richardson reminded him of germs.

"You know that stuff does more harm than good, don't you? It's killing the good germs too," I said.

"There are more than enough germs to go around." He rubbed his hands so hard I thought he was going to make them bleed. "What I don't get is why the police, instead of you, aren't looking into this."

"They have no reason to question Dr. Lang. He claims Tolzer kicked off from natural causes. But Nina is nosing around the same as I am."

"Okay. End of story. The police are taking care of it. Why should you get involved?"

"Because my gut tells me there's a big story here and I'm going to get to the bottom of it. I'm convinced the police are wasting their time if they're not looking for Lucky. That's why I'm going to see if Irene White has ever heard of him. She was there the day Lucky visited Tolzer. She may have seen something."

"What? You've got a column to write. Your first obligation is to *On-Topic*."

"This is for the column. I'm doing a piece on the role food takes in her husband's campaign. And now there's this Tolzer connection."

"You're forgetting that 'Cooking with Betty' is a food column, not a gossip piece. Recipes, menus, food-related stories. Remember?" Archie wasn't telling me anything I didn't already know.

"Not gossip," I emphasized. "Facts. I'm not interested in scandal, but if she happens to be able to give me a lead on Lucky, all the better. By the way, since you brought up the subject of recipes, I should tell you that Brooke found out I'm using her recipes once in a while."

"You're using her recipes?" He held his hands palms out in front of him. "Don't tell me anything else. If you're doing something illegal, I don't want to know."

"It was your idea to use the recipes in the box we found. You said it was poetic justice and served her right for giving me only junk."

Archie has always had a selective memory. "All I remember is that Brooke threw you out and put your things in storage. It was exactly like what happened to me, except my ex threw my stuff on the street and set fire to it."

"It wasn't the same at all. You weren't married, and you were cheating on her."

"All right, that too, but almost the same, so I understand, and I don't blame you if you are using your wife's recipes. But don't tell me about it. My father would kill me if we got into a Rupert Murdoch type scandal."

One reason why Archie is my best friend. No matter how low I sink, I still look good compared to him.

"Okay, I'm not telling you anything other than I will have the column in on time as promised. All I have to finish up is the tribute to Dr. Tolzer. You would think it would be easy, but there is more negative to say about the guy than positive."

"Keep it positive. Everyone else will have the negative. Show that *On-Topic* is willing to take the high road."

"But I have to be truthful."

"You can be truthful and still leave out the very bad stuff."

"Listen, Archie, we've been friends for a long time, you know I can't write a gloss piece."

"We're friends after five o'clock. Before then, I'm your boss."

Archie may be my boss, but I was going to write the column how I saw fit. As I left his office, he called after me.

"And another thing, Jonathan White is a powerful man, and he buys ads. You'd better get triple confirmation on every word about him—or his wife—before it goes in this magazine."

Heads poked out from every cubicle in the editorial room, but nobody dared to comment.

Chapter Fifteen

I left the office in time to catch the 4:07 Metro North home. I knew if I took a later train if I got a seat at all, I'd risk getting one next to someone who'd give me a scene-by-scene synopsis of the Wednesday matinee. As it was, even on that first peak ride of the afternoon, I had to ask a woman wearing a leather biker's jacket if she was saving the seat she had her feet on. She gave me a blank look, then pulled out her earbuds and flicked the ring in her lip.

"What?"

"This seat. May I take it?"

She took her studded boots off the cracked oxblood leather cushion and reinserted her headphones. The seat, being on the aisle, had a low headrest, not that I would have put my head against one of those seats anyway. For the next hour, I rode backward. I stared at a poster above her head advertising a fancy condominium in Stamford, to not make eye contact. When she got off in Rowayton, one stop before mine, she stepped on my foot with her heavy boot.

It was a little after five when I got off in South Norwalk, and it was starting to drizzle. Halfway home, I got caught in a full-fledged downpour, and by the time I got to my building, I was soaked. I ran into Mary Ticarelli in the lobby. She was talking to another old lady from the apartments.

"Look at you. You're all wet. What did you do? Take a shower with your clothes on?"

"It's raining, Mary."

"And you didn't even have enough sense to come in out of the rain." She turned to the other woman. "See. What was I telling you? I think he drinks."

"I wasn't drinking. I'm coming in from work." I pushed the elevator button.

"Then you must be hungry. Come on, I'll bring you upstairs for some lasagna. I made it last night. It tastes even better today."

With that, she grabbed me by the elbow and led me onto the elevator. As the doors were closing, she yelled to the woman in the lobby.

"I've gotta find this one a wife. I'm getting too old to take care of kids."

When we got off the elevator, we stopped in front of my door.

"Well?" I said.

"Well, what?"

"I thought you were going to give me some lasagna."

"What lasagna? I don't have any lasagna."

"But you said in front of that woman—"

"Oh, that Evelyn? I said that to get away from her. She had my ear for an hour. She talked so much they're hot. Feel."

She grabbed my hand and tried to put it to her ear, but I pulled away.

"Glad I could help." I unlocked my door, opening it only enough for me to squeeze in. I was relieved to see she was going into her apartment.

"I gotta watch the Ellen show. She's got Hugh Jackman on today," she said. Then, as an afterthought, "You know what I heard about that Dr. Scholl's guy?"

"You mean Dr. Tolzer?"

"Yeah, the diet man. That busybody, Evelyn, knows someone who has a cousin who goes to that diet place. They told her the doctor was killed with a cannolo."

Chapter Sixteen

When I got in, I found a manila envelope shoved through Dexter's access door. Inside, I found several pages of information on the kopi berry supplement and a note from Dr. Lang. He had been in the area and decided to drop off the information so I could use it in the column.

At first, I couldn't figure out how he found me, but then I remembered giving him my card. Those two publicity hounds, Richardson and Lang, seemed desperate to keep the institute afloat now that Dr. Tolzer was gone. Too tired to read the whole packet, I tossed it on the breakfast bar. I didn't need work at that moment. I needed the company of a sane woman, fast.

When I saw Nina at Sally's a few days before, I realized how much I missed her. So, what did I do? The next time I saw her, I accused her of following me. How stupid could I get? We were growing apart, and if I didn't make the first move, we'd never get together again. We had a good thing going, and I wanted to get it back. That and I wanted to see what she had to say about Tolzer. I called her cell.

"Estevez," she answered.

Damn. She was in police mode.

"It's Quincy. Listen, I'm sorry for the misunderstanding. Sometimes I say stupid things."

"No argument there."

"You know why I say stupid things? Because the universe hates me, that's why. I'm certain it doesn't want me to be happy."

"Or it thinks you're a narcissist."

Or it thinks you should cut me some slack once in a while went unsaid on my part.

"So, you accept my apology?"

"Since it looks like that's as close as you're going to get to apologizing, I guess so," Nina's voice told me we were cool again. I breathed a sigh of relief.

"Good. I thought dinner and a movie would be nice. What do you think?"

"Are you asking me out?"

"Of course, I'm asking you out. What do you think I'm doing?"

"It'll have to be an early night," Nina said.

That job of hers again.

"We can still make the early-bird special then." I'm glad she didn't catch my sarcasm.

"Not that early. I'll see you at seven. My place." Before I could say another word, she cut me off.

I got to Nina's house, a three-bedroom ranch with a stone front and bay window, not far from Norwalk Community College. I caught the smell of frying garlic as soon as she answered the door. She looked incredible with her dark hair down instead of pulled back tight as she wore it for work. The top three buttons of her blouse were undone, showing just enough cleavage to pique my imagination with the possibilities for dessert. Yet, when I bent down to kiss her, she turned enough so that I caught her on the cheek.

"You're cooking?" I asked both surprised and delighted by the wonderful smells from the kitchen.

"Mofongo,"

Awesome. One of my favorites. Definitely not a health food, but delicious.

"I thought we were going out."

"I said my place. Don't you listen?"

For two educated people, it was amazing how our communication skills broke down so often.

"I thought you meant to pick you up here. I would have brought the wine."

"You brought yourself. That's enough."

She already had a bottle of wine open. Without asking, she poured for both of us.

"To us," I said as we clinked glasses.

"To friendship," she said with more emphasis on the word friendship than I cared for.

I took a sip.

"Good," I said. The truth was, I would have preferred a Sam Adams.

She told me to sit as she brought her wine into the kitchen to prepare dinner.

From the sofa, I watched her use a kitchen knife to chop plantains, garlic, and green onions. It struck me that this beautiful woman could wield a Glock 45 with equal finesse.

When the mofongo was ready, Nina brought it to the table in the pilón, the wooden mortar, in which she had mashed the fried plantains. Then she served it with shrimp and a stewed tomato sauce. It was delicious. This was so much better than going out to eat. The universe wanted me to be happy after all.

The small talk ranged from the Yankees to the weather, to breakfast at Sally's, to her family back in Puerto Rico. When we finished eating, she went to freshen up. As I cleaned the kitchen, the phone rang.

"The machine can get it," she called from the bedroom.

Who even has a landline, let alone an answering machine these days? But hey, It's not for me to judge. After a few more rings, I heard her *record after-the-tone* spiel. Then I heard a voice that could have belonged to a teenage boy.

"Nina, it's Cooper. I thought you should know. The report came back from Farmington."

I knew he was talking about an autopsy report. The office of the state's chief medical examiner is in Farmington.

"Tolzer died of malignant hyperthermia. I know it sounds like cancer or something. But it means the dude's body thermostat malfunctioned and his body temperature shot up. It's consistent with a thyrotoxic crisis, otherwise known as a thyroid storm. But get this. The ME is saying it was due to overdosing on methamphetamine. I've heard of meth addicts running naked in snowstorms because their core temp has gone up so much. Ripping off his shirt is consistent with the behavior of someone hyped up."

Nina came running into the room and grabbed the phone.

"Cooper! Cooper, answer me!" There was a pause, and she put down the receiver. She gave an exasperated sigh, "Damn you, Cooper." Her face was bright red as she erased the message. "He's a rookie and doesn't know any better than to leave a message like that on a machine." Then she added. "You didn't hear that."

But I did hear it, and malignant hyperthermia due to methamphetamines was very interesting news. I knew that shirt was the key, only I thought it was an overdose of digoxin that prompted him to try to cool down. Tolzer didn't look like a tweeker; at least he didn't seem amped when I talked to him. It made more sense than death by cannoli. That is, unless someone had put the methamphetamine in the cannoli.

"The poor kid thought he was doing something good." I put on a goofy smile to lighten the mood.

"Come on, let's sit on the sofa," Nina said as a way of closing the subject. Whatever the connection, she had no intention of letting me in on it.

She fell onto the couch and patted the seat. I plopped down and cuddled next to her.

"Hold on. I'll be right back," she said.

She got up and went back into the bedroom.

"Mind if I turn on the news for a sec?" I grabbed the remote before she could answer and turned on the TV.

"Be my guest," she called from the other room.

"Sorry, I wanted to see who won the game," I said when she came back.

"It's okay."

"That was good," I said. "The dinner, I mean."

"Dessert will be better," she said.

I moved closer and kissed her. It was long and passionate, and she was responsive. It was exactly like old times.

"I was talking about the flan," she said referring to her signature dessert of creamy egg custard topped with caramel.

Oh well. I didn't regret the kiss, but she must have seen the disappointment on my face.

"After the dessert," she said in a voice heavy with promise. She kissed me again and put her hand on my thigh to steady herself as she stood up. She brought back more wine and a plate of the sweet custard, which we shared as she curled up next to me. Yet another report about Alan Tolzer on the news caught my attention.

"So what do you think about Tolzer?" I asked.

"I think he was a quack. But a smart quack."

"That's not what I mean."

"Then what do you mean?"

"Do you think it was murder?"

There was a look of genuine surprise on her face.

"Why are you still on that?"

"Because I'm thinking that someone murdered him."

"We don't know that."

She was getting irritated, but it was too late to go back.

"Why are you still not willing to admit that murder is a possibility? You heard Cooper say that what Tolzer died from was consistent with overdosing on methamphetamine. I doubt if he was a user. Someone had to slip it to him."

"And you heard him say that it's also consistent with thyrotoxic crisis. The man's physician told us he was treating him for a thyroid problem. Your theory is quite a stretch. This is police business, and I already said more than I should have. I'm not talking about it anymore."

"It is my business too, in a way, being a journalist."

"You work for a food columnist. What do you know about investigating a murder?"

"I've read Michael Connelly, and I even interviewed Sue Grafton once. I think I can handle it."

"You didn't even know Dr. Tolzer. Why would you want to get involved?"

"I've met him. Besides, I have my reasons."

"Megan Hawkins?"

"What about her?"

"I only know she was Tolzer's executive assistant," She said. "Is there more?"

"I knew her a long time ago. She's upset about Tolzer's death, and I want to help her."

Nina got up and fastened the top three buttons of her blouse.

"Is that why you came here? To get information?"

"No. At least that wasn't the only thing."

"Get this clear. Keep out of it and let us do our work."

"Well, the only thing I have to say is—"

She didn't let me finish.

"The only thing you have to say is good night."

Damn, damn, damn, damn, damn. When would I ever learn to keep my mouth shut? There is nothing lonelier than the drive home after a failed date. I thought of how hot Nina had looked and decided that a drink was in order. Instead of going home to sulk about what could have been an incredible evening, I would drown my sorrows at a SoNo bar called The Loft. I was halfway there when I reached into my pocket for my phone to check my messages. It wasn't there. I checked the console. Nothing. Then I remembered that I had left it charging on my kitchen counter.

I'm addicted to my phone the way some people are addicted to drugs. I didn't even think about it while I was with Nina. But now that the evening had gone south, I needed my lifeline in my pocket. Besides, she may have seen the foolishness of the argument and was trying to call me at that minute. I decided it would be expedient to stop by home and get it before going to the bar.

* * *

When I got to the garage under my apartment building, another car was in my parking spot. A visitor must have hogged the first available space. I drove over to the visitor's parking spots, and all of them were full. I had no choice but to park the Camaro on the street. I locked my car with the windows up but left the top down, knowing I would be right back. I'd done this many times before in my neighborhood and never had a problem.

Sure enough, as soon as I entered the door to my apartment, I spotted the phone where I had left it on the counter. I'm not one to believe in the sixth sense or any otherworldly intervention, but I admit that I did have a feeling that the course of the evening was about to change.

My heart began to race as I picked up the phone to retrieve Nina's message. It wasn't there.

So much for intuition, I stuffed the phone in my pocket. As I headed for the elevator, I could hear Mary Ticarelli's door open behind me.

"Just going out?"

I knew if I even looked at her, I would say something I would regret, so I hopped on the elevator and closed the door to get on with my lonely evening.

I remember fumbling with the car keys. There was a white-hot light. I could hear a cracking sound reverberate through my skull. I didn't feel the pain until I woke up. I don't know how long I was out, but when I touched my head, I knew my hair was bloodied.

Until I could get my eyes to focus, my main concern was that the Camaro might have been stolen. Relieved that it wasn't, I sat on the sidewalk wondering what to do next. I leaned on the car to stand, but the world was spinning. Finally, I bent over and lost the mofongo. It wasn't as good the second time around. I heard someone coming and tensed up, ready to strike out to defend myself if need be.

It turned out to be an elderly couple walking a small white dog. I don't know if they assumed I was drunk or if the blood scared them off. Whatever the case, they averted their faces and hurried away. Now that my stomach was empty, the dizziness passed, and I managed to open the car door to put up the top. Talk about freaking locking the barn door. I went into the garage to take the elevator upstairs; the strange car was still in my space. I remember thinking that thanks to this guy's thoughtlessness, I got mugged.

Asshole.

When I got off the elevator, I heard Mary's door open. I glared at her and walked to my door. As I unlocked it, I realized she was right behind me.

"What in the world happened to you?"

Mind your own business. Go away. Leave me alone. All the possible answers passed through my mind. All I wanted was to be alone in my misery.

"I fell on the steps," I told her.

Against my protests, she insisted on coming in to tend to my wound. Rather than put up a fight, I let her in. I didn't need her, of course. But if providing a little mothering would make an elderly lady feel good, who was I to deny her?

She made me sit on a kitchen chair as she hovered over the back of my head and patted the wound with gauze and peroxide.

"You've got to go to the hospital."

"No, I've got to go to bed."

"No nap. You might have a concussion."

"Then I'll watch television. I'm not wasting my time in the emergency department. They aren't going to do anything that you're not doing."

She finished washing out the cut. In the mirror that she held up, it didn't seem as big as I expected, considering the amount of blood that had come from it. She had managed to stop the bleeding for the most part, and again she urged me to go to the hospital. Again, I insisted that I was not going.

"I hope you're going to stay in now" was her final admonishment. I sent her back to her apartment with thanks and assurances that I would call her if I had any further problems.

I was glad I didn't tell Mary that I got mugged. She would have been even more adamant about reporting it to the police than she was about my going to the hospital.

I sat in a recliner holding an ice pack to my head and tried to stay awake. I thought it would be a good time to read the kopi berry packet that Dr. Lang had left for me. The packet was full of generic information and improbable claims that the kopi berry supplement would melt forty pounds without dieting, exercise, counting calories, or eating prepackaged meals. I tossed it aside. Lang had said he would hold back any information that was a trade secret, but this was garbage. I wanted the information in the missing file that Megan left on Dr. Tolzer's desk.

I tried watching TV to stay awake, switching between Jimmy Fallon, Stephen Colbert, and Jimmy Kimmel. They were all reruns. I noticed that each show aired its commercials at the same time. I wondered if the networks scheduled them that way. Every once in a while, my thoughts wandered, and I'd think about things such as how Nina seemed a little jealous of Megan. Cute, but it was a pointless worry. I still had a thing for Nina, whether she knew it or not. The one thing I didn't want to think about but kept popping up in my throbbing head anyway was that my mugging might have been related to my investigation. A mugging usually means a robbery. I had my wallet in my pocket. I check to see if my money or credit cards were gone. Everything was there. The more I thought about it, the more questions I had.

I got up, threw the icepack in the sink, and then made coffee, hoping for a caffeine buzz to keep me alert. But when I returned to the recliner, I still fell asleep.

Chapter Seventeen

The next morning, my vision was clear, and there were no signs of nausea. I took a lot more than the recommended dose of an over-the-counter painkiller and made up my mind to pretend the throbbing in my head wasn't happening. God help that mugger if I ever got my hands on him.

On my way to breakfast, I noticed that the strange car was still in my parking space. What was more important was that my Camaro was still parked out on the street. As I walked, I called Doug Sterling, the building superintendent. I left him a message with the errant car's license plate. I rushed into Sally's at a little before seven, wearing a baseball cap to cover the gauze pad Mary had taped to my head.

"I overslept," I told no one in particular as I slipped onto a stool at the counter. My coffee was there waiting for me. It was black. She knew that wasn't how I liked it. I wondered if Sally was trying to send a message.

"I'll have two eggs over easy, a bagel, and two strips of bacon, Sal."

"Egg whites on whole wheat. Hold the salt," she called to the cook.

"But that's not what I ordered."

"Right. You're lucky I've got your six o'clock," she said.

What was this with everyone trying to look out for me?

"I don't need anyone to look out for me. I'm not sixteen."

"Well, you act it. Take that hat off while you're eating."

With that, she snatched the cap off my head.

"Hey." I protested

"Wait a minute. Turn around. What's that on the back of your head?"

By the time I finished my sandwich and a second cup of coffee, she knew all the events of the previous day, from Ponds to Rob, to dinner with Nina, to my getting mugged. She had a worried look on her face the whole time, except when I told her how Rob had almost neutered himself.

"And you wonder why people feel they have to look out for you. You're a train wreck waiting to happen. Nina didn't say anything about you getting mugged when she was in earlier."

"That's because she doesn't know. And I'd like it to stay that way if you don't mind." There might have been a sip of coffee in my cup. I picked it up anyway and finished the last drop. "Did she say what she did last night?"

Sally stood there shaking her head. She still wore that worried look.

"Only that she watched a movie and went to bed early. Why?"

So watching a movie after I left was the highlight of her evening. I hoped that she enjoyed it. I looked toward the clock so Sally couldn't see what was in my eyes.

"The train. I want to catch the 7:36 to work. Gotta go."

I threw enough money to cover the breakfast and a generous tip on the counter and ran out the door. From the sidewalk, I could see the train pulling into the station. I ran into the building and then tore up to the platform. I hopped on the train seconds before the doors closed. Once onboard, I realized that I didn't have my monthly pass, which meant I'd have to buy a ticket on the train. When the conductor came around, I handed him twenty-six dollars.

"Round trip," I said.

He looked at the money in my hand.

"Too much. It's nineteen dollars."

"For a round trip? It's always been twenty-six."

"Nope. You can't buy a peak round-trip ticket on board. Twenty-six for a round trip at the window, nineteen one-way on board. New rules."

Thanks a lot, Sally. It wasn't even a quarter to eight and the day was already going shitty.

The train pulled into the Park Avenue Tunnel under Grand Central on time at exactly 8:42. I piled out onto the platform with hundreds of other commuters. Judging from their blank looks, they seemed to have the same goal of getting through the day to catch the evening train back to Connecticut. In the morning, they would all start the whole routine over again.

We lumbered up the metal stairs to the cavernous main concourse, where I stole a glance at the elaborate ceiling. I promised myself that someday I would take the time to stop and admire the beautiful backward constellations up there, even if I did put myself at risk of getting knocked over by the other commuters in their determined flight into or out of the city.

Once on 42nd Street, I grabbed a cab to West 26th Street. On a sunny day like this, I was tempted to walk, but I had the feeling I had a busy day ahead of me. I dashed into the building, signed in at Cliff's desk, and bolted for the elevator.

Once on the eighteenth floor, I marched straight through the newsroom, oblivious to anyone there. When I got to my office, I booted up my computer and worked on the tribute to Tolzer. I touted Tolzer's accomplishments in the diet industry and his contributions to the public's understanding of nutrition. I also mentioned that he had a Ph.D. but did not say that he was not a medical doctor. Anyone could deduce that. I also said there was an unofficial report that the cause of death was malignant hyperthermia. I gave a brief explanation that it was a case where the core temperature shoots up due to impairment of the body's thermostat. I further explained that there were many causes for malignant hyperthermia. They ranged from a thyrotoxic crisis to a drug-related situation. Not bad if I did say so myself, but too short. I thought I could fill it out if I included some quotes from Irene White. I had told Archie the day before that I was going to talk to her at some point. Now I had a good excuse. I wanted to find out why she was so angry on the day Tolzer died.

The problem was that you can't walk up to the wife of a gubernatorial candidate and start grilling her. For all I know, she had bodyguards to keep people like me away. I decided the best way to approach her was through another person. It had to be someone with influence, and someone who could help her husband's campaign for governor. The only person I knew like that was Betty. The campaign was in full swing, and the election was close at hand. I knew Jonathan White's campaign staff would jump at the chance for Mrs. White to talk about cooking and relate to the average voter. White's opponent, Jan Butler, was hammering on the point that the well-heeled businessman and state senator was out of touch with the everyday citizen. The latest polls showed her to be a little ahead in that area.

It was easy enough to get the phone number of the appropriate contact at White's campaign headquarters from the *On-Topic* main desk. With the plan still only half-baked in my mind, within minutes I was talking to Sheila Packard, White's campaign coordinator. I explained I was Quincy Lazzaro, Betty Green's assistant, and that Ms. Green would like to do a homespun piece on Mrs. White for the "Cooking with Betty" column in *On-Topic Magazine.*

"When would Betty like to do the interview?" she asked.

That was way too easy. You would have thought I was offering a hundred thousand votes and national exposure bankable for a future White House bid. Which I was.

"As soon as possible. Unfortunately, Betty is so busy. To squeeze the piece in for the next issue, I will have to conduct the interview. I'll be using Betty's questions, of course. Then I'll forward the answers to her so she can write up the article. It's the norm around here, since, as you can imagine, she is always on the go."

There was silence from the other end of the line, which I felt I had to fill.

"Of course, we could always put the interview off for three or four months to a time when Betty isn't so busy if you would prefer."

Again, silence. Then, "Hold on a minute." A short while later, Sheila Packard was back on the line. "You're sure Betty is going to write the article herself?"

"Of course."

"I must ask that you send the article to us for full approval before printing."

That went against my grain, but I decided it would be worth it to make headway on the Tolzer case.

"As Betty always says, easy pleasey." I hate that expression, but a woman at the magazine uses it all the time, and it seemed like a buzzword that Packard would relate to."

"Mr. Lazzaro, do you mean easy-peasy?"

"Easy-whatever. I'll send you the article as soon as Betty writes it."

"All right then. The day after tomorrow at Mrs. White's home in Pine Orchard, say three o'clock."

The day after tomorrow, that would be Saturday. I didn't want to wait that long. My deadline was Monday.

"Uh, okay. That would be fine. Let's see, today is Thursday. The magazine will be put to bed on Monday. That means there wouldn't be any turnaround time, so we'll put the piece in next month's issue. Please thank Mrs. White for me."

More dead air. "Wait. I'm looking over the schedule. I see an appearance at the Stratford Senior Citizens Center has been canceled. It was for one o'clock this afternoon. Would you be able to make it then?"

I looked at my watch. It was already 9:45. It wouldn't be easy, but I could make it. It seemed Mrs. White was very anxious to get into "Cooking with Betty." It occurred to me that if the column had that much clout, I should be asking Archie for more money to write it.

"Well, it would take some juggling of my schedule, and it will be cutting it close, but yes. I'll clear it with Betty and see Mrs. White at one o'clock. In Pine Orchard, you say?"

Packard gave me the address and directions to the White residence. I hung up with silent apologies to the senior citizens of Stratford. They would be playing a few extra games of Bingo that afternoon, thanks to me. I packed up my stuff and headed for the door.

Every head in the newsroom turned as I ran into Archie, who was coming out of the kitchen carrying a tube of disinfecting wipes.

Archie looked at the laptop case I was carrying.

"Leaving already?"

"I have to run."

"What the hell. You just got in."

One of the newer columnists, a wide-eyed young woman fresh out of

Barnard who wore a black knit scarf wound around her neck even though the office was quite warm, appeared out of nowhere.

"Archie, I need your opinion on a new idea I have for a feature. I think Mr. Monahan will love it once you help me iron out a few kinks."

She winked at me. As she distracted Archie, I took the opportunity to slip out of the door. I owed her one.

Once on the street, I grabbed a cab, and as the driver sped to Grand Central, I checked the Metro-North schedule on my phone. The next train out was at 10:07. We made it to the Vanderbilt Avenue entrance of Grand Central at exactly 10:05. I threw a twenty to the cabbie and told him to forget the change, then I ran through the grand concourse checking the board for the track number. As I got to the train, the doors were closing. I forced them apart with my hands and jumped on just before the train pulled away. At that time of the morning, it was easy to get a seat on the outbound train. I had only then settled in when the same conductor from earlier came by.

"Short day. What'd ya do—get canned?"

"Don't worry about it. Norwalk."

"Round trip?"

"I thought you couldn't buy a round trip on the train."

"Ya can't. I just wanted to know if that's what ya wanted. That'll be nineteen dollars."

"It's off-peak now."

He looked at his watch. "Yeah, so it is. Thirteen dollars. Ya got a bargain, Sport."

Chapter Eighteen

I picked up the Camaro where it was still parked on the street outside my apartment building. Then I drove thirty miles up the coast from Norwalk to Pine Orchard, an upscale residential section not far from my old home in Sachem Creek. I found the White's two-story coastal colonial house without a problem. Like the other fine homes in the neighborhood, it dated from the turn of the twentieth century. That was a time when people with names like Blackstone, Pillsbury, and DuPont found the area a convenient alternative to Newport.

I parked and walked up to the central entrance and rang the bell, all the while aware that I was on camera. Irene White answered the door herself with a cordial greeting. Nice touch, a more relaxed greeting than I had expected. She led me to a great room dominated by a large window that afforded a tranquil view of a pond. I could see the fairway of the Pine Orchard Country Club off in the distance.

She was quite pleasant, nothing like the lady who had almost knocked me down at the Westport Diet Institute. If she recognized me, she didn't give any sign of doing so. She asked me to have a seat, and as I did so, I wondered how I could ever put a down-home spin on someone of such obvious means.

I kept my questions food-related for the time being, asking about the role of food in the life of this woman who hoped to be the first lady of Connecticut. After all, I was there for a legitimate interview. If I found out more information about Tolzer's murder, hooray for me.

She was a tiny woman who, in her husband's campaign ads, was always shown golfing or skiing. She supported her husband's campaign, but she racked up accomplishments of her own. She ran a website development company. Plus, she sat on the boards of several hospitals, charities, and educational institutions. She had ambitions. That was clear. Yet she masked them behind eyes that made you think the only thought in her head at the moment was about what you were saying. Something I imagined she learned at some fancy private school like Miss Porter's.

"Mrs. White, if your husband wins the election, what special food would you serve your family to celebrate?"

"My husband is going to win. Because the people of Connecticut want and deserve a governor who will take a common-sense approach to put people to work. Jobs lost because businesses can no longer afford to stay in Connecticut, or this country for that matter, must be brought back." She paused. "You have to forgive me, that's the politician's wife in me, but to answer your question, it's very simple. Comfort food."

"I caught the reference to bringing back jobs to this country. Does your husband have higher aspirations?"

"For now, he only aspires to help Connecticut regain its past position as the best state to live in and raise a family."

"To get back to food. What does comfort food mean in your family?"

"I'd say hearty nostalgic foods, maybe a steak, corn on the cob, apple pie, something all-American."

My worries about the down-to-earth approach to the article faded. She was doing all the work for me.

"And if the election doesn't turn out as you hope?"

"Again, comfort food. A casserole is a possibility, and definitely some chocolate ice cream. But again, I'm confident that Jonathan is going to win."

"Forgive me, but I find ice cream and pie surprising given your advocacy for healthy school lunches."

She turned on a smile that could melt the heart of the Soup Nazi.

"As my husband does, I believe in a common-sense approach. That applies to politics and food. Of course, we have to provide healthy food for our children not only in school but at home as well. That's not to say that we should deny them, or ourselves, a hot dog at a ball game or pumpkin pie at Thanksgiving."

The rest of the interview continued in a similar forthcoming manner. By the end, it was clear that this intelligent, beautiful, successful woman was also a devoted daughter, wife, and mom. She seemed so good-natured and modest that I was all the more curious about why she was so angry that day at the Institute. I found she was also a wonderful cook when she invited me to stay for an afternoon snack of whole shrimp nestled in a blanket of filo pastry and smothered with pineapple, mango, and raspberry sauce.

"It's so easy to prepare. Twenty minutes tops," she said as I scraped the last bit of sauce from the plate.

I was already writing the article in my mind as we ate. I could see the banner: Irene White—A Woman of Taste, followed by the teaser: "Irene White is a daughter, wife, mom, and businesswoman. She's also hoping to be the First Lady of Connecticut. But can she cook? You bet she can! As election day approaches, she talks about dishes that have special meaning to her family."

"This is delicious. Would you share the recipe with Betty for the column?"

She gave me an odd look. "But it is Betty's recipe. I save them from every issue."

I laughed. "Well, I hope you won't tell Betty I don't always read her column."

She winked at me. I don't know if she was the perfect woman or a perfect politician's wife, but I liked her. Which made me feel all the worse when I had to make an awkward transition to the subject of Alan Tolzer.

"This is very good. I notice it's a low-carb recipe. Do you follow the Westport regimen?" I avoided the word diet. I didn't want her to think I was implying that she needed to watch her weight, which she did not.

The amiable face that had defined the interview to this point grew dark for a moment, then recovered. "I'm pleased that you're enjoying it. Perhaps it would complement the diet. I'd find that to be interesting if it did. You must be aware that Dr. Tolzer has died."

That was supposed to be my line. Was she toying with me?

"Why yes, I am."

"Of course you are. It's all over the news," she said.

Her face saddened. No sense in asking her how she knew.

"Yes, it's all over the news."

"I saw you at the Westport Diet Institute, didn't I? You were at the front door when I stormed out."

Talk about being headed off at the pass.

"Right. Like I am today, I was there to conduct an interview. With Betty so busy, I find that's often my role."

She eyed me with suspicion. "Well, we all have our roles to play, Mr. Lazzaro." She gave a deep sigh. "Unfortunately, that day, my role as children's advocate necessitated that I remind Alan he had committed to endorsing my school lunch reform initiative, and he failed to follow through. I'm afraid I do become passionate when it comes to the welfare of children. I wouldn't have pushed so hard if I had realized—"

She drew in a dramatic, deep breath. Then she went on to another subject. "I take it Betty will have enough time to write the article and get it to my people for approval before her deadline. Did I hear it had to be in by Monday?"

It was clear that lunch and the interview were over. As I had suspected, she didn't want to talk about Alan Tolzer. Archie wasn't going to be happy when he found out I questioned her about Tolzer, but the questions were food-related, and it was my job to find the truth. As she was showing me to the door, I decided to go for broke.

"Mrs. White, do you know Charles Grand? He also goes by the name of Lucky."

"Not that I recall. I meet a lot of people, though. Why do you ask?"

"He was there the day Dr. Tolzer died. I thought you might have seen him."

"If I did, I didn't know who he was."

I usually can read people well. I believed she was telling me the truth. "Okay, then. Do you believe Dr. Tolzer died of natural causes?"

It may have been my imagination, but I thought I saw a faint look of surprise on her face.

"I have no reason to believe otherwise. Do you?"

"I'm not sure yet."

"Well, when you are, I suggest you speak with the authorities. For now, I have to say, Mr. Lazzaro, that I granted you this interview in good faith. Unfortunately, I'm not sure you are operating in good faith. I really am out of time. Good-bye."

Damn. I didn't even get to ask her if she was having an affair with Tolzer.

Chapter Nineteen

It was still early when I got back to SoNo from Pine Orchard. My parking space in the garage was empty, and I parked the Camaro in it. The wound on my head was hurting, and I was stiff from the long ride. Still, I felt I needed some exercise. With no Dexter to take for a run, I decided going out in the kayak was what I needed to keep my aches at bay.

One of the reasons I took my apartment was because I could launch my kayak at the Maritime Park across the street. I bought the kayak in the Bargain Shopper to replace the Kevlar racer Brooke had chopped up before the divorce. I wheeled my carrier over and set off down the river. Within minutes, I was under the railroad tracks and passing the marina docks, headed toward the Fort Point Street drawbridge.

It had been a hectic day going into New York and then up to Pine Orchard, only to have the interview with Irene White go sour at the end. The kayak, like the car, was a perfect safety valve for my stress. As soon as I reached the harbor, I popped in my earbuds to listen to an NPR podcast of the Car Talk guys. They were old shows, but I loved their humor. They were about to give the puzzler when a computer-generated voice replaced Click and Clack's banter.

"This warning is for you, Quincy Lazzaro. Mind your business, or you will regret it. Don't be stupid. When someone warns you the plate is hot, don't touch it."

I stopped paddling to listen to it again. How the heck did that get on my device and why? The voice was distorted to sound robotic. If someone went through the trouble of disguising their voice, they must be worried that I'd recognize it. I listened a third time, trying to identify who it was. No luck.

I let the boat drift as I called my computer geek friend. Sam Goodwin helps me every time a technology problem pops up.

"I need you to tell me something about podcasts," I said.

"What kind of show do you want to do? Commentary? Music?"

"Neither. I want to know if someone can alter a podcast."

"Can an Android phone get hacked?"

"Spare me the Apple lecture, Sam. Just tell me if someone could mess with an episode I listened to."

"The altering part is easy," he said. "But whoever did it had to get it into your library somehow."

"My phone's always with me. And I download everything myself."

"From where?"

"From my work computer. I still manage my podcast library there and sync it to my phone."

Sam laughed. "You're doing it the old-fashioned way, man. Most people just stream straight to their phones."

"Are you saying I'm a dinosaur?"

"No way. Plenty of people still sync through a computer. It just makes it easier to slip in a bogus file. If someone had access to that work PC, they could've dropped in a faked episode. Next time you synced, boom, it shows up on your phone like it's legit."

"I knew that," I said.

That was not what I wanted to hear. Anyone at the magazine could have access to my computer. If Archie was correct, they all knew my password.

"Yeah, sure you did," Sam said. "Hey, give me a buzz when you want to launch your own show."

"Peace," I said and hung up.

But I felt anything but at peace. An adrenaline spike made my heart race, and my extremities felt freezing cold. I looked around to see if anyone suspicious was lurking about. No one. Receiving that unexpected message had thrown me for a loop. I continued my kayaking with the threat weighing on my mind. The fact that it happened was more frightening than the message.

As far as the message itself, I tried to list who would want to threaten me. I don't have many, if any, enemies, and for the life of me, I could not come up with a name. The threat had to have something to do with my investigation of the Tolzer case.

I imagined how I would beat the crap out of the guy who threatened me. My inner Jason Bourne soon gave way to my inner Ted Lasso, and I realized I had no one to direct my aggression toward. I did the only thing I could do, I channeled my energy into paddling faster and faster. Before I knew it, I was off Canfield Island and the Westport Diet Institute. As I looked at the beautiful grounds, I couldn't help but wonder what I had gotten myself into when I first entered its gate.

My kayaking excursion ruined, I turned around and was home before six o'clock. There was a message on the answering machine from Doug Sterling. The police had determined that the car in my space was hot.

"It doesn't make sense," the super said. "Why would anyone put a stolen car in your space?"

"It makes perfect sense to me. They wanted me to park on the street where it would be easier to mug me," I said to the machine.

When I realized what I had said, I was glad there was nobody there to hear me. I decided right then I had to check my paranoia, or I would become a nut case.

I was sifting through the mail when I got a call from Archie. Daddy Monahan wanted Betty to have lunch with him in the city in a few days. There was nothing like a call from Archie to make me realize that no matter how bad things were, they could always get worse.

"What do you want me to tell him?" I could hear the worry in Archie's voice. As I listened to him, I multitasked, glancing at the stack of bills in front of me: Visa, cell phone, department store, and health club. I made a mental note to pay the health club first. Mixed in, I found a postcard of a blue sky, tropical water, sandy beaches, and food that looked like artwork. I read the words blazoned over the pictures, Grand Case, St. Martin, The

Gourmet Capital of the Caribbean.

My aunt, who was on a Caribbean cruise, had scribbled on the back. *Having a great time. The French cuisine is out of this world.*

Perfect! "Tell him Betty is on her way to St. Martin to do a story on the gourmet restaurants in Grand Case. She'll be gone for a month," I said to Archie.

"How do you think of this shit?" Archie said. "I hope he buys it."

"Promise him a dynamite article and tell him Betty's not going to put it into her expense account. He'll buy it."

I hung up before Archie could protest any further. That was great. Now I was going to have to research the Internet for information on Grand Case to do the story.

I decided I was fine with that. With Monahan off my back for a few weeks, all I had to do was meet Monday's deadline. Then I could concentrate on finding who killed Dr. Tolzer and who threatened me using my podcasts.

My stomach growled, reminding me I hadn't eaten since the snack at Irene White's house. I went into the kitchen to look for something to munch on. I looked in the cabinets. What to make, what to make? Cereal? No, I wanted something good. Saltines? Too dry. Succotash from a can? I wasn't that hungry. How did that can even get in there? Anchovies? They would be good, but no bread.

Searching in the nether regions of the cupboard, I found what I was looking for—one lone can of tuna fish. Packed in water, not oil, which I preferred, most likely left over from one of my diet kicks. But that was okay, I could stand to keep down the calories. I washed off the top of the can. I'd been doing that since I heard a report that all kinds of critters do the cha-cha on the tins when they're in the warehouse. Then I opened it on my new deluxe combo electric can opener and knife sharpener, the only real kitchen tool I own.

Holding my thumb on the lid, I squished down as I drained the liquid into the sink. Then, taking two squeeze bottles, one of mayo and one of mustard, from the fridge, I squeezed a dollop of each into the can and mixed it with a fork.

I went back to the TV to enjoy my drink and feast on the tuna right out of the can. Ahh, comfort food. Not the same as what Irene White made, but comfort food, nonetheless.

Chapter Twenty

I still had one more person to interview. I decided I would pay Jeanette King a visit in the morning. As far as I knew, she was only a client, so I doubted she would know anything about the kopi berry file or Lucky. But I was curious about why Tolzer had her banned from the Institute. Plus, I wondered if the bad blood between the two resulted in Tolzer's murder. I might have been wrong in thinking that Richardson was the prime suspect. I hoped to find out in the morning.

But the night was still young, and I could learn some of what I needed to know right here in Norwalk. I would pay a visit to the Norwalk police to see what I could find out about Lucky Grand.

The Norwalk police station sits on a plaza at the corner of Main and Monroe Streets, a quick five-block jog from my apartment. I walked into the U-shaped brick building, hoping to get information on the whereabouts of Lucky Grand. I walked out at 9:00 p.m., much to my surprise, with him in tow.

Although I had recognized him on television from Megan's description, in person, he seemed a lot more formidable. As we left the building, he didn't seem very appreciative.

"Where's Ernie? He took long enough to send someone," Lucky said.

"Ernie?"

"The guy who usually comes down with the bail."

"I don't know Ernie. The desk said you were waiting for bail, and I bailed you out."

"You're not from Ernie's Bail Bonds? Then who the hell are you? Why'd you put up the bail?"

"The name is Lazzaro. I have questions about Dr. Tolzer."

"You got questions, ask him."

He started walking down Main Street. I followed.

"He's dead. You didn't know?"

He stopped and studied my face as if he were looking into my soul itself to see if I were lying.

"Dead. No shit. I've been in jail for a couple of days. I didn't have time to read the social columns, ya know. I hope he mailed me that last retainer."

He started to walk again.

"Where are you going? I have some questions for you," I said.

"As if it's your business, I'm going to get something to eat. If you're smart, you'll head the other way."

He stopped in front of Wethersfield's, one of the many excellent restaurants that have popped up in SoNo.

"The police don't know you're the guy who was out on the lawn with the doctor, or that you had words with him over the phone before he died."

It may have been my imagination, but he looked bigger and more threatening.

"Are you trying to say I had something to do with that doctor's death?"

"I'm saying that instead of holding you only for a bar fight, the cops might have some questions for you if they realize you had a connection to the doctor."

That may or may not have been true. As far as the police were concerned, Tolzer died of natural causes.

Lucky paused to consider the options: either talk to me or the police. He fell for my bluff.

"I was working for him. He needed me to look into a few things going on at that place. We were talking out on the lawn because he didn't want anyone to overhear. I was filling him in on what I found."

"So you're a detective."

"No shit. That's why I called him later on. I forgot to turn in all my hours.

Now I'm going in this restaurant to eat, and when I come out, I don't want you around."

"Yeah, well, here's a coincidence. I'm going in there too."

Lucky exploded like an egg in a microwave.

"In one minute, I'm going to mop up the street with you."

"Not here you're not if you don't want to end up back in jail. I have more questions. Such as, what did Tolzer need you to look into?"

Lucky must have considered the options again and decided to give me enough to get rid of me.

"Tolzer knew money was being made on the side. He didn't like it. He wanted proof so he could clean house. It's all in my report. I didn't kill Tolzer. I was working for him." Lucky stepped onto the stoop in front of the restaurant and put his hand on the door.

So, the changes Tolzer planned to make weren't in the diet but in the staff. Did Richardson and Lang know, or did they both lead me on when I assumed the changes were to be made in the diet?

"On the side. You mean someone was stealing from the Institute? Who?"

He turned toward me. His eyes went wide, and a split second later, a red spray of blood projected from his mouth. Blood covered me from head to toe. Only then did I realize that I had heard a shot. I hit the sidewalk and scrambled on my belly to an alley at the side of the building, waiting to hear more gunfire. When none came, I stole a look out.

Megan was standing over Lucky with a gun in her hand.

Chapter Twenty-One

At first, I didn't notice people coming out of the clubs and restaurants and starting to gather around. All I saw was Lucky Grand's body lying on the sidewalk, blood covering the front of his shirt and trickling out of his mouth, his open eyes seeming to cast an accusing stare at Megan.

Megan was frozen over him, tears running down her cheeks as she made little gasping sounds.

"Megan put the gun down," I said.

She held it out to me.

"No. Place it on the sidewalk."

I knew it was the correct thing to tell her, yet in the back of my mind, I was thinking there was no sense in getting my fingerprints on the murder weapon. It's funny the things that go through your mind during times of stress. She knelt to place the gun on the ground, and I helped her up. She was sobbing.

"I didn't do it," she said.

I was trying to keep an open mind, but it was hard to ignore that she had the gun in her hand as she stood over Grand's body. It was difficult as well to ignore that she had told me that she intended to get a gun to protect herself from him.

"Shhh. Not now."

"But you have to listen. I wanted to apologize for getting angry with you. I called, but it went straight to your voicemail."

"I didn't charge my phone last night. It's probably dead."

"I was worried, so I got your address from your card and went to your building. A little woman in the lobby asked me who I was looking for. When I told her you, she said she saw you headed downtown."

I recalled seeing Mary Ticarelli as I was leaving. That woman may be gullible, but she sees everything that goes on in our building and makes it her business.

"I was coming down the other side of the street when I spotted you talking to that horrible man. Then the shot. I don't know—someone ran. I thought you were shot."

Tears ran down her cheeks again. I put my arm around her. "I saw the gun on the ground, and I grabbed it to help you."

The crowd stood silent as if hoping to hear something juicy they could post on Facebook. One guy was already taping the scene with his smartphone. I pulled Megan close to me, letting her bury her face in my shoulder.

"But I didn't…"

"Not another word." I realized how harsh I sounded and said in a softer voice, "It's going to be all right. Trust me."

I hoped I was right about that.

By this time, squad cars were pulling up. I was surprised they took as long as they did, since we were only a block from the station. Once more, Nina Estevez was one of the first to arrive. She looked from me to Megan to the body on the ground. This must have seemed like a broken record to her. As when she investigated Tolzer's death at the Institute, she didn't let on she knew me. She made everyone move away and then gave the body a closer look. "It's Grand," she said to her partner, Cooper. The young cop stole a glance, turned pale, and then looked away as Nina secured the gun.

"What happened here?" I wasn't sure if Nina was talking to Megan or me.

"Not a word," I whispered to Megan.

"Lazzaro, am I going to have to run you in for interfering with a police officer?"

I guess she did recognize me.

"The girl killed him. I saw the gun in her hand," someone yelled from the crowd. Once the silence broke, a cacophony of voices filled the air. Most of them were saying the same thing.

"Cooper, get statements," Nina said, never taking her gaze from Megan. "You're going to have to come with us." She gestured toward the car.

Megan started to step back but checked herself. Her whole body shook.

"I'm going with her," I said.

"I meant you too," Nina said.

It's one thing for me to say I'm going. It's another to have a cop tell me I have to go to the station.

"Me? Why?"

"You're covered in blood for one thing." With that, they put us in separate squad cars.

* * *

I cooled my heels in a windowless room at the police station, furnished with only an oak table and three chairs. I climbed on one of the chairs and looked into the face of the clock on the wall.

"I want to see Megan Hawkins," I shouted. "I want to see her right now. Do you hear me? Right now."

I waited a bit, expecting some kind of response.

Nothing.

"Let me talk to Megan. She has her rights. I have my rights. Damn you."

With that, I hit my palm against the clock and lost my balance. I jumped off the chair, and it fell over. It was all I could do to stop myself from landing on the table. If nothing else, the crash brought a scowling, squinty-eyed cop. He stood in the doorway and stared me down as if that was going to scare me.

"What the hell is going on in here?"

"I know these rooms have a camera in the clock. Why didn't you answer me instead of making me almost break my neck?"

"Because that's an urban legend. There's no camera.

Now pipe down until we're ready to talk to you."

"I want to talk to the girl who came in with me," I said.

"Any more shit out of you and you'll be talking to the people in the psychiatric ward."

"For what?"

"Your irrational behavior."

"I don't have any irrational behavior." I was pacing by that point.

"You will after thirty days in that unit."

"You can't do that."

"Keep it up and you'll see."

After he walked out, I thought about a story I heard of an Alzheimer's patient whose nursing home always sent him to the psych ward for "observation" rather than address his behaviors. He would be out of their hair for a month at a time, his rights obliterated by the stroke of a doctor's pen. I thought better of causing any more trouble.

After another hour and a half or so, the door opened again, and a tall guy with close-cropped dark hair that I learned was Detective Gambardella from the state police special crimes unit, came into the room.

"Can I see Ms. Hawkins?" I asked.

I was very careful to control my voice so he wouldn't have an excuse to throw me in the psych unit, but inside, I was ready to tear the place apart.

"I'm afraid not," Gambardella said as Nina walked in.

"Nina, let me talk to Megan."

I'm not ashamed to say I was pleading.

If I thought my "in" with Nina was going to get me any special privileges, I was conning myself.

"Why were you with Grand?"

I realized that all cops, male or female, have the same look on their faces when they interrogate you. It doesn't make for pleasant conversation.

"I was looking into something."

"By 'looking into,' you mean 'investigating.' Why are you investigating anything?"

"You know I'm doing a story on Dr. Tolzer. Well, I had a hunch that Grand murdered him, but I only knew Grand as Lucky. I learned he was at the Institute earlier, and I had seen how disturbed Tolzer got when he received a call from him."

"You didn't know his name, and you bailed him out?"

Gambardella looked as skeptical as if I told him I could cook an egg with a cell phone.

"To see what information I could get out of him."

"I told you to keep out of this and let us do our job," Nina said.

Then do it, I wanted to say with apologies to Dale Carnegie.

"I'm trying to say it doesn't make sense that Tolzer died of natural causes." I could see from the look on both their faces that they knew it too. "I was looking at Lucky as the prime suspect."

Gambardella smirked and shook his head.

"How's that theory holding up for you? Still think he killed Tolzer?"

I knew where that was going, and I had to be careful not to make things worse for Megan.

"I don't know."

I didn't want to cloud the issue by telling them about Jordy Ponds, Irene White, or Jeanette King. I had no proof of their involvement, although I intended to follow up on each of them. By the same token, I didn't tell them about the threat I received, and besides, that was my business. One more thing I wasn't going to mention was Grand's report, at least not until I had time to find it. I wished I had asked him where it was.

"I'll tell you what we know," Gambardella said. "That your girlfriend's prints, and only hers, are all over the weapon that killed Grand."

"My friend," I emphasized the word friend and looked at Nina. Her face was as emotionless as if it were carved on Mount Rushmore. "My friend said she picked the gun up from the sidewalk. Besides, the killer could have been wearing gloves."

Nina used a much more conversational line of questioning. "Why would the shooter leave the weapon behind?"

"If he knew his prints weren't on it, he wouldn't want to get caught with it on him. Chances are the gun wasn't registered, at least not to the shooter."

Gambardella let out a breath, and his shoulders sagged for a second.

"I'm right. It's a stolen gun, isn't it? It doesn't belong to Megan."

His look told me he thought I was a wise guy. He didn't have to tell me that even if the gun wasn't registered to her, it didn't prove that she didn't pull the trigger.

"Did you see her with the gun in her hand?"

I thought for a while before I answered his loaded question.

"Well, yeah."

Gambardella gestured with his hand as if to wave me off.

"But you think your friend didn't kill Grand?"

"She said she didn't do it, and I believe her. Furthermore, I intend to prove it. And I'm going to prove that whoever killed Grand also murdered Alan Tolzer."

"Do you know what I believe? I believe that you'd better leave this investigation to us. And if you interfere with our case, you're going to jail."

First, the Norwalk police threatened to have me committed, and now the state police want to lock me up. What next? I looked at the clock, which hung crooked on the wall. It was after midnight.

"All I know is that if I'm not charged with anything, I'm out of here," I said. I got up and walked out. Nina followed me into the hall.

"A word to the wise, Quincy. Listen to Gambardella. There's more to your friend than you know."

It was well after midnight when I left the police station. When I walked past the restaurant where Grand's luck had run out, police were still around, and the area was cordoned off. I could return in the morning.

Chapter Twenty-Two

I got home exhausted. Yet, I tossed and turned in bed for most of the night, thinking about all that had happened in the last few days. Then I ended up on the couch watching TV. When I finally nodded off, I dreamt that I saw a burst of sunlight sparkling off the ax head, and for that split second, it blocked out the hell that broke loose around me. I watched in bewilderment as the blade fell on my prized kayak.

"This is because you think more of this stupid boat than me." Brooke's voice shot through the air, high, sharp, and wild enough that the ground tilted under my feet.

She swung the ax again.

"And that is for spending so much time in this damned thing!"

I threw my body across the kayak to stop her from further smashing my pride and joy to smithereens. But she raised the ax higher and brought it down hard. To avoid decapitation, I dove to the ground and hit my head.

I woke up on the floor next to the couch, my head hurting. The echo of the dream still clung to me, but as it faded, another thought pushed its way in. Nina's warning. What exactly did she mean when she said there was more to Megan than I knew? Was she trying to tell me the bullet had been meant for me instead of Lucky? By jumping from a food columnist to an investigative reporter, was I cooking up a recipe for disaster? Probably.

I dragged myself to the bedroom. The light from the Maritime Park across the street made getting around my apartment possible without the need to leave a light on when I went to bed. I was in desperate need of sleep, so

I closed the blinds in my room and pulled the drapes over them before I jumped under the covers. Even with that, a faint glow filtered down the hall from the open blinds in the living room. I was too lazy to get up to close them in the other rooms, so I pulled the sheets over my head and drifted off to sleep once more, hoping that Brooke would stay out of my dreams.

* * *

I woke up thinking I heard a noise. My first thought was that it was Dexter. But then I remembered Brooke picked him up the day she accused me of giving Betty her recipes. I looked up at the ceiling where my alarm clock projected the time in large red numbers 2:45 a.m. I wrote the noise off as someone coming off the elevator in the hall; kind of late, but in a big apartment building, it happens sometimes.

I rolled over and jammed the pillow against my ear in case there was another disruption. I tried to think of which neighbor could be coming or going at that hour, but before I could come up with a name, I was out. Then I woke up a second time. Propped up on one elbow, this time I was sure something was amiss. From the bed, I thought I saw movement in the ambient light that washed in from the hall. I could feel my heart pounding.

The thought that someone was in the place raised not only my anxiety but my anger as I tried to figure out how they could have gotten into my apartment. I knew I locked the door when I came in. I wondered if I had let my imagination overrule my reasoning. I listened. Nothing.

As quiet as I could, I lowered myself from the bed to the floor and made my way along the floor to the edge of the bedroom door.

I got up flat against the wall. I listened. I convinced myself I heard something in the kitchen. There was no question about it, I was not alone. I made every effort to be quiet, but I still bumped into a bookcase.

That's when I detected the very distinct odor of gas. I had no choice but to confront whoever invaded my apartment. I needed a weapon and felt for my hiking stick, which I knew was propped against the bookcase. With the stout five-foot staff of oak in my hand, I made my way into the hall.

"Who's there?" I shouted.

I peeked into the kitchen, where the odor was stronger still, and heard the hiss of escaping gas. I fumbled for the light switch but realized it might spark an explosion. With one hand over my nose and mouth, a useless but instinctive gesture, I found the stove and felt for the knobs. Every one of them was on. After turning off all the jets, I opened the window over the kitchen sink. With the stick ready to do damage, I checked the living room and the other bedroom and found them empty.

Confident that no one was still in the apartment, I ran into the hallway waving the stick. I watched the numbers over the elevator door click off the last three floors of its descent. Since it was no use pursuing the intruder any further, I turned to go back to my apartment. That's when I saw Mary Ticarelli standing in her doorway. She looked at the stick in my hand and hesitated before she spoke up.

"If you're going to run around here in your underwear, you might at least have the courtesy of buttoning up," she said. Then she retreated into her apartment and slammed the door.

As I entered my apartment, I realized that I had to unlock the door before I ran out into the hall. Maybe the home invader didn't come in through the hall door. I checked the slider to the balcony. It was still locked. I checked every window. All locked except for the kitchen window, which I had opened to let in fresh air. The place had been practically hermetically sealed. I would chalk up the whole incident to my imagination, except for one thing. I knew I did not leave all the gas jets on before I went to bed.

Sure, the correct thing to do was to report what happened to the cops, but common sense told me they would never believe someone came in and turned on the gas and then locked up after themselves when they left. I called the non-emergency number for the police and, without going into detail, told them I heard a noise in the hall and thought an unauthorized person might be in the building. They said they would send someone out to check. A few minutes later, a squad car pulled up, and I saw two uniforms enter the building. If anyone was still in the building, they would find him.

I watched through the peephole when I heard the elevator and saw the two cops walk up and down the hall, then stop in front of my door. Damned caller ID. One of them knocked.

"Sorry to bother you," I said from behind the closed door. "I guess it was nothing."

"Could you open the door, please?"

"Why?"

"Procedure."

I opened the door.

"I may have been dreaming," I said.

"Mind if we have a look? Procedure," he said again.

I did mind, but I was the one who called them, and they did have a job to do. One of the cops poked his head into the rooms.

"Do I smell gas?" he said.

"I was about to make some coffee but turned off the jet when you knocked," I said. "Sorry I bothered you guys for nothing."

"Better to check things out. There've been a few problems. Have a good night."

I wouldn't have felt like such a wuss if I had told them it was more than only a noise in the hall. Someone had tried to kill me. I was sure of it. Yet I couldn't prove it.

I turned the easy chair toward the door and spent the rest of the night in it with the walking stick across my lap, the second time this week I had to spend the night in that chair. The thought made the healing wound on my head, which I had been ignoring, ache again.

At about 6:30 a.m. I decided there was no sense in trying to get back to sleep. I had a lot of things I wanted to do, including going down to the police station to see Megan. I got dressed and checked my email. A message from Irene White surprised me. It was hard to believe it was only yesterday afternoon when I visited her. She said she enjoyed the interview and was looking forward to reading the copy before the publication. She sent regards to Betty. What was up with that? She wasn't happy when I left her house.

She was a typical politician's wife, changing with the wind.

And Betty. What a joke she was. Sooner or later, it was going to come out that Betty didn't exist. That would be a problem enough with Mr. Monahan, even though plenty of men have written with female pseudonyms. But the fact that I couldn't cook and that I wrote a column using borrowed recipes made me a fraud, and there would be no way to justify it. It was becoming more and more imperative that I find the killer and break a big story so I could extricate myself from that column.

Chapter Twenty-Three

On my way to breakfast at Sally's, I walked by Wethersfield's so I could check out the crime scene. I was hoping to see something to jog my memory about the night before that could make sense of this whole mess. The police were gone, and only broken bits of yellow crime scene tape remained tied to a couple of small trees by the street. A white chalk mark still outlined where the body lay on the sidewalk, and another marked where the police found a bullet casing.

I stood in the same spot I stood in when Lucky got shot. I faced up Main Street, the way Megan would have come from my building.

The chalk mark on the sidewalk indicated that the casing had fallen behind me. I recalled how Lucky's expression had changed seconds before the report of the gun. What had he seen over my shoulder? It wasn't Megan. She would have been walking toward us on the other side of the street, assuming she was telling the truth.

The killer must have followed us from the police station. Megan's story might have been true, that she spotted us, heard the gunshot, and saw someone run. When she ran to see if I was all right, she saw the gun on the pavement and picked it up, thinking she could help me. But why were only her prints on the gun?

When I walked into Sally's, as usual, she had my coffee on the counter before I even sat down. She stood there, looking at me with an expression that said she wanted to say something profound but couldn't find the words. The place was about half full, but in a little while, there wouldn't be a seat available.

"What? You're not going to call in my egg whites on dry whole wheat?"

"I already did when I saw you walking up the street."

"How did you know I didn't want only a doughnut like the other day?"

"Because I figure you've come to your senses. Almost getting killed has a kind of sobering effect."

I could see genuine sympathy in Sally's eyes and a little fear, too.

"You heard?"

"Of course, I heard. It's all anyone is talking about this morning. It's all over the papers."

"I can't talk about it here," I said, looking around the restaurant and seeing so many familiar faces, every one of whom was pretending not to listen.

Sally told Newme to cover the counter and brought me into her office. She motioned for me to sit on a sofa piled high with red plastic trays loaded with bread rolls. She often used the office to store the rolls when the bread man delivered them early in the morning. Rather than move them, I opted to stand.

"Okay, shoot." She winced at the poor choice of words and tried to soften her voice. "Tell me about it, I mean." With the gruff exterior gone, she almost seemed like a mother.

I explained everything about the shooting and how Megan and I had to go to the police station. "There's something else, too."

"Don't tell me it gets worse."

"Kind of. On top of everything else, I'm going insane. And I don't want any smart remarks out of you."

I wished Sally did have some snappy comeback, because when she didn't, it drove home how screwed up my life was. I went on to tell her the rest of the story. I started with the dream about Brooke, and then how the gas was on, and as far as I could prove, I was the only one in the apartment.

"Now I'm faced with another possibility. The bullet that killed Grand could have been meant for me."

She surprised me by giving me a theory rather than a lecture.

"I don't think so, but it's possible that a second one was, and Megan scared them away before they could get to you, so they tried to finish the job with the gas. How they got in, I have no idea, but it doesn't sound like your imagination."

"But why?"

"That's easy. You're getting too close to something."

"I wish I knew what."

"Well, it's a pretty sure bet that Grand didn't kill Tolzer. So you should be thinking about who else had a problem with the doctor."

"There's no shortage there. I already talked to Richardson and Lang, who work at the Institute. I can't see either of them doing it. Then there's Jordy Ponds, who got fired as the diet spokesperson, and there's a woman named Jeanette King, who had some kind of problem with Tolzer."

"I know you're not going to listen if I tell you to keep out of it, so do me a favor and watch yourself. Business is slow, and I can't afford to lose customers."

"No need to worry about me. I'm only going down to post bail for Megan."

"To post bond? You can't do that."

Sally sounded like she was talking to a dumb kid. "Of course I can. I posted one for Grand."

"Grand was in for a fistfight, not murder. You can't walk in and bail out someone accused of murder."

"No?"

"Of course not. She's going to have to wait in the lockup for a few days until the bail hearing. Then the judge will decide if she's a flight risk. If she's lucky and the judge does grant her bail, it'll be a million dollars. It could even be two."

"Shit, I don't have that kind of money."

"You have led a sheltered life. You don't put up the whole million, but you do have to give the bondsman ten or fifteen percent."

The percentage I knew. But I wasn't thinking when it came to the amount of bail. "I don't have a hundred thousand, let alone a hundred fifty thousand dollars."

That didn't mean I was going to sit back and let Megan rot in jail. I left

Sally's and headed to the police station to see Megan. I had to let her know I was there for her, even though it didn't look good.

Grand got shot before my eyes, and although I didn't see who shot him, I did see Megan with the gun in her hand after I came out of the alley. If I were the investigating officer, I would have booked her, too. Yet I didn't believe she did it. It was more than wanting to believe her story about picking up the gun from the street to protect me. I knew deep down inside she was telling the truth.

When I got to the station, the desk sergeant, a chubby bald guy behind a thick glass window in the lobby, was reading what looked like a tabloid. I cleared my throat to get his attention. He looked up and closed the paper at the same time.

"Can I help you?"

"Yes." I glanced at the paper, a copy of Woman's World. He must have felt a need to justify his choice of reading material.

"I like to read the 'Solve it Yourself Mystery,' " he said. "I usually guess who done it."

I leaned toward the round metal grill in the middle of the window.

"Good to know. I'll sleep better tonight."

"Thanks," he said. My sarcasm going over his head.

"I'd like to see Megan Hawkins."

"Hawkins? Let me look that up."

"Yes, Hawkins, the woman accused of shooting a man last night. How many of those can you have?"

"Hawkins, you say? A shooting?"

"Right."

"Don't see it. She must be getting processed. Want to wait?"

He motioned toward a row of blue plastic seats on my side of the window.

"I guess I don't have a choice. I'll wait."

"Make yourself at home," he said.

I sat on one of the hard seats for twenty minutes before I went back to the window.

"Was she charged?" I asked through the grill.

"Who?"

"Hawkins. Megan Hawkins."

The desk sergeant checked his computer again as if it were the first time I had asked him.

"I don't see her in the system."

"Of course she's in the system. She was brought in last night on suspicion of shooting a man. A while ago you told me she was being processed."

"Oh, you mean the girl who killed Grand?"

"Allegedly killed Grand, you mean. She's innocent until proven otherwise, as far as I know."

"I'd cool my jets, buddy, unless you want to get thrown out of here."

I took a deep breath and studied the lines in the grill until I calmed down. Mouthing off wasn't going to help Megan.

"Okay. I'll start over. I'm here to see Megan Hawkins, the woman who allegedly shot Lucky Grand last night. Would you be able to help me out?" I tacked on "Please" as an afterthought.

"Hold on."

The desk sergeant went into a back room. I heard muffled voices. When he returned a few minutes later, he sat in front of the window and leaned toward the circular grill.

"Have a seat over there, please."

It took all my willpower to control myself as I sat once more on one of the hard blue seats.

After cooling my heels for about five minutes, Nina poked her head out of a door in front of me.

"Nina. Uh, Officer Estevez." I had learned my lesson. I knew when I should use her professional name.

"Mr. Lazzaro, I understand you are here about Ms. Hawkins."

"Yes, I'd like to see her. Actually, I'd like to post bail for her if that's possible."

I said so with hopes that she wasn't actually charged with murder. I hoped that whatever she was charged with would carry a bail I could afford. Call me an optimist.

She motioned for me to go through the door, and I did.

"If you don't mind my saying so, I don't know if I'd want you to bail me out. If you know what I mean."

"Ha, ha. The officer is a comedian. I wouldn't quit my day job. Can I see her?"

Nina brought me into a small office that had only enough space for a desk and two chairs. She motioned for me to sit down. I did.

"How well do you know, Ms. Hawkins?"

"I met her a couple of days ago. Well, actually, I guess you could say twenty years ago. I told you that when we had dinner."

"Which is it?"

"Twenty."

"So, you know her pretty well."

"Hardly at all. Where is this going, Nina?"

"How did you know Lucky Grand?"

"I didn't."

"Yet, you posted bond for him."

"Yeah, about that, am I going to lose my money now that he's gone, so to speak?"

"You're out the bondsman's fee at least. What's more important is why would you post bond for someone you didn't know?"

"Because Megan thought he might have had something to do with the death of Dr. Alan Tolzer, and I'm doing a story. I told you all this."

"So, you got him out and delivered him to Ms. Hawkins?"

"Whoa. Wait a freakin' minute. If you think I had something to do with killing Grand, you should be talking to my lawyer."

"If I thought that, you would be back there in a cell."

"Well then, if you're not going to charge me with anything, this subject is closed. Now, can I see Megan?"

"No."

"Why not?"

"Because she's not here. She was gone before you left here last night. Someone came to get her while you were being interviewed."

"You released her before me? And you thought she had murdered someone? Sally said there had to be a bail hearing. You're kidding. Right?"

I could see by the look on her face that she was not.

"I tried to tell you there's more to Ms. Hawkins than you may know."

I was getting so nervous that the gash from when I got mugged was throbbing. I instinctively touched it to see if it was bleeding again.

"Who got her out? Where'd she go?" I demanded.

"I don't know the answer to either of those questions. Someone higher than me handled it. That's what I was hoping you could tell me," she said.

This was insane. I wished it was another dream. But it wasn't.

"Here's what I can tell you. I'm out of here."

Chapter Twenty-Four

When I got outside, I called the Westport Diet Institute hoping Megan would answer. Instead, I heard another young woman's voice on the other end of the line.

"This is Quincy Lazzaro. I'd like to speak to Megan, please."

"She's not here. Hence, you got me."

She spoke so fast that at first I thought she was speaking a foreign language.

"May I ask who I'm speaking to?"

"This is Stephanie. I'm a temp from the agency."

You would think the agency would train its temps in phone skills.

"Could you tell me when you expect Megan back?"

"I hope not for a long time. I could use the money."

"May I speak to Mr. Richardson then?" After a time, Richardson picked up.

"This is Quincy Lazzaro. I'm looking for Ms. Hawkins."

"That makes two of us. She didn't show up this morning. I had to get someone from an agency."

"Can you give me her home number then?"

"You don't believe in a person's right to privacy, do you, Lazzaro? You know I'm not going to give it to you. It wouldn't do you any good if I did. We've been trying to call her all morning."

"If she gets in contact with you, could you at least tell her I'm looking for her?"

"If she gets in contact with us, I'm going to tell her it's best if she doesn't come back. Her name is all over the papers. It's not good for the image of the Institute. We've had enough problems in the last few days."

Whatever you do, don't hurt the image of the corporation. That's what it was all about: the bottom line. Richardson was a first-class jerk. He didn't even seem to care that Megan was missing, yet he was pretending to worry about her privacy. No matter, a quick Internet search yielded me her phone number and address.

I tried several times with no answer. I decided to go to her place in the Silvermine section of Norwalk, not far from the well-heeled towns of New Canaan and Wilton. I found the house on a cul-de-sac of cluster homes.

I got out of the car in front of a boxy two-storied building. It had shutters and fluted columns that made it look like all the other construction on the street. I rang the bell. No answer. I knocked. Still no answer. I tried looking through the sidelights. All I could see were shiny hardwood floors and furniture like you see in the ads of the New York Times. Not my style, and just as well, considering what it must cost to live in a place like this. Tolzer must have been paying Megan pretty well.

A middle-aged lady walking a yappy poodle that I could swear was pink stopped on the sidewalk in front of the house. She squinted, and little lines appeared between her eyebrows.

"Can I help you?"

Odds were that she wasn't from the neighborhood Welcome Committee.

"I'm looking for my friend, Megan Hawkins. Might you have seen her?"

The woman eyed me with suspicion as her little dog broke away from her and ran toward me, barking like a maniac. I like dogs even though the tiny yappy ones aren't my favorite. I knelt and put out my hand, palm up, hoping the little mutt wouldn't bite me.

"Astaire! Keep away."

Like I was the one who was going to bite.

The dog sniffed my hand and then rolled on its back to have its stomach rubbed.

"Good fella."

"He usually doesn't trust strangers, but he seems to have taken to you."

Her voice was much less confrontational now.

"He's a great little protector."

I smiled at her, and she smiled back, but the smile turned to a look of concern.

"I haven't seen Megan since the day before yesterday. I read about her troubles in the paper. She's a good girl. I don't believe a word of it. Are you from the police?"

"No. As I said, I'm a friend, and I'm worried about her."

"I am too. I should have called the police the other day. I feel so guilty that I didn't."

"About?"

"The arguing that was coming from her place. Actually, she was doing the yelling, I assume at the man who left a short while later. Then everything seemed to be all right so I thought it best not to get involved."

"Did you see what the man looked like?"

"An odd fellow. Red hair. Short and wide shoulders, like a baboon, so to speak."

Grand. Megan told me she didn't know who Lucky Grand was when she saw him on the lawn. "When was this?"

"Last Sunday. About seven in the evening." That was the day before Tolzer died.

"Shit!"

I could tell from the look on the woman's face that she felt she had misjudged me, and she was sorry she had taken me into her confidence. She picked up her dog and walked away.

First, Tolzer was murdered. Then Lucky's luck ran out, but not before he told me someone at the Institute was making money on the side. If Tolzer threatened to fire that person, that was as good a motive for murder as I ever heard. Now Megan had disappeared, and it seemed she knew Lucky all along. What the hell was going on? If I had put something like this in my novel, I would have said I had written myself into a corner. But this was real life, and there had to be an explanation.

My goals changed. Not only did I want to prove Tolzer was murdered, but I had to figure out who killed Grand. I believed the killer was the same person, and it wasn't Megan. But the first step to proving that was finding her.

I remembered Megan telling Jeanette King she would call her to see if she was okay. The two seemed to be friends. I wondered if Jeanette had some idea of where Megan might be. I had a hunch that if I spoke to her, I could make some headway. I wanted to talk to her anyway. Jeanette had been angry at Tolzer. The question was whether she was angry enough to kill him. She could have a connection to Lucky Grand as well.

I knew Jeanette's address from Richardson's files. Using the Merritt Parkway, I drove the fifteen or so miles to Easton. Easton is an old-fashioned New England farming town plopped in the New York City bedroom that we call Fairfield County. I found the address without much trouble, a white two-story farmhouse with a wraparound porch.

I recognized Jeanette in her flower garden by her bushy salt and pepper hair. She must have spotted my car pulling in because she was wiping her hands on her apron and seemed to be waiting for me as I walked across her front lawn.

"Can I help you?"

Her voice was cheerful, and her question didn't hold the suspicion in the voice of Megan's neighbor when she asked me the same thing.

"I'm hoping you can. I'm looking for…"

"Let me guess. You're looking for the Helen Keller House. It's not on this road. A lot of people make that mistake."

"No, I'm not looking for directions. I was going to say I'm looking for information."

"You're looking for the library?"

"No. Actually, I'm looking for you, if you're Jeanette King." I knew she was. I remembered her from Megan's office.

She picked up a basket of flowers from the ground and held it in front of her, a move that belied her cheerful manner.

"Well, then today must be your lucky day, because you've found me. Mister?"

"Lazzaro. Quincy Lazzaro."

"You're the man who was with Megan the other day. And why, may I ask, were you looking for me?"

"I was hoping you'd heard from her. Any idea where she might be?"

She took an orange rose out of a basket and held it to her nose. For a second, she seemed lost in private thought, and then she was back to our conversation.

"Oh dear, I love her to death, but I wasn't surprised when she failed to call me. I imagine Dr. Tolzer stopped her. I warned her about him. He was a terrible person. You saw how he treated me."

Her mouth twitched as she put the basket on a small café table. I didn't want her to go off on me as she had done to Tolzer, so I backed off a bit, trying to gain her confidence.

"I did see. No matter what the issues between the two of you, he could have been more courteous."

"Courteous. That man didn't know the meaning of the word."

I wondered if Tolzer had even had a clue about how disliked he had been.

"I hear you. I caught a bit of his fury myself when I tried to interview him for my boss, Betty Ann Green. She writes the 'Cooking with Betty' column. We're working on a tribute to him now."

"A tribute to Tolzer? Good luck with that."

"What can I tell you? I like a challenge."

"Why are you looking for Megan?"

"After the police released her, she seems to have disappeared."

"Police? What are you talking about? Is Megan in trouble?"

Lady, where have you been? If she was telling the truth, she must have been the only one in the world who didn't know Megan had been arrested.

"I'm afraid so. It's all over the news. I'm sorry. I thought you knew."

"I don't own a television, and last week the cat knocked the radio off the shelf. What's happened to Megan?"

I noticed a folded newspaper on the table. I guess she hadn't read that either.

"The police think she shot a man named Lucky Grand. Did you know him?"

Jeannette seemed a little shaky for a minute, and I thought I was going to have to help her to a garden chair. "No. No, I never heard of him. Why would Megan shoot anyone? I don't believe it."

I could understand why she didn't believe it. I saw Megan with the gun in her hand, and I didn't believe it either. I didn't see why I should upset her more by sharing that little detail.

"The police took her into custody, but someone bailed her out. Now I can't find her. I'd like to help her if I can."

"Megan is the only one who has been nice to me at the Institute. She's the last person I'd want to see in trouble," Jeannette said.

"If you could help me understand what's going on at that place, I know we could figure out a way to help her."

"What is there to understand? A bunch of lowlifes runs that place."

"I could tell there seemed to have been bad blood between you and Dr. Tolzer."

"Not bad blood. We hated each other."

I raised my eyebrows.

"I have to give you points for honesty," I said.

"Oh, come on now. Do you like everyone you know?" This wasn't about me, and I wasn't about to answer. But if I did, the answer would be Rob Chase, my ex-wife's tennis pro and extracurricular partner. And not even he was worth killing.

"I like some people less than others," I said.

"Well, I'm not ashamed to say that when he got sick and died, I really didn't care."

So, she too was buying that Tolzer died of natural causes.

"Why the hatred?"

"It's all over those kopi berries."

"So, let me get this straight, you hated him over this Sumatran coffee."

"If he did to you what he did to me, you'd hate him too."

I remembered the crumpled-up letter from her that I found in Richardson's office. I put two and two together.

CHAPTER TWENTY-FOUR

"You were going to sue him over the berries. Am I right?"

"You have that only half right. I am going to sue him."

I shook my head. "I don't think so."

I could see the anger rise in her face. "Is that a threat? Because if it is, you'd better understand that I don't scare."

"It's not a threat at all. I'm saying the man is dead. You can't sue a dead person Would you mind telling me why you were suing him?"

"I am suing him. Since he's dead, I'll sue the corporation."

Ease up. Ease up on her, or she's going to clam up.

"Those are beautiful roses." I nodded toward the flowers in the basket. "I've never seen an orange rose."

"I grafted them myself to develop this color." "You're very talented. You remind me of Betty." Jeanette beamed.

"I love her column."

"Yes, her column. I know I seem to be prying, but there are going to be dozens of stories about Dr. Tolzer. If I could find a new angle, say something to do with the kopi berries, I have a shot at a job writing my own column at the magazine."

"I see. A new angle is your angle. Everybody has to have an angle. That's okay. It's what keeps life interesting."

"I like your attitude," I told her.

It always amazes me how much information people will give you if you catch them off guard, especially if they think they have been wronged. They seem to be looking for confirmation that they are right.

"I know I sounded angry before, but that's because I am. Tolzer won't recognize my rights."

She was still talking as if he were alive. I don't think his death had sunk in yet.

"The rights to the berries? How can you own rights to a coffee bean?"

"Not the coffee bean, the berries around the bean. They're loaded with antioxidants and fat-burning properties after they've been 'processed' through the civet. There is only one company that supplies those berries, which are the mainstay of the next generation of the Westport Diet. What

Tolzer can't, or I should say didn't, seem to understand is that I own part of that company."

"How may I ask?"

"I received it in my divorce settlement."

"From Dr. Tolzer?"

"Don't make me laugh. No, from my ex-husband, Stephen Richardson."

Wow, that caught me off guard!

"The lawyer from the Institute?"

"Yes, he invested in the supply company behind Dr. Tolzer's back. He knew the berries would be a major part of the new Westport Diet. The doctor wasn't happy about it, but they made some kind of deal. Of course, I was left out, and I haven't seen a penny of what I'm owed."

"How much would you say that is?"

"I've said enough already, Mr. Lazzaro. Let me know if you hear from Megan, will you?"

With that, she carried her basket of flowers into the house. I got into my Camaro more worried than ever about Megan's safety.

Chapter Twenty-Five

Somewhere along the Merritt Parkway, as I drove back to Norwalk, something brushed my foot. With my mind occupied with Megan's disappearance and Tolzer and Jeanette's feud over kopi berry supplement rights, the sensation didn't register. With the top down and the bright sun casting deep shadows under the dashboard, I couldn't see much when I glanced toward the gas pedal. I knew my imagination was getting the best of me. With two murders and Megan's disappearance all within a few days, I had shot nerves. I had to get my act together.

I fiddled with the radio and drove several more miles along the forested parkway with its amazing Art Deco overpasses. Every once in a while, I felt a light brush against my heel, probably a leaf or something rolling around under the seat. I considered pulling over to see if something was there. But that wasn't wise on the Merritt, with only two lanes, narrow shoulders, and traffic more suited to a superhighway than this scenic byway.

I drove on, enjoying the warmth of the sunshine. In fact, it was getting downright hot, and I considered putting up the top as soon as I got off at my exit. I fiddled with the dial on the radio some more to see if I could find a decent song.

Then, in my peripheral vision, I spotted something on the seat next to me. My first thought was a piece of coiled rope. A belt? I didn't put one there. It was the triangular head that made me realize I had a very unwelcome passenger.

Driving while talking on the phone is foolish. Driving while texting is dumb. Driving while a three-foot venomous copperhead snake is sunning itself in the passenger seat next to you is downright insane.

I'm not squeamish. I've jumped from planes, climbed mountains, and swum with sharks, but I hate snakes. They tell me my brother was afraid of snakes, too. If a war hero can be afraid of snakes, I had no reason for shame. It must be a family thing.

I kept my eye on the serpent as best I could while still minding the road. The traffic was heavy and moving at a good clip. With no place to pull over, I couldn't stop the car without causing an accident. No sudden moves, I told myself.

The snake started to move across the center console. No sudden moves. I glanced down. Its head was on my lap. Pissing my pants was not an option. No sudden moves. The snake slunk across my lap and then crawled down my left leg. I gripped the wheel until my fingers turned white.

I couldn't see it. I couldn't feel it. I'm not even sure if I could feel anything. I still had no place to stop, so I moved along with the traffic, my heart pounding and my hands so sweaty I could hardly hold on to the wheel. It seemed like I would never reach the next exit. Finally, one came up, and as I headed down the ramp much faster than I should have, I saw the snake's tail disappear into the dashboard. Once off the exit, I yanked the wheel to the shoulder and jumped out. There was no way I was going to get back in that car with that thing in there. I called Archie to come and pick me up. I spent the full hour and a quarter it took for him to arrive from Manhattan watching for the snake to reappear.

As Archie drove up, the snake came out of the dashboard and coiled up once more in the sun, this time on the driver's seat. I was not about to abandon my Camaro to a damned snake. I motioned Archie to stay back by his car and be quiet. From the side of the road, I picked up the longest branch I could find and touched it to the snake. The snake hissed, then opened its mouth wide. Afraid that it would slither under the seat, I worked the branch under the snake and lifted it. The serpent coiled around the branch. With one swift motion, I flipped the branch, and the snake flew writhing and hissing through the air. It landed on the hood of Archie's car with a dull thud.

"What the hell," Archie screamed as he ran away from the car. The snake coiled and made one abortive strike, hissed, slithered down from the hood, and disappeared into the grass.

"A snake," I said as if that said it all.

"I can see it's a snake. Why'd you throw it at me?" Archie's face was as red as mine must have been pale.

"You're afraid of a little snake? Come on, Archie, grow up. I threw it at you by accident. Okay?"

"First, you call me for a ride, and then you throw a snake at me, and you tell me to grow up. What's going on?"

"The only thing I can figure is that someone put it in my car."

"Who?"

Who indeed would try to kill me with a snake? Could Richardson have followed me to Jeanette's and put the snake in the car while it was out of sight on the other side of the house? Ponds? Could it have been the guy who put the message into the podcast? I started to call the police but thought better of it. They would say the snake dropped into the car from a tree. My biggest fear was that whoever did it had Megan.

"I don't know, Archie. Okay? I don't know."

"It has something to do with you putting your nose in that Tolzer situation, doesn't it? If you keep this up, someone is going to find out you write Betty, and there goes my job!"

"Your job!"

"And yours too. As your friend, I'm only looking out for you. Take my advice and don't get involved."

I looked at the seat where the freaking snake had crawled across my lap.

"Megan is missing, and someone tried to kill me. I am involved."

I called Billy, the mechanic at my local garage, and told him to pick up the Camaro and go through it thoroughly to make sure there were no more unwanted creatures. I left the key for Billy, as arranged, sitting on the right front tire, and then hitched a ride to the office with Archie.

Archie wasn't happy he had to come all the way up from Manhattan, a drive of over an hour, to give me a ride. He didn't say much on the way back to the city, which was fine with me. I spent the time thinking about recent events, and I concluded that somehow I missed the point when I was in only up to my neck and could have bailed out. Instead, I was definitely in over my head. The question was how far. I'm at my best when things are at their worst, and that snake in my car made me determined to prevail. I decided to redouble my efforts. Focus! Focus! This became my new mantra.

Chapter Twenty-Six

I recalled Amy saying that Tolzer's real name was Alan Tolzerano. And that he had taught school in New York City during the riots of the 1970s.

While Archie sulked the whole way back to the city, I used my smartphone to do a little research. I found a reference to a Tolzerano who worked at P.S. 131 in Brooklyn. The teacher had led a student march on city hall during that period. I called the school and asked if anyone there remembered someone by that name. The person who answered the phone told me to hold on and then came back with a negative reply. I was about to hang up when I heard indistinct voices. Then the woman was back on the line.

"Hold on. Mrs. Constantine walked in. This may be your lucky day."

Lucky day? I hoped she was right. I heard that earlier and ended up with a snake riding shotgun in my car. I caught Archie glancing my way every once in a while as I waited. I didn't offer any explanation about what was going on. Again, I heard muffled voices in the background, then a different woman came on the phone.

"This is Helen Constantine."

I explained that I was writing an article on Dr. Tolzer and was looking for anyone who knew him when he was Alan Tolzerano. She agreed to talk to me after school got out at 2:15 p.m. I looked at my watch. There was only one way I could make it.

"Well?" Archie asked.

"I'm doing a little research on Tolzer. Don't worry. It's for the tribute in the column."

Connecticut's Merritt Parkway gave way to New York's Hutchinson River Parkway. We passed through White Plains and Scarsdale in silence. Archie retreated into his thoughts, and I into mine.

I waited until we approached the Cross County Parkway. Archie put on his signal to exit before I let him in on my plans.

"Stay on the Hutch," I said.

"That's the long way to the office."

"Yeah, but we're going to Brooklyn."

"You might be, but I've got things to do."

"You heard me make an appointment with Tolzer's old co-worker. There's something about his background that doesn't fit. If she gives me anything good, I may prove that someone murdered him. If I do, then it breaks in Betty's column. It's a win for me and a win for you, Archie. Your father will give both of us raises."

I didn't mention that I also hoped it would get me out of the Betty column and into the investigative one.

Archie wasn't happy about it, but he threw on his left turn signal. He veered back into traffic, almost hitting another car.

We found the school in an up-and-coming section of the borough. It dated to the 1920s, judging from the two entrances, one marked Boys and the other Girls. This politically incorrect oddity aside, the four-story brick structure signaled a good, solid education.

Archie parked in a small visitor's lot and started to get out.

"Where are you going?" I asked.

"You don't think I'm staying out here after chauffeuring you all this way. I want in on this."

I didn't need him tagging along, but I didn't have much choice.

Archie made me open the door, and then he slipped in without touching it.

"I'll do the talking," I said.

We signed in at the office much the same way we signed in at the security desk in the lobby of the Ashfield

Building. Except here we both had to produce identification, state the reason for the visit, and wear name tags. Even with that, I had the impression the secretary did not trust two strange men in the building. I couldn't help thinking that this procedure would have been unnecessary back in the day when this was a new school. The world may have made a bit of progress in the area of sexual equality, but it has regressed in the area of equanimity.

The secretary had us wait while she called someone on a two-way radio. A big man in jeans and a plaid shirt arrived at the office door. She introduced him as Mr. Jenkins, the custodian, and she had him escort us to Mrs. Constantine's room.

The teacher was an African American woman. I calculated she had taught for more than 40 years, but she looked twenty years younger than I expected. I noted that she dressed more befitting of a CEO than a teacher. She smiled at us, but I could tell she wondered why we were there.

I explained that Archie was the editor of *On-Topic Magazine*, and he had given me a ride. She then greeted us with a ready smile and invited us to sit down at a long table by a bank of windows.

Archie's eyes moved from one corner of the room to another.

"Is something wrong?" she asked.

"Where are the chalkboards and bolted-down seats?"

"You'll have to forgive my friend. He hasn't been in a school building in a while."

"The building may be old, but we're state-of-the-art here. Electric whiteboards, e-readers, and laptops."

"I guess you've seen a lot of changes over the years," I said.

"Changes come and go in education. I've been in this building ever since I began teaching, and I've seen things come full circle several times. This will be my last full-time year."

"You're retiring?"

She glared at Archie, who was leaning back in his chair so only the back legs touched the floor. She cleared her throat, and he lowered it. It would have served him right if she had given him a detention.

"Cutting back. I have too much energy to retire. I'll sub once in a while.

But you're not here to talk about my plans for the future."

"You're right. I was hoping that you remembered Alan Tolzer. He's the nutritionist who recently passed away. He used the name Alan Tolzerano when he worked here."

"Yes, I remember Alan. He was on the staff when I arrived and stayed for another two or three years. He used to be very outspoken. Always butting heads with the community worker, a young girl, Rene, if I recall. Yes, that was her name, Rene Cooper."

"Butting heads?"

"Over what was best for the kids. They both wanted to start a lunch program. The children used to go home for lunch in those days. Half of them wouldn't return once they left the building. She was conservative, favoring basic foods. He was more radical. He believed in eating certain foods in combination with others to get the full benefit. He also favored less red meat and carbohydrates in favor of more fish and vegetables. He had ideas that are mainstream now but were innovative and controversial then. He was headstrong, and sometimes they would get into it."

"You got along with him?"

"To an extent. I was a rookie, and he hit on me more than once. I knew how to handle it."

"So, most of the teachers didn't like him?"

"No, that wasn't true at all. He was the kind of guy that you loved and hated at the same time. He always had one eye on moving up, kissed up to the principal. You know the type. We went out on strike that second year, and he was the only one to cross the picket lines. Meanwhile, I went to jail."

Archie was rocking in the chair again. Mrs. Constantine gave him another look. He made the front two legs of his chair come down with a loud thump.

"For striking?" he asked with a skeptical tone.

"It was against the law. Teachers couldn't strike back then."

"Why didn't he go along with the strike?" I wanted to know.

"He said he couldn't afford to. I understand to a point. Back when I started, teachers made only six thousand dollars a year. When he started, they made three. He always had a second job, so I don't know why he couldn't afford to strike. I suspect it was something more than the income. It was as if he were afraid of getting in trouble. He could have had a past for all I know."

"You say he left not long after you arrived?"

"It was at the end of my second school year. No, my third. I remember because it was around the time that I met my husband. He had recently come from Greece. In fact, Alan introduced me to him."

"Do you remember why Tolzer, or I should say Tolzerano, left?" Archie wiped his hands on his pants, ridding them of some suspected germs.

How did he get involved in this conversation?

"He got into some kind of trouble with the side job. I never knew exactly what happened with that. Then, a few years later, I heard he was calling himself Alan Tolzer. Dr. Alan Tolzer, to be exact. I always wondered if he stuck with Rene."

Archie leaned in across the table and asked another question.

"Rene, the community worker? I thought they didn't get along."

"I didn't say that. I said they butted heads often. Although the truth is, I thought they didn't get along. That is, until once I went to a party and Alan showed up. And who do you think was on his arm? Rene. And there I was feeling sorry for her."

"How's that?" I asked, taking the questioning back from Archie. I shot him a look to let him know I would do the interviewing.

Helen's eyes glazed over as she relived an event from long ago.

"You could tell Rene liked him. But from the outside, it didn't seem the feeling was mutual."

"No?"

"I told you he hit on me, and the way I understood it, every other woman in the building. Who knew Rene was shacking up with him all the while?"

"Do you think Rene knew about his fooling around?"

"Hard to say. It was the seventies. They were wild times. This was before AIDS. I guess I was naive. I didn't know what was going on for the most part. I knew a bunch of them hung around, but I didn't get into that stuff. Monday morning, they were all back in school holding the front line. You would think they were home grading papers all weekend. But somehow everyone survived. The bad ones went on to become principals. The worst of the worst became administrators in the central office. Now I realize that some of them who moved up had a hand in Alan's leaving."

Archie attempted to speak up again. "What happened—"

"To Rene?" I finished for him.

I was glad he was taking an interest in the case, but I couldn't allow him to interrupt my train of thought.

"She left about the same time Alan did. She went on to make a place for herself."

"As an administrator?"

"No, as a name on the FBI's most-wanted list. They say she bought the sawed-off shotgun that a seventies activist group used to kill a watchman at a grocery warehouse."

Chapter Twenty-Seven

"So why the sudden interest in the case?" I said to Archie when we were again in the car and headed back to the office.

"You're going to investigate it anyway. I may as well speed things up and give you a hand."

I knew taking the credit and impressing his father had something to do with it. As he drove me to the office, I reflected on what a freaking long day it had been. I got hardly any sleep the night before. I'd been on the go since six-thirty that morning, and at every turn, I had gotten more confused.

I'd found that Megan had been released from jail on the sly and now seemed to be missing. On top of that, it turned out she'd known Lucky Grand all along. Then I learned that Jeanette, at least according to her story, was a part-owner of the kopi berry supplement. Next, it became clear from the copperhead in my car that someone had it in for me. That made me wonder even more if the bullet Grand took had my name on it. And finally, I wondered whether Tolzer and René had stayed together after they left the school.

When we got back to the office, Archie went his own way. That was fine with me. I had a few things to do before I could go home to sleep. I had told Irene White that she could preview the part of the column that contained her interview. I was doing this as a courtesy. The interview was going in the column with or without her approval. I started to email the piece to her when I realized that my keyboard was sticking. That's what I get for eating while at the computer.

I was cleaning around the keycaps with a bent paperclip when Mr. Monahan stuck his head in the door. He was a big man with jowls and a pug nose that made him resemble Handsome Dan, the Yale mascot bulldog. He rarely came down to the office. He preferred to rule with an iron hand from his home in the Hamptons in the summer or Palm Beach in the winter. His son, Archie, was in charge of the everyday minutiae of running the magazine. But make no mistake about it, the end product of every edition had the old man's stamp on it.

Archie and I had been friends since our college days in Middletown. I had gotten to know his father over the years before I got the job with "Cooking with Betty." On the outside, away from the magazine, Mr. Monahan was a regular guy. He felt I was a good influence on his sometimes-shiftless son. But working for him was a different matter. He demanded that everyone rise to his lofty standards, including me.

The day had progressed into a sunny Friday afternoon. I knew right away if he wasn't on Long Island's East End, something was up. I had an uneasy feeling it wasn't good.

"Mr. Monahan. How are you, sir?"

"Am I interrupting your Free Cell card game, Lazzaro?"

"Not at all. Ah—you're joking. Right? Actually, I'm fixing the keyboard so I can get this out for Betty."

"Yes, Betty. She seems to put a lot of responsibility on you. You should take over the column."

"Me? No way. I don't know how to cook. Have no interest in it."

I realized how that sounded.

"I mean, other than helping Betty with the column."

Mr. Monahan scowled.

"My office. Bring that good-for-nothing son of mine with you."

He disappeared as fast as he had come.

I stopped what I was doing and rushed to Archie's workplace.

"Your old man wants to see us in his office. Now! Something's up."

Archie didn't seem worried.

"Leave it to me. I'll do the talking."

When we got to Monahan's office, we stood before his desk like two high school kids facing the principal. Archie whipped a small bottle of sanitizer out of his pocket and spread it on his hands.

"Why the long faces?" Mr. Monahan asked.

I gave a nervous laugh. "No long faces. We're swamped with work and anxious to get it done, that's all."

"I was thinking," Mr. Monahan said. I've learned that nothing good comes after the words I was thinking. Especially if your boss is saying them. "You boys should come out to the Hamptons this weekend. Bring dates, if you'd like. You deserve a little R&R."

I breathed a sigh of relief. I'd thought he was going to bring up Betty.

"That would be excellent. Unfortunately, I'm kind of busy with something," I said. That was true. I had a murder to solve.

Monahan grunted. "I wasn't asking. There's a charity event my wife is in charge of, and a few people reneged. She needs you both."

"It sounds very nice." I tried to sound enthusiastic, but my voice was as flat as if it were coming through cheap headphones. The boss didn't seem to notice.

"Bring Betty with you." I should have known, he was toying with us all along before he came in for the kill.

"Oh, that would be impossible, sir." My heart made the same ta-thump ta-thump ta-thump that my tires made on the bridge to Canfield Island that first day I visited the Institute. I wondered if the old man could hear it.

"Nothing is impossible. Be there. With Betty." The faux jolliness in his voice was making me nervous. I glanced at Archie and wished he would come to my rescue. Instead, he was picking nonexistent lint off his shirt.

"Uh." Think, Quincy. Think.

"I insist. I'm anxious to meet her." He was enjoying this. As for me, I was sure there was something unpleasant in my pants.

"Betty is still in St. Martin, Dad." It was about time Archie spoke up.

"Yes. She is. She should be coming back any day now with a blockbuster article on the Grand Case restaurants," I said.

"Yes. Gourmet capital of the Caribbean. I heard. You realize this is a very unusual situation, don't you?" Old man Monahan looked from his son to me making sure we understood that both of our jobs were on the line.

"Her going to the Caribbean? That's not unusual, Dad."

That's a boy, Archie. Keep going.

Monahan lifted one finger as a signal to pay attention to what he was about to say.

"Never showing her face is a very unusual situation, though. I like to know who my employees are. We're a family here, aren't we?"

"We are, sir." My gaze was fixed on his finger.

"And a family shouldn't have any secrets. Unless it's a dysfunctional family. We aren't a dysfunctional family, are we, Archie?"

"Not at all, Dad."

I almost laughed out loud.

"Quincy?"

"No. No dysfunction, sir."

"Good. As soon as she gets back, I want to meet her. She can come out to the Hamptons for the weekend. I'll send a car to get her, and her husband and kids too."

"I'll see what I can do," Archie said.

"I hope so. I'm leaving for Southampton in fifteen minutes. I'll see both of you at the house tomorrow."

Chapter Twenty-Eight

Most people in the New York area would give anything to spend a late summer weekend in the Hamptons. Not me. I fumed all the way home on the train because this weekend's sojourn was going to cut into my investigation. I had no choice, so I resigned myself to sun, sea, sand, and sexy swimsuits. On second thought, sometimes stepping back makes things clearer.

* * *

At about 8:00 p.m. I had the barbecue grill on my balcony cranked up. Fred Simmons called down from the balcony above.

"What are you doing down there, Lazzaro? It smells like the brewery caught on fire."

"Beer Butt chicken," I yelled up to him.

"You mean that thing where you stick a can of beer up the chicken's ass and then cook the hell out of it?"

"I'm experimenting with a new version. First, you drink half a can of Corona."

"I can handle that," Simmons said.

"Yeah, that's the easy part. Next, you squeeze a lemon into the beer in the can and add a shot of Bacardi. Throw in a ton of jalapeño sauce, chopped onion, some garlic, and lots of salt. Then you set the chicken on the can and put it on the grill."

"Smells wicked good from up here. Olivia went out and left me a quiche."

I was about to tell him that I'd send some up when my cell phone rang. The caller ID said City of Norwalk. I had a pretty good idea who it was.

When I heard Nina's voice, I went inside to talk. A call from her couldn't be good news. I had to watch what I said before it got ugly.

"Nice to hear from you, Sergeant Estevez. What can I do for you?"

"Look, Lazzaro, let's stop the passive-aggressive crap. I have something to share with you."

I looked at the grill through the slider. A little smoke was escaping from under the closed cover, but everything seemed to be going okay. If this experiment went well, the next column after the Tolzer tribute was as good as done.

"Why?"

"It's not because of your pleasing personality. Now, you didn't hear this from me, but that gun that killed Grand." I heard her click her tongue. "It was registered to Dr. Alan Tolzer."

Registered to Tolzer? He was already dead, so he didn't kill Grand. "Where are you going with this?"

"That doesn't bode well for your friend. Ms. Hawkins could have had access to it."

"Was the gun reported stolen? For all we know, someone took it weeks ago."

"I spoke to Mr. Richardson at the Institute. He said the gun was under lock and key in Dr. Tolzer's office. He wasn't aware of it being missing until I inquired about it."

"Or Tolzer gave it away. Did you ever think of that?" I lowered my voice before I lost control. "Can I ask you something?"

"What?"

"Why are you telling me this?"

"The reason is very simple. I got the word from Captain Brady, who got word from the mayor, to lay off on trying to link the Grand murder to

Tolzer's death. Someone in high places is putting on the pressure. I can't use the information. I'm hoping you can."

"You may have missed something, Nina. I'm rooting for Megan Hawkins."

At least I thought I was. After recent developments, it was getting harder to believe she was the angel I had believed her to be. Still, I wasn't about to share that with Nina, even if she was operating in cooperative mode.

"No strings?" I asked.

"I only ask that you keep me informed."

I took that to mean keep her informed with anything I found out from this point on. I hung up without committing myself.

I glanced out to the balcony. At first, I thought a heavy fog had rolled in. Then I realized there was more smoke out there than at a fireworks display in Little Italy. I rushed out and threw up the grill cover. The chicken sat on the can, its wings straight out from its side, with the tips in flame. It looked as if it were holding two birthday candles.

I needed a break. I called Simmons and asked if he wanted to hit the diner.

When we got down to the garage, Simmons insisted on driving his hybrid crossover.

"Like the new car?" he said as he pulled onto the street.

"Great." If you're a soccer mom, I thought. I should have insisted on taking the Camaro. Better to change the subject.

"Did I tell you what was in my car?" I asked. "A freaking snake. You believe that?"

"No shit. I hate snakes," Simmons said.

"You think I love them? I almost wrecked the car. The worst thing about it is someone put it in there."

"Hmm," Simmons said as he glanced out the side window.

"Hey, you passed the diner."

"Leave it to me, I know a good place," he said.

We passed several of the best restaurants in town. I was hungry and getting irritated. "Any of these places would be okay."

"Almost there," he said.

He took Reed Street to Cedar and crossed under the turnpike. Before I knew it, we were going up the Stevens Street hill toward Norwalk Hospital.

"Know what this is?" Simmons asked.

"The place where Harry Reasoner died?" I said as we pulled into the visitor parking lot.

"No. Well, yeah, but it's also the home of the greatest food in Fairfield County."

"Where?"

"In the hospital cafeteria, man. I eat there all the time. Reasonable prices, too. Not overinflated like every other eatery around here."

It was a big mistake to let him drive. I should have taken the Camaro. In the crowded cafeteria, I pushed my tray along the stainless-steel rail until I got to a pizza station. I ordered a slice. Then I got some cheese fries at another station. I decided that Simmons was on to something.

I met up with him in front of a toaster where he was waiting for a bagel. I toasted one too. Sally would say I was overdoing it on the carbs, but they looked too good to pass up. While I waited for the toaster, I eyed some blueberries on the fruit display. I'd heard good things about blueberries. The perfect thing to round out a healthy meal. I filled a small container, wondering how kopi berries compared in nutritional value.

"Sorry about the chicken, man," Simmons said.

"Yeah, I'm not having luck with animals. First, a snake in my car and then a phoenix in my barbecue."

"Hmm," he said for the second time that night.

I put an extra-large cup under the coffee machine and filled it. Simmons watched and grabbed a cup for himself.

"Coffee. My drug of choice," I said.

I eyed the bacon cheeseburger on his tray but decided to pass. I headed for the cashier, where I picked up a bag of chips and took out my wallet.

Simmons pushed his way in front of me.

"No, put that away. My treat," he said.

If he wanted to pay, fine with me.

We took the only table available, next to a group of medical workers wearing stethoscopes like rappers wear bling.

CHAPTER TWENTY-EIGHT

"Thanks," I told him. "You didn't have to pay."

"Not a problem," he said. "Besides, I kind of owe you for something that happened."

Nothing I would want to hear could come after that statement.

"I'm not following you."

"I'm feeling guilty. I may have made things bad for you."

"How?"

"The other night, Olivia asked me to run out to get some milk. She's always forgetting something when she goes to the store."

He was looking into space, trying his damnedest not to make eye contact with me.

"Where is this going, Simmons?"

"What I'm saying is I was walking back home when I spotted your car on the street with the top down. I knew it wasn't there when I went out."

"And."

"I saw a guy by your car; he looked innocent enough. I should have told you, though. He might have put something in the Camaro."

"Might have? Did he put something in it or not?"

"Well, I guess he did. I thought you were having him drop something off. But now that I'm thinking about it, what if it was the snake?"

What if it were the snake? Of course, it was the snake. That meant I had been driving two days with that poisonous copperhead slithering in my car. And I didn't know it. I wasn't going to waste time blaming Simmons for not telling me. First of all, it was my fault for leaving the top down while the car was out on the street. If the shoe were on the other foot, I would have thought it was a prearranged drop-off, too. Other than Mary Ticarelli, I don't think anyone else in the building would have thought otherwise.

"Well, what did he look like?"

"I don't know. He was a guy. I didn't pay attention."

"Think, man. This is important. Do you remember what he was wearing?"

Simmons gave a little shrug.

"Blue blazer, khaki pants. Does that help?"

"Yeah. A lot. You narrowed it down to half of the men in Norwalk."

Chapter Twenty-Nine

When we got back from the diner, Simmons went up to his apartment while I stopped at my mailbox in the lobby. Among the political mailings, I found a business-sized envelope from the State of Connecticut Department of Revenue Services. Bold letters on the envelope read Important. Open Immediately.

I ripped open the envelope and read it as I stood in the lobby.

Dear Mr. Lazzaro:

Your Connecticut Income Tax return(s) has been selected for review by the Audit Division of the Connecticut Department of Revenue Services. The records and information listed below are required in order to verify your tax obligation as reported on your returns(s) for the taxable year(s) 2016, 2017, and 2018.

The letter asked for copies of all W-2 forms and included a form "What to Expect in an Office Audit." I had to get the requested information in by November 15.

My state taxes were being audited. Not my federal, but my state. Whoever heard of such a thing? It seemed that someone in high places had it in for me. By the way, did I mention that it was state taxes? My first thought was Irene White. With her husband being a state senator and all, I imagine she could have pulled a few strings. Still, even though I knew when I left the interview with her, she was less than happy with me, I couldn't believe she would do something like this. But if not her, who?

I had already gotten the warning in the podcast that I had better stop putting my nose where it doesn't belong. Then the snake in the car. Now this. My questions were rubbing people the wrong way.

I didn't need the extra pressure of going through my tax records. Some of what they asked for went back to before my move down to Norwalk from Sachem Creek. I was going to need a psychic to find them. It was late, and I had been on the go since six-thirty that morning. There was no way I was going to look for my paperwork before I went to bed, and the next day I had to make the long schlep out to the Hamptons. Looking for the records would have to wait.

Chapter Thirty

After catching up on some much-needed sleep, I rolled out of bed at 10:00 a.m. with a craving for bagels and lox. Sally serves the best lox east of New York City, but I had a good two-hour drive out to the East End of Long Island ahead of me. I decided to make my breakfast instead of going to the restaurant. Of course, I didn't have lox on hand, but I knew I had some bagels in the freezer. I pried one apart with a knife and popped it in the toaster on the high setting so it would thaw. Turning to the fridge, I found a tub of strawberry cream cheese. The pink spread reminded me of the nonexistent lox. Remembering the can of anchovies in the cupboard, I decided to make a faux version of Sally's specialty. If it came out well, I could even put it in the column. Two of my favorite foods come in pop-top cans—beer and anchovies. I pulled back the ring and drained the olive oil from the anchovies can into the sink. The amazing grassy smell wafting through the kitchen filled my head. But the delightful aroma was soon replaced by the smell of something burning.

I popped the scorched bagel out of the toaster and decided I had no time to make another one. With no other choice, I scraped the burnt off with a knife over the sink, and I was back in business. I spread the strawberry cream cheese on it. Then I crisscrossed that with the little fishes. Summoning my inner chef, I remembered the half jar of capers sitting on my refrigerator door. Nina had left them behind the last time she cooked at my place. That was over a year ago. I opened the jar and sniffed. Smelled fine to me. I sprinkled the anchovies and cream cheese with the little green berries. Betty would be proud.

Mr. Lazzaro, breakfast is served!

I felt better with something in my stomach. In a better mood, I decided to make the best of the mandatory Southampton visit. At any other time, I would jump at the chance to hobnob with the likes of Christie Brinkley and Jerry Seinfeld. So why not?

* * *

Although Long Island is in clear view across the Sound from Norwalk, it may as well be on the other side of the world. There are only two ways to get to the East End by car. Both take forever. You can take a long, slow ferry ride from Bridgeport to Port Jefferson. Then you have to drive half of the island. Or you can drive down to the Bronx and then cross the Whitestone Bridge over the East River into Queens. Then drive almost the length of Long Island to Southampton. On a good day, you're talking about a two-hour-plus ride. On a nice weekend, forget about it.

Somewhere past Riverhead, when the traffic finally loosened its death grip, the usual East End landmarks started popping up. First was the giant blue-and-yellow Splish Splash water park sign in Calverton. A few miles later, the enormous concrete Big Duck in Flanders, watched over the road as I closed in on Southampton. Closer to town, the wooden Welcome to the Hamptons sign with the fancy gold lettering appeared.

It was almost two o'clock when I drove down Main Street. The center always reminded me of downtown Westport. The quaint nineteenth-century buildings of both towns had a refinement that linked them to the past.

I'd been to Southampton many times before with Brooke. She always insisted on stopping at Hildreth's, the oldest department store in the country. I thought the history of the place was cool, so I went along. But then she dragged me around the corner to every shop and gallery on Jobs Lane. Not my thing. On this day, I drove right past them all with no regrets.

At the end of Jobs Lane, I took a left onto Pond Lane. From that point on, nothing on the Connecticut Gold Coast even came close. If Westport is tony, then Southampton is á la mode with a cherry on top. For every mansion in Westport, there were four in Southampton. If Westport's car of choice was the Mercedes, Southampton's was the Bentley. As for me, SoNo was as upscale as I cared to get, and of course, Sachem Creek would always be my home.

The Monahan place was a turn-of-the-last-century gambrel surrounded by fifteen-foot precision-cut hedges. It wasn't exactly a mansion, but with six bedrooms and six baths, it was in good company with its larger neighbors.

The lawns were a hive of activity with people preparing for the evening event.

Archie, dressed in tennis clothes, came out to meet me. He shook hands and then wiped them on a towelette. He led me through the house, which was equally chaotic with party preparation, to the back porch. Leaning against a fat white column, he admitted he thought I was going to be a no-show. He wouldn't be Archie without a complaint.

He offered to get me a beer and retreated into the house. I settled into a cane-backed rocker to watch the noisy ocean waves crash on the beach. The ocean is so much more interesting than the usually placid Long Island Sound.

"What's with that?" I asked when he returned. I pointed to a large white papier-mâché creature on the far end of the lawn.

"The duck. What does it look like?"

It did look like a smaller version of the concrete Big Duck building I had passed on the way into town.

"Why?" I asked.

A young woman came through the screen door and gave me a big smile, showing off her over-bleached teeth.

"It's the theme of the fundraiser, Save the Duck," squealed Miss Bright Smile.

Did I come all the way out there to help save a freaking cement duck?

Archie was lucky he was my best friend, and even luckier he was my boss.

I didn't hide how pissed I was. He pretended it went over his head, but I noticed he stepped out of my range.

"Hey. Where are my manners?" Archie said. "This is Bo. She's a dentist."

No kidding. Looking beyond the chicklet smile, I saw her beautiful eyes and gorgeous chestnut hair.

"My folks have more or less dumped overseeing this shindig on me. I was hoping you two could entertain each other until the party,"

Good old Archie. I couldn't ask for a better friend.

*　*　*

Bo and I slipped away. We ended up at the Driver's Seat on Jobs Lane, eating lobster rolls under the umbrellas on the back patio. Never once did she say she wanted to drag me into the nearby shops. As I was ordering a second round, a Cosmo for her, a Sam Adams for me, I got a text message from Nina. We went back and forth.

Nina: White's staff asking questions ABT U.

Me: Y?

Nina: U tell me. Where R U?

Me: Going to a party for a duck.

Nina: Work or pleasure?

Me: Work.

Nina: Have fun. Don't eat the Foie gras.

Like most of my conversations with Nina lately, it was cryptic at best. There could be any number of reasons why White's people were vetting me. The most likely being that I was doing a story on his wife's cooking.

Bo sipped her Cosmo.

"I'm looking forward to tonight, aren't you?"

"Yeah, people don't do enough to save buildings shaped like ducks."

"That novelty architecture isn't done anymore, but I'm talking about the guests who will be there. Movie stars, authors, politicians—it will be so exciting."

I was sure that it would be if I didn't have a few things to attend to back home. A murder investigation and an income tax audit being at the top of the list. "Yeah, exciting," I said.

I took Bo home to change before the party. We got a little sidetracked, and the party had begun by the time we got back.

* * *

While Bo greeted friends, I wandered. A middle-aged woman wearing diamonds that made my eyes hurt cornered me. She gave me a ten-minute lesson on the construction of the Big Duck. Then she lapsed into how important it was to preserve the history of the long-gone Long Island duck farms.

"Weren't most of those farms cleared away to build homes for rich people?" I asked.

She blinked and then blinked again and walked away with a frown.

Was it something I said?

As Bo had pointed out, every celebrity in the tri-state area was there, including one I didn't expect to see.

I was standing alone between the fireplace and a set of French doors that led to the porch when a tall man on the other side of the room caught my eye and broke away from his group. As he headed my way, he straightened his jacket with an aggressive pull on his lapels as he neared me.

"Mr. White," I said in the way of a curt greeting.

"Mr. Lazzaro.

Although I had been a guest in his house back Connecticut, I never actually met the man. But he was familiar based on his constant television exposure. Since the magazine runs a fake picture of Betty under her byline, I'm far from recognizable. It was a mystery how he knew who I was.

"I'm surprised you know me," I said.

"Oh, I know a lot about you, Mr. Lazzaro."

"I'm surprised to see you slumming it on Long Island during the middle of the campaign."

"I have a place out here, as do many of my important constituents. Come."

He led me through the French doors to the porch, where a few people chatted. We walked down to the far end, where it was more private. The roar of the ocean was much more ominous in the dark than it had been in the afternoon.

"I would think all your constituents are important," I said.

"As you are. That's why I know your name. My wife has spoken of you."

"You're asking for my vote then?"

"No, I'm asking for your support."

"You want Betty's support, you mean?"

"No. I need your support in that I want you to give my family some space. I may be fair game, but my family's personal business is off limits."

So, I was striking a nerve somehow. That explained Nina's text message. And I could bet that it also explained why my taxes were being audited. I was at a loss about how I had gone over the line, though. After all, White's wife wanted me to interview her for the food column. She had even canceled an engagement to arrange it. It was free publicity for his campaign.

"That almost sounds like a threat," I said.

"It is what it is. A statement. I do not like having my family annoyed by a food columnist who has no idea of what he is getting into."

He turned away from me. I was about to ask him how I was butting into his family's personal affairs when Bo came along.

"There you are. You missed Molly Sims and Christie Brinkley singing with Alec Baldwin. I can't wait to read about that in Dan's Hamptons!" She covered her lips and looked around the room. "Opps, maybe I shouldn't say that too loud. It's not one of Mr. Monahan's papers."

Bo and I both laughed, but White took the interruption as an excuse to get away. I still wanted to ask what the hell he meant. Bo sensed a problem and stuck by me, pointing out celebrities like Paul McCartney and Billy Joel. I wasn't much interested. I went to the bar to get us drinks.

"A Cosmo for the lady, and I'll have a beer. No, make that a vodka martini, dry."

"How dry?" the bartender asked.

"Leave out the vermouth. Double the vodka."

"You got it, pal."

"Know what? Use rye."

"So, you want a Manhattan?"

"Yeah. That sounds good, and I'll take the beer too."

"Double shot and a beer chaser coming up."

I kept an eye out for White, but he was nowhere to be seen. Archie was all over the place, a real party animal, though he never came over to talk to me. Then I saw White and Mr. Monahan come from the library into the living room. They shook hands, and someone brought White his coat. I thought of going after him, but he walked out with a small group. I would never get a chance to say a word to him. Instead, I left the drinks on the bar and stomped over to Archie. I excused myself and broke into his conversation with Kelly Ripa.

"Go ahead. You two have things to talk about," she said and walked away.

As Kelly blended into another group, I pulled Archie aside.

"You didn't tell me Jonathan White would be here."

"What's the difference? He's a client, and he's a resident."

Bo joined us. "I thought you were getting drinks," she said.

"We have to talk in private," Archie told her. "Him and me." He pointed back and forth between us.

For the first time since I met her, Bo hid her pearly whites behind a frown.

"I see someone I know over there." She pasted her smile back on and walked away.

"Come with me where we can talk," Archie said.

He led me to the library and closed the doors. Hundreds of books sat on mahogany shelves that went from floor to ceiling. My guess was that few, if any, of them were ever read.

"You knew I've been looking into Irene White's connection to Tolzer," I said.

"You think she killed him?"

"I don't know who killed him. I'm trying to look into every lead. What I do know is that somebody is trying to hide something. And White told me to stay away from his family."

From the sheepish look on Archie's face, I could see there was something he wasn't telling me. Then it dawned on me.

"Your father invited us here because White wanted me to be here. And you were in on it. This whole thing, the invitation, Bo, it was all set up so White could give me a warning in person. Am I right?"

"The benefit to save the Big Duck was planned a long time ago."

In all the years I had known Archie, I don't think he had ever gotten me that pissed off.

"That's not what I asked."

"It's late, we'll talk about it in the morning."

Then he slinked out of the library like the weasel that he was.

If it weren't such a long drive home, I would have left then. I had no choice but to stay the night. I went upstairs to get some sleep.

Chapter Thirty-One

I t was about eight o'clock the next morning when I came out of my room toting my stuff. Archie must have been waiting for me because I found him in my face the instant I opened the door.

"Where are you going?"

"Back to SoNo. I have things to do."

"Look, I know you're pissed, but ya gotta move on. You know? Mother sent me up to get you for breakfast. She'll feel bad if you don't stay."

Mrs. Monahan had to be a saint to put up with her tyrannical husband and sycophantic son. I considered how she had always been nice to me and gave in. Besides, I hoped I'd learn something about why White thought I was a threat to him.

Archie went down ahead of me, and when I entered the room, he was already at the table with his mother and father.

"Good morning," I said to no one in particular.

Mrs. Monahan returned my greeting. Mr. Monahan's grunt could pass for either good morning or so I see you're still here. Archie said nothing at all.

"Nice party, Mrs. Monahan. I'm sure the Big Duck appreciates your efforts."

Mrs. Monahan, who proves that seventy is the new forty, made a waving gesture with both hands as if to say it was nothing.

"'I've loved that quirky building since I was a child," she said, then added, "I'm glad you could come."

I wished I could've said the same.

"That was quite an impressive guest list."

Archie straightened up in his seat and addressed his father.

"Q's referring to Jonathan White," he said.

Mr. Monahan poured some orange juice into his glass. He offered the pitcher to me. I waved it off. He took a drink. "Your loss. I squeezed it fresh this morning."

"I'll try it," I said.

He poured some juice into my glass. Then, acknowledging the super-sized pachyderm in the room, the old man spoke up again. "Do you know how *On-Topic* and all our other magazines stay in business?"

"The advertisers," Archie said.

"Tell Quincy again," Monahan said. "I don't think he heard it."

"He doesn't have to say it again. I know. The advertisers," I said.

He looked at me, showing surprise that I knew.

"Oh, please," Mrs. Monahan said.

Mr. Monahan glared at her as if to say he would handle it.

"Jonathan White cornered me a few days ago. He reminded me of how much money he spends on advertising in Connecticut Today. I didn't tell him this, but that revenue keeps that magazine in the black."

It's always the bottom line. I thought I knew where he was going with this.

"He also mentioned the guy who writes the 'Cooking with Betty' column. He said that guy had been causing a problem by poking his nose into his family's private business. Let me repeat that, the guy who writes the column." He emphasized the word guy.

No, that wasn't exactly where I thought it was going at all. But when I thought about it, White did call me a food columnist the night before. That he was investigating me.

In my mind, I started packing my office. I didn't want to leave behind my autographed picture of me and Derek Jeter or my Wesleyan mug. I pictured myself putting them into a cardboard box to bring back to Connecticut.

Archie opened his mouth to address the accusation, but I cut him off. I answer for myself.

"I can explain that, sir," I said.

"First of all, stop calling me sir, and second of all, I'm offended that you would think that I didn't know you wrote the column."

"You did? So, there's no problem then."

"Of course, there is a problem. There's the obvious problem of insubordination. There's the problem of deceiving the public. There's the problem of 'Cooking with Betty' being the most popular column I have. And then there's the problem of a politician thinking I will let him threaten me. Nobody threatens me. Especially not a politician. My magazines are in nobody's pocket, no matter how much they spend on advertising."

Archie jumped in, seeing an inkling of hope that he could save his skin.

"Good. Then you're okay with it," he said.

"No, I'm not okay with any of it. You're fired. Both of you!"

I have to admit that in one way it was a relief. Having no job wasn't the worst thing that had ever happened to me. I had to look on the bright side. I would have more time than ever to finish Killer View. It's funny, though. I was starting to get the hang of cooking. And I liked it. I guess the truth was that I was going to miss Betty in some weird way, almost as if she existed.

"But what are we going to tell our readers?" Archie said.

"You can tell them Betty died. Her car hit a cow. I don't care," Monahan said.

"I don't believe it. Do you want to kill the cash cow, Dad?"

"Of course not, you fool. Lazzaro, you are off the column. There was more than one Ann Landers. Why can't there be more than one Betty? Find someone else."

"Then I still have a job," Archie said. "I'll get right on it."

Well, that sucks. But what did I expect? Monahan wasn't going to fire his son and then have to support him. I put my napkin on the table and stood up.

"Thanks for breakfast, Mrs. Monahan."

Mrs. Monahan gave her husband a look.

"We didn't have breakfast yet," she said.

I shook my head.

CHAPTER THIRTY-ONE

"I'll get a McMuffin on the road."

"You should stay."

"I have a lot to do today, starting with finding a job," I said.

She shot another look at her husband.

"Bull hooey," she yelled. "You have a contract. I want you to get to the bottom of this damned story before someone else does."

"But I was fired."

"You work for *On-Topic.* That's my magazine, as are most of the others. Connecticut Today is the only magazine Marion brought to this marriage. That makes me the decider."

Mr. Monahan's first name was Marion? Imagine that.

"You're giving me the investigative reporter job?"

Again, Mrs. Monahan looked at her husband. It was he who spoke.

"You've got this assignment for now. Be grateful. We'll take it on a per-column basis."

"I can live with that."

"And you'll continue with 'Cooking with Betty' until Archie finds a replacement."

"That will be fine for a while. I can use the extra money."

"We're not talking more money until your contract is up. And don't say I can't do that. Read your contract."

So, I was going to be doing my dream column as well as my nightmare column, all for the same money. At least I had a job. I suppose Betty would say half a sheet cake is better than none.

I had my breakfast, and then I got out of there while the getting was good. I had mixed emotions as I drove the Long Island Expressway. Most of all, I was happy to be going home. Which reminded me, my first order of business when I got there would be to look for my tax records.

Chapter Thirty-Two

"Are you getting in from a bender?" Sally asked when I walked into her place at 4:00 a.m.

"No. I'm on my way to work."

"Hold on, I must be dreaming. You aren't that motivated to get up this early."

Sally made a big production of pretending to pinch her arm to wake up.

"I was up all night looking through my tax records. I figured I may as well get down to the city and get some work done."

I covered a giant yawn with both hands.

"If you ask me, you would have been better off with the bender. You look like hell."

"Skip the commentary. I'll have a coffee and something to eat."

"Newme! Bring Sleepy some coffee before the rest of the Seven Dwarfs show up. I'll rustle up something for him to eat." She turned back to me. "We're hardly set up. We don't open for almost an hour, you know."

When Sally went into the kitchen, I caught Newme's eye and motioned toward the bakery case.

"Boston Cream," I mouthed.

She placed a plate with a huge chocolate-topped doughnut in front of me. Nothing in the world smells as good as a Boston Cream doughnut. I reached for my wallet, but Newme waved me off.

"For all the grief Mom gives you, you deserve it," she said.

I sucked the thick vanilla custard out of the fill hole as I read The Norwalk

Citizen. An unbelievable story about a mountain lion killed by a car on the Merritt Parkway caught my eye. The Connecticut Department of Energy and Environmental Protection used DNA to prove it had migrated from South Dakota. That's a long way from Fairfield County. As I wondered to myself how the DEEP could justify a test like that in a poor economy, Nina sat down beside me.

"I guess it's true," I said.

"What?"

"A cop can smell a doughnut a mile away."

"Cute. I never heard that one before."

I stuffed the rest of my sweet treat into my mouth. Nina glared at me, but to her credit, didn't chide me. I washed it down with a big gulp of coffee. "Did you read about this mountain lion? The driver said it seemed to be attacking the car." I pointed to the article.

"Don't believe everything you read," she said.

I noticed some Boston Cream on my finger and licked it off. "Are you always that cynical, and do you always get here this early?"

"Usually. I have a job to do," Nina said.

"And you're good at it."

"But do you know what happens when you're too good at something? The big guys get nervous and start asking questions about your friends." The look on her face was not a happy one.

"Are one of the higher-ups giving you a hard time about me?"

"I thought you should know," she said.

I knew she crossed into a gray area of ethics when she sent me that text message.

"I appreciate the warning. At least I wasn't surprised when Jonathan White himself later told me to back off."

I thought Nina would be as outraged as I was, but she surprised me.

"You should be more careful who you hang out with."

"Listen, Grand wasn't a friend of mine. I didn't even know him."

"I was talking about Megan Hawkins."

"Megan? What are you getting at?"

"Do you know where she is?"

"No. Why do you think I'd know where she is? You're the one who released her."

"She got released on bail. She's not supposed to leave the area."

"Well, like I said." I licked some chocolate off my fingers.

She stared at me, and I braced for more questions. She was wasting her time. I had no idea where Megan was. I wished I did.

"Have you thought about what I told you about the gun?"

"That it belonged to Tolzer? Yeah. But I still don't think Megan killed Grand. Her story may be true. Someone else shot Grand with Tolzer's gun and then, knowing their prints were not on it, tossed it to the sidewalk."

"And you believe she saw it and picked it up."

"To protect me. Yeah. I do."

"Are you sleeping with her?"

What I was hearing couldn't be correct. Where did she get off asking about my personal life when, as far as I could tell, she wanted nothing to do with me?

"What would you say if I were?"

"I'd say it was icky."

"Icky? How? We're both adults."

"Icky. You're almost twenty years older than her."

"She's not a kid."

"But you knew her when she was a kid. You told me so."

"What right do you have to check up on me?"

"That's the second time you've accused me of that. I'm doing my job. That's all."

A few customers had entered while we were talking. Newme scurried over with her finger to her lips.

"Don't you two realize that everybody in the place can hear you?"

My first impulse was to talk louder so that everyone knew the police were trampling on my rights. Instead, I calmed down and lowered my voice to a murmur.

"You have no right to be looking into my affairs."

If she took the word affairs wrong, that was her problem. I didn't have to explain that my interest in Megan was paternal. Nothing more. Megan and I hadn't done a damned thing.

Nina spoke in a low voice as well.

"I didn't look into your affairs, as you put it. I made inquiries about Hawkins. That led me to your hometown. Your name came up as part of the investigation." I wasn't buying it.

"You came right out and asked me if I was sleeping with her. Was that part of your investigation, too?"

Nina's face turned red. "That wasn't official business. I was curious."

If I didn't know better, I would say Nina was jealous.

"Do me a favor then. Be inquisitive about somebody else."

* * *

I left without taking my breakfast and rushed over to the station where I hopped on the 4:52. Fifty-five minutes later, I was in Manhattan. Things were pretty bad when you had to go into the city to get away from the madness. It was a little after six o'clock, and the autumn sun had still not risen when I got to my building.

During the day, the Ashfield Building is a madhouse of activity. But when I arrived a little after 6:00 a.m. I found the lobby empty. I thought it odd that Cliff, the security guard, was not at his post. I figured he had taken a quick break for a smoke, thinking no one would be coming in at that hour. I signed in so he would know I was in the building and headed for the elevators. I wanted to put the final touches on the column and have it on Archie's desk before he got in.

With my deadline met, I would be able to readjust my strategy. Up until then, it was work first, sleuthing second. Now that I had the official go-ahead, if not the blessing, of Mr. Monahan. Thanks to his wife, I could put my all into finding the truth about Dr. Tolzer's death. And the sooner I did that, the better. Until resolving the case, I didn't stand a chance of getting back with Nina.

Once on the eighteenth floor, I let myself into the On-Topic offices. The lights were on in the reception area. But the corridor beyond was dark except for a blade of light from a half-opened door. As I walked down the hall, I realized the beam was coming from my office.

Someone was in my office. My heart raced, and I stopped to listen. Not hearing anything, I told myself to calm down. It was only a case of the cleaning crew ignoring the company's energy conservation policy.

My desk faced the window so I could take in the views of the Hudson and the Hoboken piers on the other side of the river. When I stepped through the doorway, I could see the back of a figure who was at my computer.

"Hey, what are you doing?"

The guy snapped off my desk lamp. In the time it took for my eyes to adjust to the darkness, he pushed me down and ran into the hall. By the time I got up and got my bearings back to follow him, all I caught was a glimpse of his blue blazer and khaki slacks. He was dressed the same as the guy Simmons saw throwing the snake into my car.

The guy charged through the door to the stairwell.

"Stop!" I yelled.

He didn't. Not that I expected him to. It doesn't work on television, and it doesn't work in real life.

I bolted down the hall, hit the panic bar, and flew through the door. I could hear the ring of footsteps on the stairs. Down or up? I listened. He was going up. Odd, I thought. I would go down if I were trying to escape. If he was going up to the next floor, it was to confuse me. He'd then take the elevator down. Guided by the dim light of the stairwell, I pursued him up the stairs. Then I realized I couldn't hear footsteps any longer. Was he lying in wait to jump from behind the pipes that ran along the inside corner of the stairwell? With the smell of the damp concrete in my nose, I stopped at the nineteenth floor and opened the door. I looked down the passageway. Two men I recognized from around the building were talking in the hall.

"Did you see anyone come in?" I called.

CHAPTER THIRTY-TWO

"From the stairwell? No," one of them answered.

I ran up to the twentieth and checked that floor. A cleaning lady was pushing a wide mop down the hall.

"Did a guy come in here?"

She shook her head and kept mopping. So whoever that guy at my computer was, he seemed to have outsmarted himself. Not being able to use the elevator on the nineteenth or twentieth floor, he had only one place left to go, the roof. I ran up the last flight to the roof and opened the stairwell door with caution.

Only in New York would you see a nineteenth-century water tower perched atop a modern twenty-story building. They're actually wooden water barrels on legs. This building had five of them, each separated by air conditioning units that hummed and percolated in the morning air. In the predawn, the towers and huge condensers offered plenty of places for my assailant to hide. Meanwhile, the lights of surrounding buildings made me a prime target, so I tried to stick to the shadows as well. Could it be I had lost him? Had he gone over the side? Doubtful at twenty stories up.

Being careful not to drop my guard for a second, I edged toward a cooling tower. Then I felt the weight of someone on my back, knocking me to the rooftop. The huntsman had become the quarry. That mountain lion on the Merritt Parkway came to mind. I sprang at my attacker like a wild animal, causing him to fly against the parapet. To my astonishment, he tried to scramble over the wall. Knowing it meant certain death for him, I lurched at him to pull him back.

We struggled some more. He went over, holding on to the rail. Things were happening fast, but somehow I knew this was no stranger. Who? I clasped his wrists and tried to pull him back. His weight was pulling me over. Finally, I pulled him onto the safe side, and he landed face down on the roof, gasping for breath. I helped him to his feet, and he pushed me away. I hit the pipe railing on top of the parapet with my stomach. My torso hung over the side as my feet lost contact with the rooftop, making me a human seesaw.

Below, the city was waking up. I could see a few people on the illuminated sidewalks below, oblivious to what was going on over their heads. It had to be sheer adrenaline that stopped me from going over as I grasped the pipe railing.

I settled myself on the rooftop, winded and angry. Then I caught a glimpse of him running toward the stairwell. As he got to the door, something made him turn and run for the furthest of the water towers. I wondered if he heard someone coming up the stairs.

I ran to the tower and jumped for the iron ladder. After pulling myself up, I climbed after him. As I got close, he began kicking toward my head, and I grabbed his leg, and his shoe flew off. It landed in the huge whirring fan at the top of a cooling unit below us. There was a shredding sound, and bits of leather and rubber pelted my back. He kicked again, and I jerked my head away.

My feet slipped, and I hung on to the rung above my head for dear life as he stamped on my fingers. I managed to get my feet back on the ladder and grabbed his leg with one hand. I knew I could fling him off now, and he would meet the same fate as his shoe. That would be an extreme punishment for going on someone's computer. But I had no intention of getting chopped and diced myself. I decided to try to reason with him. My breathing was heavy, and it was a struggle to get the words out.

"Listen, man, this is going to kill one of us. Let's get the hell off this tower before that happens."

He stopped kicking when a bright light from below lit up the side of the water tower.

"Come down from there. Now! The both of you!"

What a clown. You'd think we were high school kids painting graffiti on the water tower. Didn't he realize this was a life-or-death situation?

"Sounds good to me. How about getting the light out of my eyes so I can see?" Then I directed my anger at the other guy. "And you up there don't even think of kicking again, or I'll make sure you end up in that fan."

The light moved away from my face, and I inched my way down one rung at a time. I tried to keep an eye on the guy above me to make sure he didn't try to knock me off again. When I got to the bottom, Cliff, the security guard, was waiting with a flashlight in one hand and a gun in the other.

"Mr. Lazzaro. What the hell is going on here?"

I bent over with my hands on my knees and took a minute to catch my breath. I was getting too old to chase people down and fight with them on top of skyscrapers. Something told me eventual middle age was going to suck.

"Ask him," I finally managed to say. Cliff was acting like I was the bad guy here, and I wasn't too happy about it.

"You mean Tommy?"

"Tommy? Who's Tommy?"

I took the light from Cliff and shined it in the young guy's face. It was Cliff's nephew, Tom Baylor, the office intern.

Chapter Thirty-Three

From the way the guy acted, I'd assumed he was planting threats on my computer. I had no idea it was Tom Baylor at my desk. He always seemed like a nice enough kid, and Archie did say everyone in the office hopped on my machine. Still, why would he overact like that if he was just using it?

Speaking of overreacting, I almost got both of us killed by chasing him up to the roof like that. I didn't like the way this investigation was making me act. I had to watch out or something bad was going to happen.

Cliff's hand was shaking, and it was making me nervous. I'm not used to having a gun held on me.

"You can put the gun away," I said.

Cliff looked down at his hand. I don't think he even realized he was pointing the weapon at us. I knew he wouldn't use it, but still, I'd feel better with it in his holster.

"We're only horsing around. The kid here bet me he could get to the top of the tower before me." I figured it was my advantage to play this down for now.

Tom shot me a glance as if to say thanks. Cliff, on the other hand, didn't seem impressed.

"If you don't mind my saying so, Mr. Lazzaro, you're a little old for that kind of foolishness."

"Yeah, what can I tell you? It was a challenge."

"Do you guys know what kind of position you've put me in? There are security cameras all over up here. I have to call this in."

That wasn't good news. If he called it in, the police would get involved, and I didn't want to deal with them. It might come out that I'm Betty for one thing. For another, Nina might get wind of it, and then I'd get another lecture about staying out of police business.

"I don't think that's necessary, Cliff."

"It sure as hell is. My job could be at stake."

"Okay. Do what you have to." If he wanted to explain how I got into the building without his seeing me, that was his business, but I felt I should warn him. "I didn't see you at the desk when I came in."

"You did sign in, didn't you?"

"Well, of course. I didn't want you getting into trouble for not being at your post."

Realizing that he had as big a problem as I did, Cliff groaned.

"Thank God you did that at least."

Tom took the opportunity to chime in. "Look, Uncle Cliff, nobody is going to look at those security tapes unless there's a problem. As long as you don't make this a problem, no one is going to ask to see the tapes."

"I've got a trainee covering downstairs, and I can't leave her there on her own too long," Cliff said.

Tom raised his eyebrows at his uncle. "Her? I didn't see any trainee, unk. I didn't see you either. Why were the two of be away from your post?"

It was clear what Tom was thinking. He didn't have to say anymore. His uncle got the message; the kid might mention to his aunt that he and the woman trainee were MIA for a while.

"I want you two clowns off this roof. Grow up and any more of this crap from you, and I'll throw both of you over the side myself."

Good old Cliff. I'm sure he wouldn't have been as lenient if the circumstances had been different. Lucky for him, we weren't terrorists. He'd have a lot of explaining to do about why he and the trainee weren't at their post, even if it was so early in the morning. He escorted us to the On-Topic offices.

"Make sure this doesn't happen again is all I have to say." Then he got on the elevator, and the doors closed.

When I turned from the elevator, Tom was sneaking down the hall. I ran after him and grabbed his arm.

"Not so fast, you." I dragged him into my office. His face was white as copy paper when I pushed him into a chair.

"What?"

"Why did you run?"

"I knew you'd be mad that I was on your computer. I was right, too."

"So you ran to the roof and up a water tower. That doesn't make sense."

"It's a good place to hide. I go up there for a smoke all the time."

The kid had an answer for everything. "I want to know why you were fooling around with my computer."

"I was looking at laptops online. I'm buying a new one."

"You came in during the middle of the night to use my computer to look for a laptop. I don't buy it."

"I'm supposed to be here early. It's part of my job to have certain things set up before everyone else gets here."

True enough, but I still had my suspicions. I switched on my computer to see if I could find any evidence that I was not overreacting. I looked to see the last program run on the computer. I found it was iTunes. I opened the program.

"So I like music," Tom said. "You have a problem with that?"

"We'll see."

I clicked on the most recently added item.

A computerized voice came on. "Lazzaro, this is your last warning. Lay off."

"Well?"

Tom held his breath for a second or two.

"It was only a joke."

"A joke? In my book, murder is not funny."

I didn't think it was possible, but Tom's face grew even whiter.

"I don't know anything about a murder! Honest. Someone paid me to put a couple of messages in your podcast queue for a joke. I didn't see anything wrong with it."

I had a pretty good idea of who put the Baylor kid up to putting threats on my computer.

"Who put you up to this? Was it Stephen Richardson? You put a snake in my car, didn't you? The guy who did it was wearing Khakis and a blazer." Tommy pulled back a little.

"Dude, you're nuts. I hate snakes. And a million guys wear Khakis and a blazer. All I did was put a little joke on your computer. It was no big deal. Why are you flipping out?"

"If I don't get some answers soon, you're going to see how I can flip out."

"Okay. Okay. It was a guy from a tennis club called ACE."

"ACE."

"Yeah. He called here and asked to speak to an intern."

"Did he ask for you specifically?"

"Yeah. He asked if I wanted to make a little extra cash to play what he called a joke on you."

"How did this guy know you?"

"I don't know. Someone must have told him I work here. The guy offered me some free lessons, then he tells me he wants me to play a joke on you. He said you'd think it was funny."

Ponds. Of course. He had the motive to kill Tolzer after the doctor canned him as the spokesman. I could see why he wouldn't want me poking around.

"You're talking about Jordy Ponds."

"The owner of the tennis club? No. Why would he do that? The guy is a tennis instructor named Rob."

Brooke's boy toy. And I thought I had everything figured out. Then the realization hit me that those threats in my podcasts had nothing to do with either murder. I was so fixated on connecting the threats to the murder that I never even considered that Rob would be involved. It was nothing more than a childish trick. How freaking frustrating. I was nowhere.

Just then, Tom's cell phone rang. He glanced at it, and a weird look came over his face. He ignored the call. I grabbed it just before he could slip the phone in his pocket. I hoped it might be Rob. I was ready to give him a piece of my mind if it was. I looked at the screen and read the name on caller ID.

Megan Hawkins.

Chapter Thirty-Four

"Hello," I yelled into the phone. I don't know if Megan recognized my voice or not, but I was certain she realized it was not Tom. She hung up. When I called again, it went to voicemail. She had switched her phone off. No big deal. I wanted to talk to her face-to-face if I ever found her.

I was about to confront Tom further about the snake and Simmons's report when the magazine's art director appeared at the door. The day was just beginning, and she already looked like a frazzled wreck.

"Ah, there you are. Tom, I need you to bring a package Uptown right away. Follow me to my office. Excuse me, Quincy."

She was gone before I could protest. Tom shrugged his shoulders and put on a stupid smile.

"Guess I have to go," he said.

"Go. But we're not finished by a long shot." I pushed the cell phone across the desk a little harder than I should have, and it went over the edge. Tom caught it before it hit the floor. He looked at the caller ID.

"I don't know who that was," he said. "Honest."

The guy was a pathological liar, and I wanted answers, but people were already filing into the office, and the last thing I needed was a scene.

"Out!"

He left without another word.

I paced my office like a tiger in a cage. Control. I needed control. After my divorce from Brooke, I'd sworn I would never again let circumstances dictate how I acted, no matter how pissed off I got.

I'd once heard a golf psychologist recommend cataloging the vertical and horizontal lines in your environment to calm down. "Don't count them," she'd said. "You only have to notice them." The act was supposed to be soothing. So I looked out the window.

The sun was well above the horizon now, and the New York skyline filled my view. To the east, the Empire State Building poked above the others. Lines. Plenty of lines. To the south, the jumble of lower buildings, old New York, spread out in shades of stone and brick. Deep breath. It was working. I turned west to the High Line, that ribbon of calm built on the old, elevated train tracks. More lines. Slow the breathing. That's it. Quincy is in control. A traffic helicopter skimmed along the West Side Highway, and beyond it I could see the Hudson and New Jersey.

If I had to face that Megan was somehow involved, I needed to look at it rationally. I could do that. My eyes settled on the fluid glass forms of a Frank Gehry building by the Chelsea Piers. Not a straight line in the damned place. Not. One. Damned. Straight. Line.

I picked up the Wesleyan mug holding my pens. There had to be an explanation for why she was calling the guy who was putting threats on my podcast list. I hoped it was a simple one. I contemplated the mug. Not. One. Damned. Straight. Line. I was in control. I would get to the bottom of this. Period.

Then I smashed the mug to the floor. Pens and ceramic shards sprayed across the office like shrapnel. What the hell was she up to?

Chapter Thirty-Five

My tsunami of temper receded, leaving me with a mess to clean up. It included not only the shattered remains of my college mug but the loose ends of my life. I didn't need stupid devices like finding straight lines to gain control. I needed to take care of business. My first order of business was to meet my deadline for the column. Without that hanging over my head, I knew everything else would fall into place. The office was getting down to work and despite questions about Megan weighing on my mind, I took advantage of the quiet time to get some work done.

I was proofreading the column when Archie came into my office. I caught a glimpse of him in the window—his reflection beaming from ear to ear like he'd just won the lottery.

"So. All's well and all that stuff," he roared behind my back.

"If you thought that was going to startle me, you're crazy," I said.

"The man has nerves of steel. Look at that. Didn't even flinch." Archie headed straight for the bottle of Purell on my desk.

"I'm busy here," I said.

"You know," he said, squirting a dollop into his hands, "some people might say you're antisocial, sitting with your back to the door like that."

"You almost have to be antisocial to work around here," I said.

"Didn't I tell you my father would be cool with the Betty situation?"

"He never even asked why I was writing the column," I said.

"Don't worry about it. I explained it all to him."

"How did you explain about Betty?"

"I told him the truth. She was set to do the column. But then her car hit a cow in St. Martin, and she was killed. They scattered her ashes on Orient Beach. When I told you I was in a bind, you insisted on me giving you a shot at the column.

"That's not what happened."

Archie knew that full well, but I felt I had to set the record straight.

"I had to tell him something," he said.

"He bought it?"

"Yeah, but it bummed him out. It seems he and Betty went way back."

"What the hell? That's what Tolzer said too. Are these people delusional, or am I going nuts?"

Archie lifted his shoulder in a half shrug. "Turns out there really was a Betty Ann Green. I must've heard the name somewhere, and it floated up when I dreamed up the column. She was a food writer back in the sixties; some kind of hippie version of a cougar. Who knew?"

At least there's some closure for Betty, I thought. I guessed even fabricated people needed closure.

"Well, at least it's out in the open," I said.

"Hold on there, buddy. There's nothing out in the open," Archie had this serious look on his face.

"Your father knows I've been writing as Betty."

"Right. But that's as far as it goes. Nobody else is to know. No-Bod-E!"

"I didn't hear him say that yesterday," I said trying to be as serious as he was.

"You signed a confidentiality agreement when you took the job. He had the lawyers look at it. It covers this situation."

I should have known that Monahan was going to protect his interest. The column was a moneymaker, and he couldn't risk a scandal. That meant I still had the burden of doing the column and hiding that I was Betty. Plus, I had to do a separate piece if I proved that Alan Tolzer's death was a murder, all for the same pay.

"I'm looking for less work, not more. I'm this close to finishing my novel."

I held my thumb and forefinger about two inches apart. Archie wasn't impressed.

"There's one more little thing I have to reinforce with you."

Not only did I not want to hear it, but I also wanted to get out of there before I ended up with even more work. I shut down my computer and stood up.

"I have a feeling I'm going to hear it whether I want to or not."

"Go where the story leads you with my father's blessing. But be a little discreet when you're dealing with the advertisers."

Why didn't that surprise me? I didn't blame Archie. He had done what he had to do to save his ass and mine, too. It was no more or no less than I expected of him. After all, he was Archie. I kept in mind that when I was out of a job and broke, he gave me a job, even if he did trick me into it.

"Tell me one thing. Did White have my income taxes audited?"

Archie gave his hands another shot of hand sanitizer.

"My guess would be…"

"What?"

"My guess would be a guess. So why bother?"

He gave his hands another shot of sanitizer and left.

I took that as a yes. In that case, I decided to forget about emailing my piece to Irene White for her approval. I'd deliver it to her in person and confront the Whites in their home. I'd deal with Monahan when he found out. Besides, Irene might have some idea of where Megan was. I had a few questions for that young lady as well.

Archie had no sooner left the office than my cell phone rang.

The caller ID said, Unknown Caller. I answered out of curiosity.

"It's Megan. Was that you on the phone before?" she asked.

Her voice caught me off guard, and I hesitated before I answered.

"If you mean on Tom's phone, yes. Where are you?"

"Why did you answer his phone? What's going on?"

"What's going on is that I'm confused. My ex-wife's boyfriend hired our office intern to send me threatening messages. It was a childish prank and had nothing to do with the murder of either Dr. Tolzer or Lucky Grand as far as I can see. It should be case closed. But is it? No. Because while I'm trying to scare the hell out of Tom Baylor, his phone rings, and who is the call from? You."

"And your point is?"

"My point is, what the hell is going on? How do you fit into this business with Tom Baylor?"

Megan's voice was almost a hiss. "I'd feel a lot better if I knew exactly what you are accusing me of."

I had to hold back my temper. I spoke with measured words as I tried to sound calm.

"I'm not accusing you of anything. But I'd like to know how you know Tom Baylor."

"If you must know, I met him at ACE. He's been taking tennis lessons there. We're friends, and he understands where I'm coming from."

True, she told me that Ponds gave her a free membership to ACE. And Baylor said he got lessons from Rob in exchange for putting the stupid messages on my computer. So that made sense. She could have met Tom there; a lot of the younger people use the tennis facility as a hangout. Megan's friendships were none of my business. But knowing what Tom was capable of made me wonder if there wasn't a sinister side to their friendship. I thought it best not to make further accusations and listen to her explanation.

"I shouldn't have questioned you," I said.

"No, you shouldn't have."

"It's that this thing has me crazy because I thought the threats had some connection to my investigation. Tom and I got into a fight on the roof of this building. We both could have gotten killed."

"Is he all right?" I could hear the alarm in her voice.

"He's fine. Me too, thanks for asking. Then, when I saw your call to him, I didn't know what to think."

Megan grunted, indicating she at least understood where I was coming from.

"Tom and I got to talking in the juice bar at ACE one day. He mentioned he was an intern at *On-Topic.* I asked him if he knew you. He said that not only did he know you, but you two were great friends."

"I got him a job as a favor to his uncle. That's about the extent of it."

"Well, we hung out at the juice bar several times, and my impression was that he considered you to be a mentor. Then one day, he mentioned that he and another friend of yours were playing a running joke on you. He didn't say what."

"A friend? If you mean that tennis instructor, we are definitely not friends."

"I didn't realize what was going on until last night. You mentioned before that your ex went out with a tennis pro named Rob. Then it dawned on me that they might be the same person. I realized that this guy was using Tom to give you grief. I couldn't wait until this morning to call Tom to tell him to lay off on the messages."

"That's when I saw you on his caller ID."

"And you thought the worst."

And why shouldn't I? The guy even lied about knowing her.

"Can you blame me?" There was silence on her end of the line.

"I said I'm sorry,"

"No, you didn't."

"I should have, then. Tell me where you are. I'm worried about you."

The phone went dead.

Chapter Thirty-Six

On my way to the showdown with the Whites, I made an unexpected detour to Brooke's house in Sachem Creek. I was in the area, but the real reason was a need for simplicity, something I had to do to clean up my life before everything else began.

As I approached Brooke's front door, which had once been my door, my pulse hammered. My stomach did those old, familiar flip-flops, just like when I used to pick her up for a date when we were kids. A voice screamed in my head: *You're nuts. Turn around. Leave.* I ignored it and rapped the brass clamshell knocker, a housewarming gift from my aunt, a lifetime ago.

Brooke looked as surprised to see me as I was to be there. Judging by her Nike sports bra and running shorts, she'd been ready to hit the Trolley Trail for a jog.

"Quincy." Her voice held no welcome for her ex-husband.

I nodded. "In the flesh."

"Why are you here?"

I held up her recipe box. "I came to give this back to you."

She looked at the wooden container as if it might bite. "You could have mailed it."

"I could have. But I was driving through, and it felt like something I needed to return in person."

Her mouth tightened. She didn't buy my story for a second. "What brought on this sudden change of heart about giving it back?"

I held her gaze. "I guess when I realized it meant so much to you that you had Rob send that intern to leave messages on my device."

"Rob thought he was helping me. I had nothing to do with it. Believe me, I'm furious with him for doing that. He regrets telling me about it as much as he regrets having that kid mess with your computer."

"I can believe that," I said with the thought of her destroying my kayak in mind.

Brooke's eyes narrowed, and for a minute, I braced myself for the familiar explosion.

"Here we go again," she said, but the words carried no harshness.

"The point is," I continued, "I could have gotten that kid killed, chasing him up the water tower. All over this stupid box. It's not worth it."

She seemed to be struggling to say something. Holy crap, was she actually going to express gratitude?

"You're welcome," I cut in, sparing her the trauma of having to speak the words aloud.

"Rob knows a lot of people down in Fairfield County," she said, shifting gears entirely.

Now that she had my attention, I tried to find out what was on her mind. "I guess he would, working at ACE," I said.

He also knew Megan, but I kept that to myself. I'm not a troublemaker, even with Rob.

"Well, he didn't want me to tell you what one of the women at the club told him. But he owes you, after what he did. Jonathan White was putting the screws on Alan Tolzer. His goal was to close down the Westport Diet Institute."

This was better than a thank you. Everyone has their own way of expressing gratitude, I guess.

"Why would he do that?" I asked.

"For the same reason you and Rob don't get along."

I knew why Rob and I didn't get along. He hooked up with my wife while I was busy elsewhere. The divorce followed, and ever since, any time one of us could get the other's goat, we did. But what did that have to do with Alan Tolzer and Jonathan White?

"What are you talking about?" I wasn't up for games, and my tone was short.

"Don't be dense, Lazzaro. Irene White was once Alan Tolzer's wife."

I stared at her, blindsided.

She took the box, our fingers brushing for half a second before she pulled it back. "This isn't you going out of your way for *me*. It's you avoiding whatever you should be dealing with. Same as always."

Then she turned and shut the door. It wasn't a slam, just a clean, definitive click that said she'd been waiting years to do it.

Well, that went well.

For a moment, I just stood there. "You're wrong," I muttered to the brass clamshell knocker. "I'm not avoiding a damn thing."

Chapter Thirty-Seven

I didn't hear that right. I couldn't have. If what Brooke was telling me was true, then my investigation was going to go in a whole new direction. Would Irene profit in some way if Tolzer were dead? What about Jonathan White? How would he gain from closing down the Westport Diet Institute? Sure, it could have been for pure spite, but there could have been something else.

Within ten minutes, I arrived at the White's home in Pine Orchard. This time, a housekeeper answered the door. She had me wait in the great room with the view of the pond and the country club fairway.

The views would have made it a pleasant wait if I hadn't been so wired. I found myself pacing the floor. Ten minutes later, Irene entered the room. She was not the same congenial woman who had given me the interview. She had a look that bordered on annoyed and curious.

"I didn't expect to see you here today. Do you need another recipe?"

"I finished the column," I said. "I know you wanted to see it before it went to press."

"You could have emailed it."

She kind of sounded like Brooke. Did nobody want to see me today?

"I wanted to give it to you in person."

"Leave it. I'll look at it later. I'm rather busy." There was a distinct chill in the room.

"Actually, I did have another reason to come here today. I was hoping to talk to your husband."

"He's not here. You'll have to call his campaign coordinator, Sheila Packard. She can set up an appointment."

"I didn't want to wait. My state taxes are being audited, and to be frank, I suspect your husband has something to do with it."

Irene walked over to her desk and shuffled through some papers. She found what she was looking for and held it up. It was a letter from the state that looked like mine.

"As are mine. And seventy-five percent of the taxpayers in the state. Do you read the papers? A hacker got into the system, and everyone's taxes are getting a second look. What makes you think Jonathan has anything to do with your audit?"

That was embarrassing, but I wasn't convinced.

"Your husband pressured my boss to stop my investigation of the Tolzer and Grand murders."

"What he did was remind your boss that he spends a lot of money on advertising in his magazine. And if you're going to get into personal matters, then he might reconsider how much of his budget will go to *On-Topic*. Would you do business with someone who was trying to muddy your name?"

I admit that I was wrong about the audit. But she was wrong about me trying to get into personal business. I had no idea what she was talking about.

"I'm not trying to muddy anyone's name. I'm only trying to find out who had a motive to commit murder."

"Well, I can assure you, no one in my family did."

"I want to believe that. I'm not lying when I say I do. But questions keep popping up. For example, my column. I had a heck of a time typing it. It seems that the letter I on my keyboard sticks."

She put the letter from the Department of Revenue Services back onto her desk. Then she tidied up some papers while she was at it.

"I'm afraid I can't help you with your keyboard."

"The last time we spoke, you said I could call you Irene. May I still call you Irene?"

"Where is this going?"

"Well, you see, I was sending you an email, Irene, and the keys were sticking on my keyboard. You see what I'm saying?"

"Not at all. As I said, I'm very busy this morning."

"The I, every I, came out as a blank. And when I read it back, your name came out spelled r-e-n-e." "How interesting," Irene said.

"It was interesting. Because that made me recall that a Rene Cooper once worked with Dr. Tolzer back when he was Alan Tolzerano. In fact, they were lovers."

"The late Dr. Tolzer's love life doesn't concern me." She started to walk toward the door as if to lead me out.

"It did concern Rene Cooper. It seems Alan Tolzerano was a serial philanderer, and that led to problems."

"I'm late for an appointment," Irene said.

She opened the door.

"Hear me out. Imagine how surprised I was when I found out a little while ago that you were once married to Alan Tolzer. Then it fell into place. Rene is a nickname for Irene. You were the Rene Cooper who worked with Alan Tolzerano in the New York City school system back in the 1970s. You bought a sawed-off shotgun in 1973, two days before an activist group used it to hold up a grocery warehouse. They killed a night watchman."

"That's not true. she corrected me. The watchman was wounded in an unfortunate accident. Where did you hear that?"

I wasn't about to throw Mrs. Constantine under the bus. "That's what the word is out there."

"Alan tried to live down that rumor for years. Which is one of the reasons Alan changed his name. "It was an unfortunate accident that wasn't supposed to happen. And I don't suppose that you heard that we used the food we took to feed starving inner-city kids. Food earmarked to go to them in the first place but was being held up by red tape."

"Which factored into your acquittal. But it still doesn't look good for a politician's wife to have been on the FBI's Most Wanted List. Especially if her ex-husband used the information to drum up publicity for a new book. Tolzer bragged about a sure-fire publicity gambit. At the time, I thought he was talking about the Betty interview. Now I know better."

She shook her head as if she couldn't believe how dense I was.

"You're barking up the wrong tree, Mr. Lazzaro."

"I don't think so. You lied when you said your argument with Tolzer was about school lunch reform. You argued because you didn't want him to reveal that Renee Cooper and Irene White were the same person. You were at the Westport Institute to beg Tolzer not to embarrass your husband, the husband who wants to shut down the Westport Institute."

"For someone who researches for a major column, you get an awful lot of facts wrong," she said.

A personal attack on me. I must have hit a nerve.

"How is that?"

"The fact is that Jonathan proposes a luxury tax on all spas. To say he wants to close the Westport Institute is an exaggeration. Yes, it would affect the institute but not close it. What is true is that Alan was dragging his feet on support for the school lunch initiative. But it was because he felt the Westport Diet Institute should be exempt from spa status. That's what we were arguing about. I told him that was Alan Tolzer talking. Alan Tolzerano would never turn his back on his old ideals for the sake of making a profit."

Chapter Thirty-Eight

"Mother, go ahead and tell him. He's not going to stop until he knows everything."

Megan? Here? I was halfway out the door and stepped back in, closing the door behind me. Megan was standing on the second-floor landing. Her hair was messy, and she had bags under her eyes.

Mother? It couldn't be. I knew Megan's mother.

"Did you say mother?"

Megan gave me a wistful look as she walked down the stairs.

"I always knew about my adoption, but I didn't know Irene was my birth mother until a few years ago."

Birth mother? Irene? "How did you track her down?"

Megan gave the same shake of her head that Irene had done earlier, one that seemed to say she couldn't believe how dense I was. At that moment, I picked up the resemblance in mannerisms.

"I didn't track her down. I always wondered who my real parents were. But in this case, Irene found me."

If that was true, it was a very brave thing to do, considering Irene's husband was running for governor.

"Surprised?" Irene said.

"That you're Megan's real mother? Yes. That you tracked her down, not at all."

I recalled how forthcoming she was during the interview. Also, how she deflated my sails by bringing up sensitive subjects before I could. I could understand her wanting to get it out in the open before the press could make a scandal out of the situation.

"I can imagine what you are thinking. You think that I did it to head off an embarrassing political situation. But the fact is that I was looking for Megan before my husband decided to run for governor. I found her four years ago. Her adoptive mother was ill and preferred that I not become a part of Megan's life until she passed. I felt I owed the woman that much."

I was thankful Irene had done that. The woman I remembered as Megan's mother was a wonderful person, and she deserved as much.

"You may as well know the rest," Megan said.

It wasn't hard to guess the rest.

"Dr. Tolzer was your biological father? Did he know?"

"Not until a little before he died. I got the job at the Institute after my mother died three years ago. I had intended to tell him when the time was right," Megan said. "But the time never seemed right. Then, about a month ago, Irene and I confronted him."

"You have to realize how this looks," I said.

Irene stepped in front of Megan. She could be a daunting character when her back was against the wall.

"Exactly how does it look, Mr. Lazzaro?"

"That, for one thing, either or both of you had a motive to kill him because he wouldn't acknowledge that he was Megan's father."

"But neither of us did."

Irene's voice was angry and loud. I spotted the housekeeper peeking in the doorway and then scurried away.

"Don't get me wrong, I'm only saying."

Megan came around her mother as if to say she could speak for herself.

"At first, he agreed to a blood test as long as we didn't make it public until he decided the time was right. That was good enough for me," Megan said.

"But then he reneged, and that was why Mrs. White argued with him the day I came to do the interview,"

Irene spoke up again. "He decided not to have a blood test."

"He reneged," I said.

"No. Alan realized he was Megan's father. He didn't need a blood test."

At least now I understood why Jonathan White felt I was interfering in his family's affairs. He thought I would uncover the secret of Megan's relationship to his wife and Dr. Tolzer.

"You believe us, don't you?" Megan asked.

"I'm trying hard to believe you, but up until now, you haven't been honest with me."

"But I have been."

"What about Grand? You told me you didn't know his name, but I found out you argued with him the day before Dr. Tolzer died."

Megan's eyes turned to slits and her mouth set in a hard line. Her voice was low and controlled. So controlled that I wondered if she was holding herself back so she wouldn't explode at any moment.

"All right. I wasn't as honest about him as I could have been. He came to my house asking questions about the Westport Diet Institute a week ago, Sunday. He never gave his name."

From my brief encounter with Grand, I could imagine him operating that way.

"Go on."

"I thought he was a reporter. I didn't want it sensationalized that Dr. Tolzer was my father while my mother's husband was running for governor. What a mess that would be!"

Irene went over to Megan and put her arm around her. "She's right, but we could have handled it."

"I told him I wasn't going to answer his questions. He kept insisting, and I told him several times to get out. I guess it got loud. I thought the man wanted to blackmail the doctor about his relationship with me. I felt frightened."

I would have felt the same way if I were in her shoes.

"That's why you didn't tell the police?"

"Yes, and when you came along with your theory of the doctor's murder, I got confused. What if you were right and that man had done it? I couldn't find my key card. I keep it on my key chain, which was by my door. If he stole it and used it to get onto the grounds, that might implicate me."

The part about the key card could be true. I remembered she said she had Richardson buzz her in the day after the murder. At that point, I didn't know what to say.

"Why not tell me?"

"I was going to tell you when I went looking for you at your apartment. But then I came along as Grand was bleeding all over the sidewalk. I was stupid to pick up the gun and get myself accused of killing him. I knew I had to keep his visit to myself. I know I made a mistake by not being straightforward, but I didn't know what else to do. I told you about the man on the lawn. Why would I do that?" I felt I had to play devil's advocate.

"To point the blame at Lucky Grand. Megan's eyes were wild.

"You don't believe that?"

"I'm telling you how it looks. Especially since the Whites used their political connections to get you out of jail."

Irene took great offense at that.

"Nothing was illegal about Megan's release. We posted bail as any parent would. Yes, there were some considerations made to ensure our privacy. But nothing that anyone else wouldn't receive. We wanted Megan out of there before the press found out whose daughter she is. There would have been a media circus that turned public opinion against her. And why? Because she had the misfortune of two people in the public eye conceiving her."

She had a point. Though I don't often sympathize with people who seek publicity and then complain of a lack of privacy.

I could see the agitation building in Megan. Finally, it must have reached the point where it was too much to handle.

"I thought you were on my side. You're not looking into this to help me. You want a good story to help yourself get a better job."

With that, Megan bolted from the house. Irene and I both followed her.

"Believe it or not, I'm trying to help," I yelled after her. "Come back, Megan. We have lawyers to handle this."

Megan paid no attention to me or to her mother's pleas. She hopped into a car in the driveway and sped away.

"This is my entire fault," Irene said. "I should have never told her that Alan was her father."

"Do you have any idea where she may be going?"

Irene shook her head. "None."

I was about to go searching for her when the housekeeper came out.

"Mrs. White, I may know where she's going."

"Where, Emma? Tell me."

There was a quiver in Emma's voice as she played with a small pin shaped like a monkey she wore on her collar.

"Megan was on the phone early this morning, and I heard her talking to someone she called doctor. She said she was going to see him later today."

"What doctor?" I asked.

Emma shook her head.

"It has to be Dr. Lang," Irene said. "She trusts him. She has to be going to the Institute."

"Yes, the good doctor, Lang," Emma said.

"I hope she doesn't run into Richardson," I said.

"Why?" Irene demanded.

I yelled over my shoulder as I ran to my car.

"Because if Megan is Dr. Tolzer's daughter, she stands in the way of him taking over the Institute."

Chapter Thirty-Nine

By the time I got to Canfield Island, it was dark. As I had expected, I found the gated entrance of the Westport Diet Institute closed. If Megan was in there with Richardson, who knew what kind of danger she could be in? Pressing the button on the call box wasn't an option. Following another vehicle in as Jeanette had done on the day Tolzer had died wasn't likely at that time of night. I could think of only one way to get through that wrought iron barrier. I almost chucked the plan, but I told myself it was the only way.

I took a deep breath, and then I floored my beloved Camaro, my only connection to my brother. The gate exploded open with a discordant metal-on-metal sound. An echo of the sound that Jerry's plane made that day it crashed in Vietnam. I hoped he wasn't hearing it from beyond.

I watched in horror as the heavy iron escutcheon with the letters WDI flew in the air, flipping end over end. It crashed through the windshield and landed in the seat beside me. Yeah, Jerry heard all right, and he was watching over me.

I don't know if safety glass was standard in 1968, but I was thankful the windshield held up. As I brushed pebbles of glass from my hair, I sped up the Copper Beech tunnel, making apologies to Jerry.

My heart raced when I saw Megan's car parked by the main building, confirming my fear that she was there. I had to find her, or I would never forgive myself for confronting her and driving her away in desperation.

If the driveway had been any longer, the Camaro would not have made it. I jumped out and hesitated only long enough to steal a glance at the damage to The Car. With lights and windshield shattered, a crumpled hood, steam chuffed from the radiator. No time to worry about it now. I ran up the boxwood-lined path to the oak door with the rounded top. I tried the doorknob. Locked. I turned away almost in a panic, realized what I had to do, and then spun around and gave the door a swift kick. It popped open. I wasn't naive enough to think that because I didn't hear an alarm go off that one didn't. I had to find Megan fast before the place was crawling with cops, or worse yet, Richardson realized I was there. I ran down the corridor, checking her office and every unlocked door I could find. Nothing. I headed toward Dr. Lang's laboratory, hoping against hope she was with him and not Richardson.

"Halt!"

Not the cops; they couldn't have gotten there so soon. I stopped.

"Hands up. Turn slow." My heart sank to my soles as I recognized Richardson's voice. I kicked myself for not thinking out a sensible and less conspicuous way to get in.

I turned with raised hands. Richardson stood with his feet planted apart, his knees bent. He held a gun with both hands, pointed at my head, as if he were on a shooting range.

"Very impressive," I said. "What cop show did you learn that from?"

He smirked, unimpressed by my bravado. He came closer.

"You'd better have a damn good reason for being here," he said.

"If I don't?"

"I'll have to consider you an intruder and shoot you. You were the last outsider in Dr. Tolzer's office. How do I know you're not the killer? After seeing on the security cameras how you busted your way in here, it seems a likely possibility."

Security cameras, I should have known there would be security cameras.

"What did you do with Megan?"

"To my office; start walking."

He motioned with his gun for me to head down the hall.

"She's there, in your office?"

"Shut up and walk. I don't have time to listen to your nonsense. You're drunk or insane or both to break in here. Either way, I have every right to shoot you."

"If you've hurt her, you're going to wish you had shot me when you had the chance."

"I still have the chance. Walk."

Without a thought for the stupidity of my move, I pulled my keys from my pocket, spun, and flung them at him. They caught him below the eye. He reeled, and the gun flew from his hand. I dove for it, and Richardson grabbed my leg. We scuffled. He was stronger than I thought, and he bashed my head against the floor. I saw a flash of light that seemed to surround an image of Jerry. That vision was enough for me to summon the strength to kick Richardson off. He landed against the wall, and I picked up the gun again and pointed it at him. Richardson laughed. If he thought I wouldn't use it, he was underestimating how angry I was.

"The gun's empty," he said. "I never put bullets in it. Someone could get killed."

Like some cartoon patsy, I looked at the gun in disbelief but continued to keep it aimed at him.

"Yeah, sure."

The man would have to be an idiot to pull an empty gun on someone.

"Go ahead, pull the trigger."

I had seen a movie with the same situation, and when the guy pulled the trigger, a bullet shot out of the back of the barrel. That was fiction. I aimed the gun at the ceiling and pulled the trigger. Nothing happened. I tried again.

That proved the man was an idiot. Case closed.

"Why would you have an empty gun?"

"To scare intruders like yourself. I'll ask again. What are you doing here?"

"I'll ask again, where's Megan?"

"How would I know?"

"Stop playing games, Richardson. I know you invested in the kopi berry supply behind Tolzer's back."

"You're very perceptive. But I didn't break any law."

"You did when you killed Tolzer. Did he find out and threaten to kick you out of the corporation?"

"Yes, he did. But you got a glimpse of how the doctor was—a loose cannon at times. But when he cooled down, he realized I was protecting the supply for our supplement."

"You also became the director of the corporation when Tolzer died. Now you have it all."

"Ah, but that's where your theory falls apart. Dr. Tolzer was the Westport Diet. Can you imagine what Scarsdale would have been if Tarnower had lived? It's the same thing. We'll survive, but I'm losing a fortune."

"Don't give me that. Are you trying to say you won't make money?"

"You're damned right I will."

"Well, there you go."

"And Megan will make more."

"Megan?"

"I already said too much. Lawyer-client relationship."

"It's a little late for you to start worrying about ethics. Are you saying Dr. Tolzer left Westport to Megan?"

"I drew up a new will for him a week ago. All I can tell you is that I will be the director for at least ten years. At that time, my contract gets extended, or I get bought out for half the value of the business. I'll make a fortune, but I guarantee you I would have made more money if he had lived."

So, my theory that Richardson killed Tolzer to gain control of the Institute wasn't worth a pile of tofu.

"Megan and I both would be better off if the good doctor were alive."

The good doctor. Richardson was referring to Tolzer, but the White's housekeeper, Emma, had used that same phrase in reference to Lang.

"And Lang?"

"Dr. Tolzer had some reservations about him. I don't know what. He seemed to have had some kind of problem with Dr. Lang. He said he would be making up his mind soon, but something was definitely troubling him."

I thought immediately of the investigation that Lucky was doing for Tolzer.

I had assumed he was investigating Richardson, but what if it had been Lang?

"We've got to find Lang," I said.

"We don't have to do anything. You broke in here. Remember? I'm calling the police."

I didn't have time to wait around for the police. Lucky had told me he emailed the report before he got into trouble at the bar, not knowing that Tolzer was dead.

"I'm telling you we have to find Lang. I'll prove it to you. Pull up Tolzer's email account on your computer. Do you know Tolzer's password?"

"No."

It was hard to believe that a control freak like Richardson didn't have everyone's password.

"Listen, man, this is no time to pretend you're virtuous. If you expect me to believe your half-ass story, you'll give me that password. It may be the only thing that proves you didn't kill Tolzer and Grand, too."

"I can defend myself. I'm a damned good attorney."

The smug son of a bitch. He was only looking at how it would affect him. He didn't care that Megan might be in danger. I was seeing red. Even though he had a few pounds on me and was all muscle, I picked him up by the collar and pinned him against the wall.

"The password. Now. Or you may not live to regret it," I said through clenched teeth.

It disgusted me that I had become desperate enough to do major damage to that sleazy lawyer. Losing my cool wasn't going to help Megan.

Richardson grimaced and started to say something. If it was another snide remark, we would have both regretted the consequences. He seemed to think better of what he was about to say. I waited.

"I am a god," Richardson said.

I shook him, although not with as much conviction as before.

"I am a god. One word; no spaces; it's the password," he said.

Wanting to keep up my mean persona, I stifled a smile. "Why am I not surprised?"

I watched as Richardson entered the password into Tolzer's account. The fight seemed to have drained out of him, and I knew he wouldn't give me any more trouble.

"Move, let me do that," I said as I took his seat.

I found the email from Lucky Grand. I looked at the time stamp—7:23 p.m. on the day Tolzer died. According to the time stamp, Lucky was telling the truth when he said he sent it a little before he went out on his binge. Of course, he had no way of knowing Tolzer was dead.

"I already read it. You're wasting your time," Richardson mumbled.

"I'll be the judge of that."

I opened the message, which had no subject line, and read: *Received payment. Report delivered as agreed.*

Tolzer had delivered the extra money Lucky had asked for during the interview. Judging from the time frame, Tolzer made a bank transfer to Lucky's account sometime before he died. The police would be able to verify that.

"I told you. There's nothing of value there."

I had to agree with Richardson. There wasn't much there other than Grand claiming that he sent the report.

"But where is it? There's no attachment. Did it come in a separate email?" I asked Richardson.

"No."

"How do I know you didn't read it and then delete the email?"

"Do you doubt everything people tell you?"

In Richardson's case, the answer was yes.

"He didn't sign it, but a lot of people don't bother with signing emails."

At that point, I was talking out loud, waiting for a sensible thought to enter my head. Then I noticed that although the whole message was on the screen, the scroll bar was high on the vertical track on the side of the screen. Was there more? I scrolled down the page until I came to

Lucky's automatic signature block. Charles Grand, Private Investigations. It was way down the page and off the screen. Why was that? Had the message been longer and then erased? No, the signature box would have moved up the page to below the message. Using the scroll bar, I went to the top of the page and read the message again. "Report delivered as agreed." But there had been no attachment. How did Lucky deliver the report? I went through the email one word at a time, highlighting as I often do when I need to read with care. "Received payment" appeared in blue. I nudged the cursor forward. "Report delivered as agreed" illuminated next. Then I guided the cursor down to the signature at the bottom. Then I realized the entire area between the word agreed and the signature block was in blue highlight. I hit the font button—white. That whole section of the email was in white font on a white background. I clicked the box for black font, and there was Lucky's report. I saw how paranoid Tolzer had been. I wasn't surprised he had Lucky resort to this childish trick.

Richardson seemed anxious, and he started pulling at his collar.

"Don't even think of trying anything," I warned him.

"Sit over there in front of the desk where I can see you." He did as he was told.

I read the report. No wonder Tolzer wanted Lucky to investigate what was going on at the Institute. He wanted proof that more than diet supplements were being produced there. The report spoke of a "super caffeinated" drug. I knew caffeine was a cousin of cocaine and amphetamines. But what the report described sounded dangerous. There could be only one person at the Westport Diet Institute who could be behind that—Dr. Lang.

"Megan's car was outside," I said. "Are you sure you didn't see her?"

"I saw her for a brief moment. Then she went to see Dr. Lang."

"I was afraid of that. Take a look here. What do you know about this?"

Richardson stood beside me. I don't think he had two lines read when the door to the office opened, and Dr. Lang walked in with Megan. As I had suspected, she had turned to her trusted friend when everyone else seemed to be against her.

"What are you doing here?" Lang asked.

"Megan, come over here," I said.

Megan hesitated. I took her by the arm.

"What are you doing? Let me go."

She twisted away. There was more than a little irritation in her voice. I kept my eyes on Lang as I pulled her to my side again.

"The doctor here killed Tolzer and Grand, too."

"No," she said. "Dr. Lang explained everything to me. It was him." She pointed to Richardson. "He owns the company that supplies the kopi berries for the diet supplement. Now he stands to make millions."

"Old news," Richardson said.

"He's a crook, but he's not a killer," I said.

"Hey, watch it," Richardson protested.

I waved him off and directed my attention to Megan.

"I read Grand's report. Lang had a pretty strong motive to kill Dr. Tolzer." Lang's face reddened.

"You're crazy, Lazzaro. Get your facts straight," he yelled.

Megan shook her head as if she didn't believe a word I was saying. Why was she being so headstrong?

"I don't believe it," Megan said, "You'll say anything to make it look like you solved this case. You want to make yourself look good so you can get that job at the magazine you want so bad."

Megan's accusation hit home. At first, the job was my primary goal, but somewhere along the line, I realized there was more at stake. The truth counted for something in my book. But Megan didn't know that Mr. Monahan knew about my charade, and this was not the time to tell her.

"It's the truth," I said. "Dr. Tolzer suspected something was going on and hired Lucky to investigate. Lang was producing diet pills in the laboratory."

"Diet pills aren't illegal," Megan said.

"They are when they're an addictive and dangerous drug. While Lang was working on the kopi berry supplement, which had a mild pick-me-up, he made a discovery. A slight modification of the formula could change it into a super-intense stimulant. Yet it was easier to make and twice as intense and habit-forming as methamphetamine."

Megan looked doubtful. "How do you know this?"

"It's all in Lucky Grand's report. When Dr. Tolzer met with him on the lawn that morning, Grand explained what Lang was doing. The Doctor said he had some business to straighten out. What he meant was that he was waiting for the report from Grand."

"I have to hear it from Dr. Lang," Megan said.

Lang pulled a gun from his pocket and looked like a man possessed. His lips pulled back in a snarl, his eyes wide and fixed on us, he almost dared us to make a wrong move. He grabbed Megan and held her in front of him. He held the gun to her side.

"I assure you that, unlike my wimpy lawyer friend's, this is a loaded gun."

Megan tried to step away, but he pulled her closer.

The look of disbelief on her face was painful to see. She could hardly get the words out.

"Dr. Lang, what are you doing?"

"I don't want the same thing to happen to you that happened to Grand. Don't push me."

Megan's expression didn't even twitch. "You killed him, and let me take the blame? How could you? This doesn't make any sense. And why would you make drugs?"

"Tolzer was making all the money. Why, he didn't even believe in the protocol. Whoever heard of eating cannoli on a diet? I was working my butt off, and I wasn't making anything. My wife's medical bills were out of sight, and I was going broke. I had to do something."

"So you killed Dr. Tolzer when Grand found out what you were doing."

Lang was matter of fact.

"I had to kill Grand before anyone found his report."

"I can't believe it," Megan said.

Lang had a gun to her side, and he was confessing, yet she was still trying to defend him.

"Believe it, because we're going to be next," I said. "Emma's monkey pin helped me realize Lang has already tried to kill me."

"Very perceptive on your part," Lang said. On that point, he couldn't resist showing us how clever he was. "I couldn't let you go digging around in my business. I planned to get rid of you when I went to your place with the kopi berry information. I knew you'd discover Grand's report sooner or later. When I didn't find you at home, I spotted the dog door. I came back with my wife's service monkey. That animal is so clever that it was simple to command it to go through the door and turn on the gas jets."

"And I'm willing to bet you were responsible for my whack in the head and the snake in my car, too."

Lang smirked, and I knew I was right. My guess was that he paid someone to follow me and throw the snake into my car when it was out of my sight at Jeanette's house. His expression turned to anger as Megan tried once more to wrench away. He drew her back.

She remained calm as I went on. "He slipped Dr. Tolzer an overdose of the kopi super-caffeine drug that he was making."

"Kopi super-caffeine, I like that. It has a nice ring to it," Lang said. "But I told you, I didn't kill Dr. Tolzer."

"There was enough of the amphetamine-like drug in his cannoli to kill a horse. This is why the autopsy showed Tolzer died of extreme hyperthermia. The drug caused an excessive rise in his body temperature," I said. "That's what caused him to strip off his shirt before he died. The kopi super-caffeine had the same effect as methamphetamine. No wonder the police assumed he overdosed on meth."

"I always told him cheating on his diet would be the death of him, so don't blame me," Dr. Lang said.

"I didn't know any of this!" Richardson protested.

"That's because you're nothing more than a half-assed lawyer," Lang shouted.

"Is he telling the truth, Dr. Lang?" Megan demanded.

"I had to do something. I overheard Tolzer talking about his new will to Richardson. I knew you were going to inherit the business someday. And while you would be fairer, I couldn't wait forever to make some real money." Megan looked stunned.

"It's true," I said. "Richardson had drawn up a new will for your father. You were going to get almost everything. Right, Richardson?"

I turned toward Richardson. He had slipped toward a door next to the closet where Tolzer had retrieved his cell phone from his jacket that day. Lang's face grew scarlet with anger as he noticed what Richardson was doing.

I took the opportunity to rush the doctor. We wrestled, and Megan broke away. Lang held on to the gun. It went off. I heard a scream. Was Megan shot? No, it was Richardson.

Even as I fought to avoid getting shot myself, I could see Richardson clutch his bleeding arm. When he grasped the doorknob, he smeared the door with blood. He managed to get it open and fell through. Meanwhile, Lang was trying his damnedest to get the gun to my head as we struggled. We bumped into Megan, and she fell. Then she jumped into the mix, kicking and flailing. If she was trying to help me, she wasn't succeeding. Finally, she fell away, and Lang and I went lurching over Richardson's body and through the doorway. I found myself tumbling head over heels down a flight of stairs to the basement.

When I finally landed at the foot of the steps, my head struck the cellar floor. Every bone in my body ached. The gun came bouncing down the steps after me and landed somewhere in the darkness. I felt something sticky on my neck and realized that blood was flowing from my ear. For the second time in a week, my scalp felt like a baseball bat had hit it. Despite the chill outside, it was tropical down there. The cellar was dark, and at the top of the stairs, I could see Lang silhouetted in the light from the office. He turned on the switch.

My eyes wouldn't focus, but I could make out a low ceiling of heavy beams that was doing its best to close in on me. My eyes darted around the space, looking for something to defend myself with. The gun had landed by a massive boiler behind me. I willed myself to inch toward it despite the pain. But Lang had other ideas. He leaped down the steps and landed on me. I lost what little breath I had in me.

I was stunned. He half lifted, half dragged me toward the old boiler. I resisted with all my strength as he tried to push my face onto its iron faceplate. Through its vents, white-hot light and a low roar escaped. I grasped a pipe, hoping to use it as leverage to push myself away. It singed my palms, and I yanked my hands away.

Growling and hissing, Menu came out of nowhere, spitting and clawing as he landed on Lang's back. With the help of the courageous cat, I managed to cast Lang off. The doctor landed against the steps with such a thud that I was sure he broke his back. As I stared at his motionless body, I picked myself up, shaking my burned palms. Lang sprang up with a roar befitting a wounded beast and charged at me. I managed to duck and then flip him over my back. He landed in the hot furnace pipes, screamed, and then rolled to the floor. Knowing the pain I felt in my hands, I didn't envy him.

"Hands up. Turn around slow."

I did as I was told. Nina was standing gun in hand, similar to Richardson's stance earlier.

"Bull, Nina. That is the second time I heard that tonight. How did you know I was here?"

"Megan called after she arrived."

"Then it took you long enough to get here."

Nina glared at me. "I would have been here sooner, but I can't fly."

Several other cops sprinted down the stairs and assessed his injuries before picking him up. He was alive but would sport permanent reminders of the Westport Diet Institute's power plant.

"Where is Megan?" I asked.

"Upstairs, giving a statement to Gambardella."

"I'm afraid she was involved in the murders," I said.

"More like duped into letting Lang know that Lucky was in jail, from what she told us when she called for help."

"You believe her?"

"Not for me to decide." Nina pulled a small tape player from her pocket and pressed the button on the player.

"I have to hear it from Dr. Lang."

"I assure you that, unlike my wimpy lawyer friend's, this is a loaded gun."

"Dr. Lang, what are you doing?"

"I don't want the same thing to happen to you that happened to Grand. Don't push me."

Nina hit the stop button.

"I guess that counts for something. And what it doesn't count for, I'm sure the Whites' lawyers will take care of."

"You wired her?"

"We had nothing to do with it. This is amateur stuff. She did it herself. She knew Tolzer wasn't happy about something that was going on. She narrowed it down to Lang."

"That may not hold up in court," I said.

"What you witnessed here is a start. We know for sure that Lang shot Richardson and attacked you. Now that we know he did it, we'll get a legal confession out of him about Grand."

"Is Richardson dead?" I asked.

"He'll live. Guys like that don't die easy. God doesn't know what to do with them. Hey, we've got to take care of those."

She pointed to my hands. I didn't even realize I was still shaking them to cool them to ease the pain.

I nodded to both sentiments, and we headed up the stairs. I remember getting to the landing. Nina was ahead of me. She turned toward me, and her face looked like one of those Picasso paintings. I think she grabbed for me and yelled out my name. Then everything went black.

When I came to my head ached like hell, but I still gave Nina a hard time about sending me to the hospital. "I'm fine."

"You were seeing double, and you blacked out."

"You fall down a flight of stairs and then fight for your life and see if you don't black out," I told her.

That's when she put the fear of all things holy in me. She told me I had the classic symptoms of a subdural hematoma. I only had a vague idea of what that was, but I knew it wasn't good.

"I told you I feel great. Look."

I attempted to do a little dance but stopped when I realized that I felt like crap. If she noticed, she didn't let on.

"You might feel fine now, but in an hour or two, you might end up dead."

I know you can get bleeding under the skull after a blow to the head. But I also know they drill holes in your noggin to release the pressure on your brain. That was exactly why I didn't go after getting mugged. This time, though, I put up only enough fuss not to look like a wimp. I'm glad I didn't tell her that I felt like puking my brains out, or she would have sent me in an ambulance. As it was, I was pissed I had to go in a police car, which she claimed broke every rule in the book.

The officer dropped me off at the Norwalk Hospital emergency room, and Nina got there minutes later and took care of all the admitting procedures for me. Neither the MRI nor the CT brain scan showed any sign of bleeding in the brain. But they told me I definitely had a concussion and three broken ribs as well. To my chagrin, they admitted me.

They put me on a morphine drip, which I have to confess made me feel kind of nice. That first night, in my relaxed state, I tried over and over to put my finger on something that was eluding me. I finally gave up and slept. And it is a good thing I did get some rest because the next day I had a parade of well-meaning visitors. One after another, they came by despite hospital rules to guarantee my rest and privacy.

I got through it by pushing the button on the PCA pump. I knew it wouldn't give me any more morphine than programmed to give, but it helped, nonetheless.

Megan showed up; I knew she would. Brooke also showed up; I had no idea she would. I was glad because it was time that we buried the hatchet. She told me Rob sent his regards and then, as an aside, mentioned they would be getting married. God bless Rob. No one deserves it more.

Irene White stopped by without her husband. I had the feeling it was more to check out the giant bouquet they had sent. It was a nice bunch of red, white, and blue flowers, even if interspersed with campaign buttons.

Archie didn't come in person, but he did make a video call. He tried to explain that he would have liked to have been there, but he was swamped with work. I don't know if he didn't realize that it was obvious he was in the Hamptons. I didn't care. I knew hospital germs would freak him out anyway. At least he took the time to call. He said his mother's event raised a ton of money for the preservation of the Big Duck. She wanted him to thank me for going to the party. He also told me that Mr. Monahan said they would run reruns of "Cooking with Betty" while I recovered. I tried to pin him down on whether the investigative job was permanent or not, but he was evasive.

Then there was dear old Mary Ticarelli. She showed up above the moon excited with the news she had adopted Menu. That made me happy. I'd become attached to that cat. True to form, Mary brought me a giant plastic bowl full of chicken soup and a box of cannoli. I couldn't even look at the cannoli and gave them to the nurses when she left.

I was most surprised by a visit from Tommy Baylor as visiting hours were about to end. I spotted him while he was still in the hallway. Ashamed by my overreaction that could have killed both of us, I closed my eyes and pretended I was asleep.

I could hear his soft footsteps as he entered the room. I imagined him all meek and humble for putting those threats on my computer. It would have been fun to see if I weren't so exhausted. I hoped he would leave soon so I could get to sleep for real.

I opened my eyes a slit to see if he had gone. He was still there, right next to the bed, messing with my morphine pump. In one swift motion, I grabbed the telephone with my left hand and smashed him on the side of his head. Blood immediately covered his face, and he fell back against a recliner. I let the phone drop to the floor as I pulled the IV needle out of my arm before I died of a morphine overdose. Then I pushed the call button.

The minute the nurse saw Tommy sprawled out in a bloody mess, she called security. In no time, the room was a chaotic mass of security guards. Not to mention several nurses and doctors attending to the man who tried to kill me. It wasn't until I pointed out the PCA pump to one of the doctors that they listened to my story. The digital readout was set to the maximum level. They worked on Baylor until they controlled the bleeding. By that time, Nina and several other officers entered the mix. They wheeled him out to parts unknown to me. Nina stayed behind. She didn't look happy.

"What is with you? You can't stay out of trouble even when you're confined to a hospital bed. What happened here?"

"I've been thinking all day that something doesn't fit. Now I know what it is. Lang didn't kill Dr. Tolzer. Baylor did."

"You must have been hit on the head harder than I thought. Did you forget that Lang landed you in here? Plus, we have the taped admission. We're this much away from getting a formal confession out of him."

She held her thumb and forefinger about an inch apart to show me.

"Dr. Lang said he killed Lucky Grand so the investigation would never come to light. He never said he killed Dr. Tolzer, and he never will."

Nina glanced toward the bloodstained overturned chair Baylor had landed on.

"So you're saying Baylor killed Tolzer. What's the motive? He had no connection to the Institute."

"But he did. He was friends with Megan, and they both belonged to ACE. She said he understood her. My guess is she poured her heart out to him, thinking she had a sympathetic ear. On her part, they were only friends. She didn't realize his obsession with her. I witnessed his irrational behavior when he attacked me and climbed up a water tower.

When she told him Dr. Tolzer was her real father, and he wouldn't acknowledge her, I could see Baylor going insane with anger. In his twisted mind, he thought he had to punish Tolzer for the hurt he was causing Megan. What turned out to be the real irony was that Tolzer had recently included Megan in his will."

"Let's suppose I buy your theory, which I don't so far. How did Baylor get into the Institute?"

"With Megan's key card. He probably stole it from her when they were hanging out at the juice bar at ACE. No one questions a car that comes through the gate with the use of a key card."

I could see Nina was starting to buy into my theory, or at least consider it. She thought for a minute.

"So, you think Megan told him about Tolzer's penchant for cannoli, and he got the idea to poison them. It's kind of an old-fashioned way to commit murder. Poison is too easily detected with modern technology."

"Exactly. Not only was Baylor going for the irony of killing the diet doctor with a poisoned high-calorie pastry. But he wanted the poison detected so he could pin it on Dr. Lang. His next move would have been to reveal that Lang was making the amphetamine-like drug from the kopi berries."

Nina had a puzzled look on her face.

"I still have a couple of problems with it. One, how did Baylor know that Dr. Lang was making drugs, and two, how did he get his hands on some?"

"I was thinking about that myself. Of course, my first thought was Megan, but she seemed surprised to learn of Lang's illegal drug operation. But then I realized that Baylor had another connection to the Institute through ACE. Rob had given him a membership to the tennis club, and he certainly had met Ponds there. I think you'll find that Ponds was peddling Lang's super amphetamine from ACE, and Tommy Baylor had been a customer."

"You didn't hear this from me," Nina said.

"What?"

"That day you accused me of following you to ACE, I wasn't there to have your back. I didn't even know you were at the courts. It was part of an investigation. We've been watching Ponds' place."

"Well, there you go. I'm on the right track. Tom Baylor had a ready supply of Lang's kopi super-caffeine because he was a user. Baylor saw a chance to kill two birds with one stone. Due to his obsession with Megan, he saw Tolzer as an enemy, but he was jealous of Lang because Megan felt so highly of him. So he used the amphetamine to kill one doctor with the hope of exposing the other doctor's illegal drug operation."

With that, I got out of bed and put on my clothes.

"Where do you think you're going?"

"Home. Enough is enough. I've had it." I checked myself out of the hospital against the doctor's orders and went home. I needed to sleep in my own bed. When I got in, I took the landline off the hook and turned off my cell phone.

Chapter Forty

I sent an email to Archie telling him I was going to take six weeks off on doctor's advice. I'm sure the doctor would have agreed if I had given him a chance. Archie agreed and said that he would use reruns of the column along with a note that Betty was on vacation.

For the first three days, I worked on my novel during the day and watched old movies on TV at night. The first day, I wrote about two thousand words and rewarded myself by watching *The Big Sleep*. The second day, I racked up twenty-one hundred words, followed by *The Maltese Falcon*. On the third day, I deleted a thousand words but added eight hundred new ones. *The Third Man* for the third day was appropriate compensation. By around four o'clock on the fourth day, I had another twenty-five hundred words. I was feeling pretty damned proud of myself. If I could keep up that pace, I'd have the book finished in a couple of weeks. I decided it was okay to reconnect with civilization for a while.

I no sooner turned on my cell than it started playing "I Fought the Law and Law Won." My ringtone for Nina. I didn't want any sympathy or questions about my head, so I cut her off at the pass.

"So, would I make a good cop or what?"

"I'd say as a cop, you'd make a good cook. You were lucky this time. Next time, let me do my job."

Of course, she was going to say that. But there was something in her voice that told me she knew I did a damned good job.

"So, I take it you didn't call to congratulate me. What's up?"

"I was thinking dinner was in order," she said.

I had been planning to watch *The Asphalt Jungle* that night. But dinner with Nina sounded a whole lot better.

"Mofongo?"

"Get real. I cooked last time."

"Okay, we can go to Wethersfield's. What time?"

"You are still not listening to me. You cook, your place."

I glanced toward the pile of recipes that I had copied from Brooke's recipe box. I thought about Nina coming to my apartment and what might happen after dinner. I'd have to look for something we could eat quickly.

ACKNOWLEDGMENTS

I wish to thank my wife, Annette, for her unending encouragement and support. She is my inspiration, my anchor, and my constant cheerleader.

As always, thanks to my family—Rosemarie, Sam, and Melody; Michael, Michelle, Joey, and James; Joanne; and my cousins Annette and Dennis for always being there, in ways big and small.

I am profoundly grateful to my writing group, Chris Falcone and Roberta Isleib (Lucy Burdette). Over the past twenty-five years, they've read countless drafts of my work and offered invaluable guidance at every turn. Special thanks also to Lynn Sheft, whose keen eye helped me improve this story in countless ways.

I can't forget my friends Bev and Tony Nunes, who reintroduced me to SoNo. Starting our tour at a brewery was pure genius. Thanks also to my friends Rick and Sue Lundin for their support and encouragement along the way. And, of course, to my wonderful agent, Nadia Lynch, whose guidance, insight, and support have been invaluable.

This brings me back to Annette and to remembering all the wonderful times we shared in Westport so many years ago. Annette, you are the beginning of everything.

About the Author

Ang Pompano is a writer, editor, blogger, and publisher. He's the creator of the *Reluctant Food Columnist Mysteries* and the *Blue Palmetto Detective Agency* series. His first mystery novel, *When It's Time for Leaving*, was a finalist for the Agatha Award, and his short fiction has appeared in numerous award-winning anthologies.

A past recipient of the Mystery Writers of America's Helen McCloy Award, Ang is the co-founder of Crime Spell Books and co-editor of the *Best New England Crime Stories* anthology. He also blogs about food at Mystery Lovers' Kitchen and serves on the board of Sisters in Crime Connecticut.

You can connect with me on:
- http://www.angpompano.com
- https://www.facebook.com/ang.pompano
- https://www.instagram.com/angpompano

Also by Ang Pompano

Novels:
When It's Time for Leaving
Blood Ties and Deadly Lies
Anthologies:
Best New England Crime Stories (co-published and co-edited)
Bloodroot
Devil's Snare
Snakeberry

www.ingramcontent.com/pod-product-compliance
Lightning Source LLC
Chambersburg PA
CBHW020757310726
48969CB00002B/582